fight *for* me

Fight for Me

Cover Design:
Sommer Stein, Perfect Pear Creative

Editing:
Ashley Williams, AW Editing

Proofreading:
Michele Ficht & Janice Owen

Formatting:
Alyssa Garcia, Uplifting Author Services

Cover photo © Brian Kaminski

The Arrowood Brothers Series

Come Back for Me
Fight for Me
The One for Me
Stay for Me

fight
for me

NEW YORK TIMES BESTSELLING AUTHOR
CORINNE MICHAELS

For Natasha Madison, there is no overrated without you ... meh.

one

Eight years ago

"What the hell do we do now?" Jacob looks at me, wanting answers I can't give.

"I don't know," I say, staring at the wreck in front of me.

My heart is pounding, and I feel as though I'm watching a movie instead of the horrible reality.

"He has to pay for this," Connor says, his hands are still shaking.

None of us thought the night would go this way. It was supposed to be filled with celebration and laughter. Finally, all four of us would be out of this godforsaken town and away from our drunk, abusive father.

I was finally going to ask Sydney to marry me.

She's the only reason I breathe. She's all that matters, and now, I have to let her go. One moment was all it took. That car going into the ditch, the sounds, the smell of death. I can't stop replaying it in my mind.

Staying on the side of the road isn't an option. My brothers will take the fall for what he did, and I can't let that happen.

"We go."

Three sets of eyes turn to me, all filled with disbelief.

"And leave them here?" Connor yells, his hands pointing at the wreck.

"We have no choice, Connor! We can't stay. We weren't driving, and it'll look like we were!" I yell, gripping my youngest brother's shoulders. "We'll come back. We'll make sure that, tomorrow, he confesses."

"No." Connor, the one with the biggest heart, shakes his head. "No. We weren't driving, and we can't leave these people."

Jacob sighs and touches his shoulders. "Declan is right."

Sean looks to me, realization flashing in his eyes. "My car was the …"

"I know, that's why we have to go. It was your car that hit them."

Connor seems to just catch up with what the issue is. My father may have been driving the car, but he was in Sean's vehicle while he did it. Who will it most likely lead back to? Sean.

"Dec …" Sean's voice shakes. "We can't leave these people. Connor's right."

I nod. "We go home and tell him we're going to turn him in. Connor's right. He pays for this. But we can't be here."

I feel sick to my stomach. Everything has gone wrong. My father was drunk, trying to pick a fight with Connor, but since my brother isn't a kid anymore, Dad was put in his place. As much as he wants to start with the rest of us, he won't do shit in front of me. Not because they can't hold their own but because he knows I'll fucking kill him if he touches any of us again.

However, right now, it feels like the first time he beat me. I'm paralyzed by the fact that someone I came from could be so awful.

I look to the car, wheels up, smoke coming from the under-carriage, and I have to fight back the nausea.

One instant and my entire life has changed.

"Let's go," Jacob says, dragging Connor toward the car.

"This is wrong!" he yanks his arm away and heads back.

I feel the same, but I have to protect my brothers. "We can't do anything, Connor. They're dead, and we are the ones standing here. It was Sean's car, and we have no idea if Dad made it home. We have to go after him, damn it! What if he's hurt? I promised Mom. I have to go."

He looks torn, and guilt assaults me so hard it hurts to breathe. All of this could've been avoided if we hid the keys like we always did, but it's been almost four years since I've lived full-time in Sugarloaf. I was careless. We all were.

I should've known my father would take the car. I'm the oldest, the one who has always saved my brothers, and now I failed them.

However, I will not ever allow any of my brothers to suffer the consequences for my stupidity.

After a few seconds, the four of us get back into the car. No one speaks. What could we say? I think about the people we left behind. Were they someone's mother and father? Were they good people who my father took from this world?

When we get back to the house, the four of us are somber and unsure. We find our father passed out on the couch as if he didn't just kill two people. I kick him because I'm so angry and I don't care, but he grunts and goes back to sleep.

"Now what?"

"Now, we stay here until he wakes, and then we send his ass to jail."

The morning comes, and I'm the first to rise.

I feel restless, so I head out of the house and to the cars, checking to make sure I didn't dream the events of last night.

But there are the scrapes and the dent on Sean's bumper, the red paint has blue streaks down it, and the bumper is hanging off. I close my eyes, hating that, once again, there is a mess that I don't know if I can clean up.

I think about my mother and how disappointed she'd be. She was an angel who was taken too soon. Her warmth, love, and devotion to her children were unparalleled. We've been on our own since she passed away, and her last wish is the only reason I'm here.

I made her promises while she lied there dying. I told her that I would protect my brothers, make sure they turned out okay. I gave her my word, and look at where that has gotten them.

I fall to my knees, staring at the damage and praying that the man who has only ever thought about himself will do the right thing this one time.

That's when I hear rustling behind me.

"Dec?" Connor's voice is quiet, but it sounds as if he's shouting in the still morning air.

He's looking to me for answers.

"It really happened," Jacob says.

"Yeah …" I wish it weren't the truth, but here is the proof.

When Sean opens the door, his face is haggard, and it looks as if he's lost years off his life. "I can't look at that car."

Before I can speak, my father strides out, running his hand down his face. He knocks into Sean and then rights himself.

"What are you four idiots doing?" he slurs.

"Do you remember anything about what you did last night?" I prompt.

I struggle to look at him because this isn't the man who raised me. He's an imposter, a drunk, and an abusive prick who thinks we need to be the outlet for his anger.

"You're going to confess what you did." My voice leaves no room for discussion. "You killed two people last night, and you put your sons in harm's way—again. I'm done protecting you."

My father looks over at the car and then to us. We stand ready to fight him no matter what.

"The hell I am."

"You're a worthless piece of shit!" Sean yells and heads toward him. My hand grips his arm, pulling him to a stop. "You've destroyed everyone's lives! Mine, theirs! I won't let you do it anymore! You're going to confess!" he screams.

Sean has always been the calm one, and Mama used to call him her "Sweet Boy." He has a tender heart, so to see him outraged has the rest of us speechless.

Dad takes a step closer, his chest puffing out and spit forming on his lips. "You going to make me, Boy? It is your car that has the damage. It was you four who were out joyriding last night, wasn't it? I'm sure everyone in town knows the Arrowood brothers are back and that truck makes a lot of noise. Are you sure no one heard you?"

Anger like I've never felt starts to build. "You were driving."

His evil grin spreads. "No one knows that, Son."

"I'm not your son."

"You four should think about what it would look like. You're all back, Sean's car has damage on it, and you said two people are dead ..."

Connor's breathing grows louder, and I see him clenching

his fists. "You're disgusting."

"Maybe so, but you seem to have gotten yourselves into a mess. If I were you, I'd keep your mouths shut so you don't end up sending your brother to jail. And no one will let a convict in the military." Then he turns his gaze to Sean. "It'd be a shame to see you lose that scholarship, wouldn't it?" He smirks at me and then walks inside, leaving the four of us stunned.

"He can't do this!" Jacob yells. "He can't pin this on us, can he?"

They look to me, always to me, and I shrug. I don't put anything past him. "I don't know."

"I can't go to jail, Dec," Sean says.

No, he can't. Sean is going places. We all are, and it's far away from this town. I can't do this to Sydney either. I can't saddle her with the burden of what happened last night and destroy the future she so desperately wants. What kind of a life could I give her if he ever made good on that threat? How would she go on to law school being married to a man who left two people dead on the side of the road?

And if I can't have her, then there will never be another.

There's only one option: a vow between the only three people who matter more than my own life.

"We promise each other right now," I say with my hand extended and then wait for each of my brothers to circle around me and link together hand to wrist. "We vow that we will never be like him. We will protect what we love and never get married or have kids, agreed?"

It means I give up Syd. It means I ruin every fucking dream I have, but it's the only protection I can give her. She'll find another man—a better one—and be happy. She has to be.

Sean bobs his head quickly. "Yes, we will never love because we might be like him."

Jacob's voice is as hard as steel when he says, "We don't

raise our fists in anger, only to defend ourselves."

Connor's eyes fill with anger. His hands are like vices, squeezing tighter as he stares at me. "And we never have kids or come back here."

In unison, we all shake. The Arrowood brothers never break promises to each other.

A few hours later, we've moved the car into the abandoned barn in the back. We're all tired, broken, and exhausted. Jacob, Sean, and I are leaving tomorrow, but Connor has a few weeks before he leaves for boot camp.

"Dec?" Sean grips my arm as I pass him.

"Yeah?"

"You don't have to do this, you know?"

"Do what?"

He sighs and then pushes his hair back. "Break her heart. I know what we said, and while it works for the three of us, we all were … fucked in the head. You love Sydney."

I do. I love her more than anything in the world, enough to let her go. Enough to give her a better life than I ever can. And I love her enough to know that breaking her heart is the best gift I can ever give her.

"I can't love her and think to weigh her down with all of this. I can't give her a future, and I won't break my word." My heart is breaking just thinking about it, but I have to stay strong. "If I stay with her, we will always be tied to this town. I can't do it. I have to leave, start a new life, and give her the opportunity to do the same."

Sean pinches the bridge of his nose. "She'll never let you go."

I shake my head, blowing out a low breath. "She doesn't have a choice."

I walk away because there's nothing more to say. At this point, all that is left is the hurt and pain from the decisions we've made. I have to spare her. From this point on, I have to hold on to the fact that what I'm doing is right. No matter how much it kills me to do it.

After everyone is asleep, I head out of the house and down through the fields. I could walk this in my sleep and find my way to Sydney. She's always been the pull that keeps me moving forward. When we met, we were little more than two kids with horrible fathers, but we found a closeness I never knew was possible. Now, I have to sever it.

When I reach their modest farmhouse, I climb the oak tree that gets me close enough to her window that I can knock four times.

After a few minutes, the pane lifts, and I feel like I can breathe.

Sydney's long blonde hair is in a braid, and while she may have been asleep, her eyes are bright and full of life.

"What's wrong?" she asks immediately.

"I'm leaving to go back to New York tonight."

"I thought you were staying the rest of the summer?" I can hear the disappointment in each word.

I have to let her go. I love her too much to drag her down with me. "I can't stay."

She releases a heavy sigh. "Go to the barn, I'll meet you down there. I don't want to wake my mother."

Before I can reply, she slides the window closed, leaving me no choice. I can either get out of the tree and leave without meeting her, making me even more of an asshole, or I can do as she asks and let her know this is really the end.

When my feet hit solid ground, Syd is there, wearing my letterman jacket pulled tight and a pair of sweatpants.

She's never looked more beautiful.

I take a step toward her without even thinking.

"Why are you leaving, Dec?"

I lift my hand, brushing back the stray hair that came loose from her braid. I'll never touch her face again. I'll never see the way she smiles or feel her in my arms. So many last times have already passed. I can never get them back, but I'll hold them tight.

"I have to."

"Your dad?"

I nod. "The thing is, Syd. I'm not ever coming back."

Her lips part, and she sucks in a breath. "What?"

"I'm done with this town, and I can't be here anymore. All of this ... the small-town life, I can't do it."

She blinks a few times and then clutches her stomach. "What about all the promises you made? What about how you swore you'd never abandon me? You know I can't leave here. My mother and sister need me, and I love it here."

"And I love New York."

"And do you love me?"

More than anything. More than I can ever tell her.

"Not enough to stay."

I watch the hurt dance across her face as she steps back. "Not ... enough?" Then her eyes narrow. "What the hell is going on, Declan? This isn't us. This isn't you. You love me. I know you love me!" She moves closer, her hand grabs my wrist, and she places my palm to her chest. "I feel it here. I know you better than anyone. Don't lie to me."

I need to end it quickly. She does know me better than anyone, and I have to protect her from my father's fallout. I vowed to do what I have to in order to protect my brothers, and that means breaking two more hearts tonight—hers and mine.

"You don't know me!" I almost roar. "You and I ... we've been fun, but I'm tired of it. We were only fooling ourselves by thinking we could make a long-distance relationship work. Plus, we're not even out of college yet. No one meets the person they're going to marry in high school. Promises are broken, and I'm over trying to force myself to make this work. You want to stay here, that's fine. But I will never spend another night in this fucking town as long as I live."

Sydney turns her back and nods. But that isn't my girl. She's a fighter, and when her blue eyes find mine, there's fire in them. "I see. So, to hell with me? Screw the fact that for the last *seven* years I've loved you? It doesn't matter that I've *waited* for you? Been here for you all this time? I mean that little to you, Declan?"

She's the world, but I can't tell her that.

"I don't care about you like that, Syd. I've been pretending for a while. I never want to get married. I'll never have kids. And I'll never love you like you want."

Her mouth drops, and she shoves my chest—hard. "Fuck you! Fuck you for saying that to me! I've given you everything, and this is how you repay me? You know what? Just go. Go and love your city life. Go and run away from everything we've promised each other. You'll be alone and sad, and you know what? You deserve it. I hate you! You're as bad as my father, and we both know how I feel about him."

Then she turns and runs, leaving me alone to hate myself more than she could ever hate me.

two

Present

Oh, God, Declan is here. He's in this town, which he swore he'd never be in again, and I feel as though a million needles are pricking at my skin. I pride myself on being brave, yet here I am hiding like a coward because I can't do it.

Seeing him almost seven months ago was hard enough. We didn't talk at his father's funeral, but I felt him in my soul. I stood, watching him with his brothers and taking in the looks of relief they each wore. He was even more handsome than I remembered. His chestnut-brown hair fell back, but it wasn't slick, and he filled out that suit like it was made for him. Hell, it probably was. Declan Arrowood has done very well for himself. I've followed his career because I'm a glutton for punishment, and he's impressed me at every turn.

However, I still can't find it in my heart to forgive him or talk to him.

He broke my heart that night, but each day he stayed away or refused to contact me has decimated that organ beyond repair.

I lean down, grab a flower that is growing on the edge of the pond, and hold it, remembering how he used to make me feel. He promised me that at the end of college, we'd find a way.

Two years he said after we finished our sophomore years.

Two years my ass.

I throw the flower into the pond and watch it float. It's funny that it's exactly how I feel about my life. I'm just ... drifting. I don't sink, I'm much too strong for that, but I'm still in this pond, allowing the current to take me where it deems I should go.

One would think that, after this many years, I'd be over it. And I was. I got my law degree, am a volunteer EMT, and have great friends, but there's still a gaping hole in my chest from when a stupid boy ripped my heart out and never gave it back.

Now, the same stupid boy is in Sugarloaf, and everything I buried is bubbling up.

My phone rings, and it's Ellie, my best friend who I've been avoiding until Declan disappears again.

"Hey," I say as lightheartedly as I can.

"Hey, are you not coming to the party?"

I bite my lip and try to think of a way to break it to her. "I can't, Ells."

"Because he's here?"

Yes. "No."

"Then why, because Hadley is asking for you. She told us you said you'd be right back, and that was over two hours ago. She won't let us sing happy birthday or eat cake or open presents or do *anything* until her auntie Syd is here." Her voice quickens over each word.

I am such a damn coward. I dropped Hadley off, and when she ran inside, I ran away. I'm not ready to be in the same room with him. It'll be too awkward and too … us.

Still, I can't disappoint Hadley. "I'm on my way. Just … if it gets to be too much …"

"I'll cover for you," Ellie finishes what I wasn't able to say.

"Thanks."

"Just get here before she drives us all crazier."

I smile, knowing that's exactly what Hadley will do, and I leave the sanctuary to head back to hell.

As I walk, I try to recall the bad things. If I'm angry, I won't feel like some lovesick idiot around him. I think about the night he told me we were done. The weeks after where I begged him to come back to me so we could work it out. All the heartache I endured, thinking he would change his mind.

He didn't.

He dropped me as though I were nothing and never gave me any reason.

Jerk.

I walk through the field, passing the tree-mansion Connor has built Hadley. Seriously, that kid doesn't have him wrapped around her finger, she has him wrapped around her whole hand. It's cute though, and it's made me wonder if I'm being silly by letting my dating life fall to the wayside.

I've given up on love. There's been guys, but nothing that has had any true meaning. All because the fear of having my heart broken has been stronger than the desire to love again. Declan didn't break my heart though—no, he stole it from my chest.

I trudge up the steps, holding onto the anger and resentment he put in my heart all those years ago, and open the door.

As soon as I turn, he's there.

"Syd."

"Asshole," I reply and cross my arms.

He runs his hands through his thick hair, pushing it away from his face, and then looks down. "I deserve that."

"We have something we agree upon then."

He looks at me from under those thick lashes, which no man should possess, and grins. "You look good."

So do you.

No, no, Syd. He does not look good. He looks like the devil who broke your heart and never looked back.

I have to remember all that. If I don't, I might not be able to ignore that he still makes my heart sputter or that I have never felt more secure in another's arms—not that I've spent eight-fucking-years trying to find a man even half as perfect as Declan Arrowood. More than that, though, is that I have to keep some distance between us so he won't get the wrong idea and start thinking that there's a snowball's chance in hell of a reconciliation.

Screw me once, shame on him. Screw me twice, I'm a fool who needs to be punched.

"I'm sure we also agree that we don't really need to do this. We have six months to get through, and then we can go back to pretending the other doesn't exist."

Declan moves a bit closer, and the cologne, which he's worn since he was seventeen, creeps around me. I bought him his first bottle of it for Christmas. It was musky and strong, which was how I felt about him. My heart aches with the knowledge that he still wears it.

"That's not what I've been doing."

I shake my head, not willing to listen to lies. "Six months, Declan. I'm asking you to avoid me, pretend I don't live here, or that you don't know me for the six months you're stuck here."

"I hate my father for this."

We all hate his father. When he died, his four sons should've inherited the Arrowood farm. They should've been able to sell it and move on with their lives. But Declan's father was cruel and selfish, even in death. The stipulation in the will was that each of the four brothers must live on the farm for six months. At the conclusion, they can do what they want with the property.

That means that, even after they swore they'd never come back here, they have no choice if they want their inheritance. And now I have to see the man who I have never gotten over.

"Regardless, you owe me this much."

There's a flash of hurt in his eyes, but he looks away. "You always have been beautiful and irresistible when you don't hold back."

Right. Sure I am. Enough that he could leave me so damn easily. I'm not going to let my heart read more into it. I have to protect myself because loving Declan has never been my issue. I've spent my entire life doing it as naturally as breathing.

My shoulders straighten, and I glare at him. "Well, I'm sure my boyfriend will appreciate you thinking so. If you'll excuse me, I have a birthday cake to consume."

I shoulder past him and pray my knees don't buckle.

When I turn the corner, all hell breaks loose, and I don't have to worry about my legs because I'm lifted into the air.

"Sydney!" Jacob grabs me, turning me around in his arms. "You fucking gorgeous woman. Look at you."

I smile. Here's another Arrowood I can like. "And look at you!" I slap his shoulder playfully. "You're all famous and shit."

Then Sean is there. "Give me that girl." His deep voice is filled with warmth. "I've missed you, Syd."

I wrap my arms around him and squeeze. "I've missed you guys too—well, some of you."

Sean and Jacob both laugh. "The better brothers, at least."

We all laugh, and they both wrap an arm around me, tucking me into their protective embrace. I'd forgotten how much I loved them all. Each one always made sure no one hurt me. They were loyal and adopted me as a sister they never had.

When my father ran out on us, it was these guys who took up the role of protector.

"You came back!" Hadley rushes forward, a big smile on her face.

"Of course I did! I just needed to get your present."

"Did you know that Uncle Declan promised to get me a *pony?*" She screams the last word with eyes bright.

I want to say a biting remark about the man not honoring promises, but I don't. Hadley doesn't deserve it, and my opinion is shrouded in years of bitterness. Plus, if I'm going to keep up the fake boyfriend bullshit, I need to appear like I don't care.

"That's wonderful. I hope it's a *really* expensive one. You should ask him for two. Horses want a friend."

She giggles. "I hope it's white and has long hair and loves to go for rides and maybe can fit in my tree house!"

Connor comes up from behind her and rests a hand on her shoulder. "We're going to talk about the pony."

Hadley looks up at him from over her shoulder, lip jutted out while batting her eyelashes. "But, Daddy, I really want it."

Oh, he's so fucked, and she called him daddy.

Tears fill my eyes. "Give her the damn pony, Connor."

He smiles at me. We both know he's never going to deny her a thing.

Then Ellie comes out of the kitchen holding the cake. "No

pony. Not now, at least."

He winks at Hadley.

"Okay, Mommy. Not *now*." The girl knows what she's doing.

"Can I help with anything?" I ask loudly, making my way to Ellie. I need to keep moving and avoid him like the plague.

Ellie shakes her head. "An hour ago, sure, but now, we're good."

I glare at her as she smirks.

"Is your boyfriend coming, Syd?" Declan's voice causes my stomach to drop.

Connor and Ellie look to me, and I shake my head with a soft smile. "No, he's working today."

Ellie watches me, eyes saying what her voice doesn't: *We're so going to talk about this.*

However, my favorite kid who ever lived jumps up when she sees the cake. "Time for cake!"

And I'm saved from having to expand on my stupid lie.

three

"Stupid girl!" I grab another handful of wildflowers and throw them into the pond. "Stupid heart. Stupid, stupid, stupid!"

I knew that party would be hard, but I didn't think it would almost kill me.

The entire time, I tried to avoid his gaze. I talked to everyone but him, and now, I'm so frustrated and keyed up that I can't sleep, which brought me back to this place.

My mother moved off the farm two years ago. My sister got married, had kids, and moved three hours west of Sugarloaf to a new farm. This land has been in my mother's family for over a hundred years, and I love this place so couldn't let her sell it, so I ended up taking it over. Well, I sort of took over.

We've had the same staff since I was a kid, and they'll probably stay on board until they die. They run it even though my name is on the deed.

"What are you doing out here, Bean?" Jimmy, the foreman

and my godfather, asks.

"Thinking."

"About the Arrowood boy I'm guessing since I ain't seen that look in a long time."

I turn with a sad smile. "He's back."

"I heard rumors he would be, but thought there was still time."

Yeah, we all knew, but it doesn't make it easier. It's like when a hurricane forms off the coast. Everyone stands by the television, watching it build and move. Predictions come in, and all anyone can do is wait and pray it doesn't hit. Then the turn comes and … *bam.*

I'm in the eye.

"Yeah, a few weeks. But, it's no big deal. I really don't care when he comes back since I don't plan to see much of him."

He lets out a low chuckle. "Sure, so now you're lying to yourself?"

I roll my eyes. "It's better than admitting the truth."

"Maybe so, Sydneybeans, but you're much smarter than that. Lies like that never end well. It's better to cut the head off the snake now."

The imagery of that makes me laugh. "I thought, by now, it wouldn't bother me so much. I figured that I would be over him or that being close to him wouldn't make me want to throw myself into his arms and beg him to love me again."

He rests his hand on my shoulder and squeezes gently. "Only way to get over it is to finally deal with it. Go on to bed and rest. You'll think better in the morning. He's a fool if he doesn't see the treasure you are."

Jimmy is like a father to me. He's been here each day since I was a little girl, and when my father took off fifteen years ago, Jimmy was who gave me paternal advice. When my father never came back, called, wrote, or sent smoke signals, it was Jimmy who made it hurt just a little less.

Although, no amount of love from him could save me from the pain I went through when I lost Declan.

"I wish I could say that any man felt that way, but they always leave."

Jimmy shakes his head. "Not all, Bean."

"You're paid to love me," I joke.

"Not nearly enough considering the trouble you get into. I seem to remember covering tread marks in the snow a few times when you snuck out."

I smile, recalling that night. It was impossible to resist going to see Declan. At night, when I felt alone, it was his warmth I craved. I would cry, wishing my dad would come back and love me, while Dec held me close.

And then there were other times I simply wanted to make out with my very hot boyfriend. Still, Jimmy kept my secrets from my mother and then scolded me later.

"I'm not a little girl anymore, and you're still here."

He chuckles. "Now it seems I can't imagine being any-where else. Go on back to the house and sleep."

My hand covers his and I nod. "I'll head in soon."

Jimmy knows better than to push. He pulls back, and I'm alone again. Maybe he's right. I need to face Declan and be honest with him and myself. He broke me, and I'm not doing myself any favors by pretending otherwise.

I sit on the cool grass as the sun starts to come up over the tree line. Time passes as I watch the sky become painted in warm pinks and reds as the blues and blacks fade away and I let the new day wash over me. I can do this.

I'm smart, and I've gone places in my life too. For a small-town lawyer, I'm accomplished, and I help people. This farm helps people, and I do it all on my own.

"I am a treasure. I'm a good woman who loves you still. If you don't see that, then screw you, Declan Arrowood!"

"Well, I'm sure we could arrange that," he says from behind me.

No, no, no this isn't happening.

I get to my feet, needing the height even though he towers over me. He has always been so tall and strong. It was what I loved. I was precious to him, and he always did what he could to make sure I knew it.

"It wasn't an offer."

He grins. "I know. I'm just trying to make light of it. Can we talk?"

All the bravado I had about being honest is gone. "I can't. I have to get to work."

"Just a few minutes, Syd. I know I don't deserve it, but I'd like to talk. We have a lot of time coming up that we'll have to be around each other, and I'd like us to be civil."

Like that's ever going to happen.

"I don't know that we'll manage that."

"Maybe not, but we can at least try."

I release a heavy sigh. "Maybe."

"I really did miss you," he says, and a part of my cold heart thaws. "I know you're worth everything, and ..."

"And you let me go."

His eyes close and then he clenches his fist. "It wasn't what you thought."

"It was exactly what I thought. You were done with me, and you threw me away! Just like my father did! You were exactly like him, Declan!"

"No! It was nothing like your father!" I see the devastation in his eyes and turn away.

It is the same thing. When he was through with me, he tossed me aside. "You say that, but you did exactly what you promised not to. You left without ever coming back."

"I needed to!"

"Why? Why did you need to?"

I find myself inching closer to him as my anger grows.

"It doesn't matter now."

God, that's where he's wrong. "It matters to me. Do you understand I've spent years trying to understand it? There are no answers. No clues as to why. Just one day, you show up and decide we're over."

He shakes his head, seeming to grapple with whatever is on his mind. "I did what I had to."

"What you had to? What the hell does that mean?" I yell and shove at his chest, but he steps with me, as though we're two magnets being pulled.

Declan's hand grips my wrist, thumb stroking tenderly over my rapid pulse. His voice is soft, but there's a strain in the syllables as his eyes bore into mine. "I couldn't hurt you again. I couldn't ... I had to stay away. But now ... now, I can't."

"Now you have to," I remind him.

"Tell me you don't feel this, Bean."

I close my eyes, knowing that I can't see him when I lie. "I feel nothing."

"Do you know what I feel?"

I still won't look at him, but I'm not resisting as much as I should considering I still haven't pulled my arm back.

He speaks quietly in the cool air as we stand at our pond, the place where everything began for us. "I feel like my heart is going to burst from beating so hard. I feel as though every nerve that has been dormant for years is awake. I feel the warmth of your breath, the way your pulse is quickening now, and God, Sydney, I know I should stay away from you, but …"

My eyes open, and those piercing green eyes stare back at me. I know what's coming. He's giving me an out, but I'm unable to take it. His arms wrap around me, and then Declan kisses me.

His kiss feels like home. It's as though every old memory is passing between our breaths, full of hope and forgiveness.

Every piece of anger and frustration I had is gone. I can't remember why I hate him. I can't think of anything but how for eight, long years I've wanted this.

Declan's hands cradle my face, tilting my head to get the right angle. Each brush of his tongue against mine wipes away another piece of the hurt. I'm a fool, I know this. Even in the back of my mind, I hear the little voice telling me to stop him, but I silence it.

I've needed to touch him and have him. He's the only man I've ever made love to.

It's been so long—far too long, and God, right now, I want him more than self-preservation.

He moves his hands down to my neck and then my shoulders, pulling me closer to his chest. My fingers grip his shirt, refusing to relax even an inch. I won't let him go this time. I can't.

I wasn't lying when I told Ellie that I've dreamed and hoped he and I would find a way to have each other again. And if this is all I'll ever get, I won't waste it. I kiss him back, pouring every emotion I've felt since the day he left into the kiss.

"Declan," I say as I slide my hands around to his back. He is solid and sure. I need this. "Please."

"Don't beg, Syd. I can't …"

Our foreheads touch as we struggle for breath. "I'm not begging, just asking."

His beautiful green eyes find mine, searching for something. "What are you asking for?"

I know better than to ask for his heart, and I'm smart enough to know that this … this will never work. We're too broken and too much time has gone by. I may always love Declan, but I can never trust him not to hurt me.

I think about what it is I need—goodbye.

"Love me for right now so we can finally let go."

I consider myself a smart woman. I usually make good choices and follow a set of morals that my mother worked very hard to instill in me.

Right now, I'm the dumbest girl who ever lived. Here I am, on the grass by this stupid pond with our discarded clothes as a blanket, and I'm naked—with Declan.

The only other possible excuse is that I'm in a second dimension and this isn't really happening.

Yes, that must be it because there's really no other reason to explain why Declan is on top of me, struggling to catch his breath after we had sex.

God, I had sex with Declan.

What the hell is wrong with me? What was I thinking?

I wasn't thinking, that's for damn sure. I convinced myself this was, what? Goodbye sex? Some weird version of closure and not because I'm lonely and miss his stupid ass? I know better than this.

Maybe this is a dream? A really vivid one, but maybe I didn't do this …

I lift my fingers and pinch him. "Ouch! What was that for?"

Yup, he's real, and this really happened. "Checking if this was a dream."

He looks down at me. "It was real."

I shove him, and he accommodates me by moving to the side. "Great."

This was a mistake, and I need to get out of here. I grab my shirt, which is cold from being on the ground, and pull it back on before turning to look for my pants.

"Syd." His voice slides over my name.

"It's fine. We're fine. It'll be fine. As soon as I find my pants." Seriously, did they disintegrate when he touched them? I get to my feet and start to look around, hating the tears that burn in the backs of my eyes.

I'm so angry that all it took was one kiss for me to lose my mind completely and conjure all kinds of excuses as to why this was okay. He's never going to stay in Sugarloaf, and I'm sure as hell never leaving. Not that he's offering anything anyway.

Jesus, get it together, Syd.

"I came here to talk … I don't know how we …"

I turn quickly, my hair fanning out and then slapping me in the face. "How we what? Ended up naked and screwing like teenagers in the freaking wide open?"

He runs his hand down his face, looking disheveled and irresistible. "I was going to say ended up here, but that's fine too."

I glare at him and then go back to my task.

My hands are shaking, and I refuse to think about what any of it means or what the hell I did. I have to work today. Plus, I wanted closure, so I'm going to take this as my opportunity to slam the proverbial door and leave.

"It's not like we haven't done this many times here at the pond before. It always worked when we were teenagers."

"You know what doesn't work? No pants!" I yell as my emotions boil over. "I need to get out of here and call a shrink because I'm clearly having a mental breakdown."

"Because ..."

I turn, glaring at him. "Because I'm smart. Because I don't do this. Because I ..."

"You have a boyfriend."

Great. I forgot about that. I cheated on my fictional boyfriend. "I have that too, but mostly, I have regret."

Hurt flashes in Declan's eyes. "We need to talk about what just happened."

I shake my head. "No, I need to go, and you need to let me."

Declan leans down, grabs something, and then sits back up. "Here," he says, holding my aforementioned missing pants out to me.

I take them and pull them on, neither of us say a word. What can be said anyway? We both made a huge mistake.

He dresses, and we both stand here, looking at one another.

"I know you said you didn't want to talk, but hopefully, you'll listen. I didn't come looking for you to end up like that. I came because I didn't want us to be enemies and hoped that maybe we could find some common ground. I was young, and I know I hurt you."

"You destroyed me," I correct him.

"I was stupid."

I will myself not to cry. I won't give myself over to the flurry of emotions that are swirling inside. Yes, there's anger, but more than anything, there's hurt. I'm in pain because looking at him, touching him, and hearing his voice has brought it all back again.

When he was inside me, I felt whole.

A missing piece of me was found and back in place. And that is the biggest lie I can ever allow myself to feel.

He isn't going to stay or put me back together. He'll leave.

"Are you going to stay in Sugarloaf?" I ask, already knowing the answer.

"Now?"

I laugh once and roll my eyes. "Don't be stupid, Dec. I mean after your six-month sentence. Are you going to come back home, fall back in love with me, and stay?"

He's silent.

"No. You're not." I don't need him to say the words. It's written all over his face. "You'll go back to New York, once again leaving me wishing I were worth more to you."

"Sydney, stop."

"No. I'm not going to stop. I'm never going to stop wishing you were still the man I fell in love with when I was a little girl."

Declan steps forward, his hand gripping the back of his neck. "Why does it have to be so complicated?"

I feel the moisture building in my eyes, but I hold it back. I need to say this so I can walk away from him with my head held high. "Because you promised a ten-year-old little girl that you would love her until the day she died. At thirteen, you gave that girl a ring you made out of a spoon and promised her that you'd replace it with a diamond. Then, at sixteen, you held her in your arms, kissing her as though she was the sole reason for your existence, and she gave herself to you. Do you remember that? Do you remember how we snuck out to the barn with candles, blankets, and made promises?"

His green eyes are intense and unwavering. "I remember it all."

"Then you must remember when you broke that promise, right? Did it slip your memory that you came to that same girl who would've done anything for you and told her that you were over trying to force yourself to make this work? You want to know why it's *complicated*, Declan? Because you fucking ruined that girl."

And then, just like the scene so many years ago, I turn my back on him and walk away, leaving the remains of my shredded heart at his feet.

four

Two Months Later

This is the moment of truth. I walk into the bathroom where my pregnancy test sits on the counter. Ellie and I are both late and … I don't know … I'm hoping I can find out I'm not pregnant and then suddenly start bleeding tonight.

I pull in a deep breath and walk over to my test. "No matter what, it'll be fine," I whisper.

My hand trembles as I reach for the innocuous little white test, and I lift it.

No.

No. This isn't … it can't be.

I can't be … pregnant.

Oh, God. I'm pregnant.

The breath whooshes from my chest as I drop onto the toilet seat. This isn't possible, right? I can't be pregnant. It was the one time. Just one time with Declan at the pond.

Tears prick my eyes as I stare down at it.

Maybe I grabbed the wrong test. Maybe Ellie switched them accidentally. Yes, that has to be what happened.

I reach for the other test on the far side of the counter. It's positive too.

Ellie is going to have a baby … and so am I.

I hear Connor's deep voice outside the bathroom, and I push down the nausea that bubbles up. I can't do this right now. I can't face Connor, or any of the Arrowood brothers, for that matter. I need to get out of here, go home, and think.

I'm going to have a baby.

Declan's baby.

A child that is ... ours.

My mind can't seem to think in more than six-word increments.

I will myself to grab my test, slip it into my back pocket, and count to five. After that, I will walk out of here and keep myself together.

When I push open the door, Ellie and Connor turn to me. I try to smile softly because my best friend is going to have a baby with the man she loves. There is joy there.

I see the questions in her eyes, and I shake my head, not sure if she'll interpret that as a, no, I'm not pregnant or, no, I can't talk about it. Either way, she and Connor deserve this moment. I hand her the test she took and kiss her cheek.

My eyes meet Connors, and I grin at the unmistakable look of fear in his eyes. He's a good man, and he loves Ellie. I'm happy that out of the two of us, one will be happy. "I'll see you guys tomorrow. I need to go."

"Syd?" Ellie calls my name.

The tears I've been fighting to hold back are pooling. If I speak, I'll surely break down. Instead, I touch her arm, squeeze just a bit, walk outside, and then drive away.

Only, I don't get any farther than the end of their driveway before I have to pull over. I lean my head back against the headrest, feeling alone and scared and completely confused, and breathe through my nose.

Okay, I can do this. I have a good life, money, a great job, and I'm going to take another ten pregnancy tests so I can prove this one is faulty and I'm late because I have a tumor.

I let out a soft chuckle.

It's a sad day when I'm wishing I had a tumor instead of being pregnant, but that isn't what I really want.

The truth really slaps me in the face. I want this baby. I have spent my entire life wanting to have a family with Declan. I've dreamed of it, imagined a daughter with blonde hair and those green Arrowood eyes. The little boy with his mischievous smile and my brains.

It has been my fantasy for so long.

I just didn't want this baby this way.

My hand falls to my belly, and I rest it there. "You can't be real," I whisper. "I may want you, but I can't have you."

I can't have a baby with Declan when he'll never want it. He isn't going to stay in Sugarloaf. He's planning to get back to his fancy life in New York at the earliest possible second. He knows I know that, which makes me wonder if he'll think I planned this.

Not that I asked him to come to my pond and fuck me senseless, but still, I didn't stop him.

God, I *begged* him. I actually begged.

My hand hits my forehead, and I groan.

I need a plan.

I drive home and find Jimmy waiting by the barn, arms crossed over his chest and the cowboy hat he's had since I was six on his head. I push down all the crap floating in my head because Jimmy has this weird way of seeing inside my mind. Right now, I don't need anyone knowing what I'm thinking.

"Hey, Jimmy."

"Bean." He dips his head. "Have a good day?"

I force a smile onto my lips. "It was ... enlightening."

I'm not lying, but I'm not elaborating either.

"Same here. We lost another farmhand today."

I release a heavy sigh. It's nothing new, but it's irritating nonetheless. I don't have time between my job and volunteering with the fire department as an EMT to manage the farm. That's what Jimmy does.

However, when I took over, I knew I would need to have some involvement, and since I'm pretty good at reading people, the hiring and firing became my thing.

"Who was it?"

"The new guy."

I laugh without humor. "They're all the new guy to you."

We have thirteen employees on the farm, and even though some have been here for twenty years, to Jimmy, it doesn't matter.

I'm pretty sure he came with the farm a hundred years ago.

"Well, he was the one you hired as the project manager to oversee the repair of the dairy buildings. He was supposed to be the best in the business, not that I don't have fifty-plus years."

This guy came from another farm and was able to increase the milk production by tenfold. We needed that knowledge. He was overseeing much more than Jimmy knew. Damn it.

"All right. I'll take care of it." Not that I have a clue as to what I'm doing at all. I feel as though I'm falling apart and have no idea how to stop it.

I head inside, looking at my childhood home with new eyes. Could I stay here and raise a baby? There is so much to unpack in my mind that I don't know where to start. My life isn't built for kids. I work a lot and the rest of the time I'm volunteering.

However, I don't have much choice in the matter. I'm having a child, and I'm going to have to do whatever I need to.

My phone pings with a text. I know who it is already because I left Ellie without giving her an answer.

And how could I? Her reaction to finding out that she's having a baby is the opposite of mine, so she would have ended up feeling guilty for being happy, or upset that I didn't share her joy.

Ellie: Hey, you okay?

Me: I'm great.

Ellie: You know I'm dying here. Are you pregnant?

And now I'm going to lie to my best friend.

Me: No. It's all good.

Ellie: Oh, thank god! I know you didn't want that, and it would have definitely put a kink in your plans to avoid all things Declan.

She can say that again.

Me: For real. I'm happy for you though! A baby! How is Connor?

Maybe if I can turn the conversation to her and Connor, we can forget about me. Focusing on anything other than my current problems is preferable.

Ellie: He's beside himself. Call me tomorrow?

Me: You got it.

Not that I have a clue what I'll say tomorrow.

five

"A tiny house? You? That's rich." Milo Huxley laughs as he grabs his scotch.

"I don't have much of a choice. Not all of us find the woman of our dreams, marry her, get the job we want, and get to live in luxury."

He raises his glass and nods. "That might be so, but you're forgetting the part where I lost the job, moved back to London without the girl, and have a wanker for a brother who made me an assistant for quite a while."

"I've got three of those," I toss back. "And I'm moving back to the town where I have to try to avoid the girl."

It's been two months, and I can't get her out of my head. I've dreamed of her, woke with the memory of how she felt in my arms again, and would swear I could smell her perfume at times. All of it torturing me more than ever before.

When I left her, I knew I would never be the same, but when I went back, I had no idea it would be worse than when we were kids.

"Well, I don't envy you, that's for sure."

I ignore Milo and drain the remnants of my drink. "Why did you want to meet up? Just to remind me of all the shit I'm going to have to deal with?"

Milo was one of the first investors I acquired when I branched out on my own, and he has been with me for six years. Now, he's more of a friend than anything. The two of us have been through highs and lows and always had each other's backs.

"Because I'm only in New York on holiday for a few more days, and I figured you missed me. Plus, I knew you were going back to that dreary small town where you're likely to go out of your mind with loneliness and boredom."

Sydney's face flashes in my mind, and I know I won't be bored. But I will be lonely, that much is true.

"I'll be fine."

He chuckles. "You're a bloody fool."

"Maybe so."

"You really think you can be around the woman you've lusted after for the last decade and not fuck it up?"

I regret telling him about Sydney. "I'll be fine," I say again.

He leans back in his chair and grins. "Do you remember what you said when I met Danielle?"

Milo met his wife when he was trying to get her job—his job. He couldn't resist her. I knew the first time he told me about her that he was completely fucked.

"Yes."

"Don't be so chuffed about it. All men have a weakness, and it's usually a woman. Lord knows mine always was."

I close my eyes, lean my head back, and mentally slap myself for agreeing to this. Milo knows me too well, and I'm not going to get out of this dinner without listening to more of his shit.

"We're not all you, Milo."

"Thank God for that." He lifts his glass. "My wife can barely handle one of me, imagine a world full of good-looking, smart, funny, and spectacularly fantastic lovers running around. It would be interesting, that's for sure."

"And don't forget to add how humble you are."

He smirks. "That is not one of my traits. But, we're not talking about me since I happen to have my life in order. It's you who is a fucking mess."

He has no idea. "I had sex with her," I blurt out.

Milo chokes on his drink and then slowly lowers the glass. "In your dreams?"

Might as well get this out now. I could tell my brothers, but they'll probably side with her like they always did. Sydney made everyone's life better. She was the sunshine in our darkest days. We had shelter when we were near her, and we craved it.

After my mother died, she sort of stepped into that role as I stepped into being the patriarch of the family. Dad was too busy drinking himself stupid to care about my brothers, so I did. At eleven years old I learned how to do it all. I made lunches, helped with homework, and beat up anyone who picked on them.

As we got older and became a real couple, she was always there to help. Sydney would bake them birthday cakes and would bring soup if they were sick.

She was my world.

She was my heart and soul and I let her go.

Now, I've fucked up again.

"No, when I went for my niece's birthday. I saw her at the pond we used to meet at, and … I don't know, I had to kiss her."

"And then you managed to what? Slip your cock in at the same time?"

I release a heavy sigh from my nose. "I don't need your shit."

"I think you do. For years, you have been telling me about Sydney and how you walked away from her to save her. How you can't imagine how it ever would've worked. Then you went on to say that you were done and you moved on, married your work, and never gave her another thought. I'd say you're either a liar or a bastard."

"I'm both."

I'm a liar because I never moved on from her. How could I? My losing her wasn't how it was meant to be. That future was taken from me, ripped out of my hands without any warning.

Now, I've tasted her again, and I crave more.

I'm a bastard because I'll still walk away in six months without a pause.

Milo nods and then twirls the liquid in his glass. "I don't judge you, you know? I was no better chasing after a woman I didn't deserve."

"And you do now?"

He laughs, gets to his feet, and slaps me on the back. "Not in the slightest. My wife is a million times better than I am. I'm just not stupid enough to let her go. Speaking of her, I have to get back to the hotel. Think about what I said and figure out if you're going to continue being a bloody idiot or finally get your head out of your arse."

Milo walks out of the bar, leaving me alone with a half-drunken bottle of scotch. My head is a mess, and it has been since she walked away from me that morning. If he only knew the truth about why I gave her up all those years ago, he'd understand.

The only difference between then and now is that there isn't a big secret any longer. The truth was exposed, and I could tell Sydney, and I would if I thought it would matter.

But then I wonder how I could really confess it.

I still grapple with the guilt of it all. If she knew maybe we could be friends again. Maybe she would see that my leaving was for her.

Why couldn't I tell Sydney and let the chips fall?

Before I go too far into that line of thinking, I remember why I won't ever pick up the chips to begin with. Because it isn't just about me. There are three other people who also hold the secret. If Sydney knew, would she forgive me? Would she accept that we did what we thought was right?

No, she will never understand the choice I made. She would've stayed on the side of the road that night, consequences be damned. She wouldn't have run, hid the truth, and then cut all ties with anyone who mattered to her.

No, that was me, and the path I took eight years ago hasn't changed that.

I'm driving on Route 80, passing the smaller towns in New Jersey as I make my way to Pennsylvania. I already hate every goddamn second of this. I'm going to miss New York City. The city has embedded itself inside of me. Each day, I became less country, and it gave me my true feeling of home. The smells of pretzels and trash, the sounds of horns honking, people yelling, and trains passing by are normal and what filled me when I was empty.

Now, I'm leaving it, and it feels ... weird.

Six months is all I have to endure, and then I can go back to where I feel at ease.

My phone rings, and I swipe the button over to answer Connor's call. "Hello, Jackass," I say with a smirk.

"Nice greeting."

"What can I say? I call it like I see it."

He snorts. "What time are you coming in? Your ... trailer-house-thing is all set up."

I regret making that offer more than I can say. However, last thing I want is to be stuck in that fucking house with my brother and his family. I don't need a daily reminder of what I could've had. I do enough self-loathing in my sleep. Still, now I'm in this "luxury tiny house," which I know I'm going to want to burn to the ground after a week.

"Did you go inside?"

"Of course I did. Now Hadley wants one, thanks for that."

I grin. "You should get the girl whatever she wants."

"Right, because even if I say no, it's not like her uncles won't go behind my back."

"Please, we all have years to make up for, and it's not like the three of us are in a hurry to start a family."

Connor snorts. "Yeah, you'd need to find a girl willing to put up with your shit." Then he drops his voice to a near whisper. "Or forgive you for being a total fucking prick."

"What was that?"

"Nothing, brother, just can't wait to see you."

"And I can't wait to undermine your authority."

His daughter owns him, and I love that my brother has found a way through his hell, and while Jacob begrudges him a little, I don't. Connor has struggled with the way our lives went more than anyone. He had my mother the least amount of time, and I've always wished it could've been different for him.

"Well, don't think she forgot about the pony you promised her."

"I didn't forget. Sean is working on that with the guys in Tennessee. Apparently, his buddy Zach owns a horse ranch and has some ponies coming. Don't worry, Hadley will have what I promised."

I won't break my word to that girl.

She's the closest thing I'll ever have to a child.

Connor clears his throat. "Why don't you come for dinner tonight? Ellie is cooking, and she cleaned the spare room in case you look at that ... living thing ... and decide you'd rather stay in the house."

There is no chance of that. "I'll be fine."

"I don't care if you're fine or not, she does."

I snort. "Asshat."

"Whatever. Just come for dinner. Make Ellie and Hadley happy."

"I knew you missed me." I look down at the GPS and see I still have another hour in the trip. "What time is dinner?"

"In about an hour and a half. Just get here, we'll wait for you."

I release a deep sigh because there's no point in fighting it. Ellie will marry my brother someday, which means she's already family. I owe her more than I can ever repay, so if she wants her annoying-as-hell new brothers-in-law around, then who are we to begrudge her that?

"All right. I'll see you soon."

The rest of the drive is peaceful. I spend the hour watching the towns drift by, remembering all too well how it felt when I left and the promises I made as I did. It's different driving *into* Sugarloaf.

It feels like prison.

When I get to the entrance of the driveway, I stop. I'm, once again, lost to a time when life was easy, people were alive, and secrets weren't an issue.

"Why doesn't Jacob have to answer?" I whine as I punch my brother in the arm.

My mother turns in her seat, eyes narrowed and lips pursed. "Because your brother knows how to behave in public. Do you want to sit here all day?"

"No, ma'am."

"Then answer the question before the frozen food defrosts."

I'm smart enough to know that means I'll have to go back to the grocery store with her, and I hate food shopping. Hate. It's stupid and annoying and Jacob got candy because he didn't get caught when he hit me. But I did, and now I'm stuck in the back seat with my stupid brother as he eats his Hershey bar.

Jacob turns to me, chocolate on his lips as he smirks. "What's one truth about an arrow?"

That it could pierce your heart.

I don't say that. "A true second shot will split the first arrow and create a solid path," I say without thinking about it.

I've said this same phrase a million times.

Mom grins. "Yes, and why is that important?"

Same follow up. Different day.

"Because I usually screw up the first time and need the second shot."

She leans over and touches my hand. "My darling, that's life. We often don't know the right path and wander the wrong way, but if you're smart and focus, you can always correct your path."

What I wouldn't give for that to be true. I've taken too many wrong turns, and I'm not sure there are enough arrows in the world to create the right path.

I drive up the long pathway, and the white farmhouse, which is freshly painted and glowing with the warm light inside, comes into view.

Once I stop the car, I see a silhouette standing in the open doorway, and it isn't my brother or Ellie.

Fuck. I'm never going to survive this.

six

I'm going to murder my best friend. She lured me over for dinner, saying she wanted to talk. Despite the fact that all I wanted to do was stay curled up in my bed, crying about the current status of my life, I came. Then I come to find out that it's some kind of family dinner and Declan was fucking coming.

Of course, she doesn't relay this piece of information until his car is turning into the driveway and it's too late for me to escape.

He parks close enough to the house that I can see him in the driver's seat, but he doesn't move to get out, as if he's waiting for something.

"Is Declan here?" Ellie's sweet voice asks from behind me.

"Yes."

"Are you going out there?"

I turn to her with lips pursed. "Whatever you're up to, I

don't like it."

Her hands rise in mock surrender. "I'm not up to anything. All I'm doing is forcing the two of you to deal with your crap. He's going to be my brother-in-law, and you're my best friend. You guys need to find a way to at least be nice to each other."

I roll my eyes. "I love you, Ells, but I'm going to have to kill you."

"I'll take my chances. You couldn't hurt a fly."

"I'm going to go out there first," I say, not wanting to continue this.

I'm not ready to tell him about the baby or anything really. I still don't know what I'm going to do, and while this is his baby, it isn't his life that'll be completely changed. I want to go to the doctor first, make sure everything is okay, and then decide on a plan before I tell him.

I don't know what my plan is yet, but I do know that it won't include him.

Not because I don't love him but because he doesn't love me, and I won't let myself be broken again.

"You know, the sad thing is that you're both nervous about being around the other. I don't know why you're fighting it."

I glare at her. "You can't imagine the level of hurt he's caused me. He loved me and walked away. He was supposed to be the one person who would never leave me. There isn't a memory in my childhood that doesn't star one of these Arrowood brothers and then ... one day ... they were gone. Like. That"—I snap my fingers—"I lost my family, my heart, and my future. I'm fighting because, if I allow even an inch of hope, it'll run away, and I'll be lost."

Ellie bites her lower lip, her hands wringing as she nods. "I understand."

Damn it. I shouldn't snap at her. She means well, even if she isn't helping. I've only told her bits and pieces because the whole thing is too much to handle.

I want the two of us to possibly be amicable so we can untangle this mess we're both in, if that's even possible. Ellie is being a good friend, and I should be thanking her, not biting her head off.

"I'm sorry for being such a bitch."

She steps forward quickly. "You're not. No, I'm being an idiot and not realizing that just because Connor and I found a way, that doesn't mean you can as well. I'm the one who owes you an apology."

I look back out the screen door to find him still sitting there. "Let me go and make peace. I know you guys have a big announcement tonight, and I don't want you to worry about my and Declan's fucked-up past."

Before she can say anything, I push the door open and make my way down the steps as he's exiting his car.

"Syd."

"Dec."

"I didn't know you'd be here." He runs his hands through his hair.

I give him a soft smile. "I didn't know you'd be here either. We were apparently kept in the dark."

He glares up at the window and I follow his gaze to find Connor there with a grin. Asshole.

"About the last time I was here," Declan says, but I'm already shaking my head.

"Not now. Not here either. There's a lot to say, but this isn't the time."

Declan nods once. "All right."

Regardless of my feelings for Declan, we're going to have a child. I can blame him, hate him, and all that, but that isn't the life I want for my child. I grew up unwanted by my father. I watched him walk away, saying things that no child should hear her father say about her mother. My father hated my mother, and since my sister and I were part of her, he hated us by default. I will do whatever I can to protect a child from feeling that level of pain and that means that Declan and I have to figure out a way to get along.

"I didn't want for us to see each other for the first time since that night to be in front of them, so I came out here."

He releases a heavy sigh. "We have a lot of history, and I want to say that I'm sorry about what happened between us a couple of months ago."

My eyes lift, studying his. "What about it?"

"That I hurt you again," Declan says quickly. "I should never have come to you when I had no intention of staying after my time was up. I should've ... fuck, I don't know. I never should've let things go so far. I'm sorry."

He has no idea how far things are. "And what now?"

"What do you mean?"

I steel myself, knowing what the answer will be and hating myself for asking it again, but time might have changed things. God knows my life has changed since taking that test. "Is there any chance you'll stay in Sugarloaf?"

"No. I will never stay here."

"Not for anything?"

I'm not being fair. He doesn't know all the reasons behind why I'm asking.

Declan's jaw tightens, and he shakes his head. "There's nothing that could hold me here. This town ... it's filled with things I can't be near."

Things like me.

"Maybe one day you'll change your mind," I say and then turn.

"Syd."

I shake my head, spinning back to face him. "Don't. I'm not asking for it to be me. I'm really not. What happened a couple of months ago was meant to be a goodbye. I know where you stand, and you know where I stand."

I also know that the next six months will prove a lot.

"You two going to make out?" Connor calls from the top of the porch.

"Keep it up, and you'll have a house full of ducks," I warn.

His grin falls, and I mentally pat myself on the back. He's so easy to rattle. Connor is the only former SEAL I know who is afraid of a freaking farm animal, and I'm not afraid to use it.

"Let's not forget I know your fears too," he replies with mischief in his voice.

Declan and I climb the stairs, and the two of them embrace. "Good to see you, Duckie," Declan slaps his brother's shoulder.

"I already wish your six months were up."

"Me too."

"Me three," I tack on.

Connor laughs. "She's a pistol."

"Always has been." Declan's voice is smooth like whiskey as he stares at me.

I will not let it warm me. I fight the pull to put his lips to mine and take a slow, long sip until his fire burns through my veins. However, I know what happens when I play with fire ... I end up with a baby.

Dinner is … tense.

No matter how hard I try, I can't ignore the brooding man beside me. Ellie and Connor are sitting, hands held on the table, and my heart aches a little. That used to be Declan and me. We were the couple so deliriously in love that we were unable to resist touching each other.

Now, we're both sitting, ram-rod straight with our hands clasped in our own laps.

I smile at the right time and answer the questions that are asked, but I feel as though I have my hand on an electric wire, waiting for the first current to electrocute me.

Not even Hadley could lessen the tension. As soon as dinner was done, she begged her parents to let her go out to her tree mansion. I look over at the clock for the fortieth time and note it's only been two minutes since Hadley disappeared. It would be rude to leave before seven, which means I only have twenty-three more minutes of torture to endure.

Ellie wipes her mouth, not removing the grin from her lips as though she knows what I'm thinking. "Dessert will be in about a half hour," she says.

"I'd love some dessert," Declan states.

My eyes narrow at Ellie. "I don't know that I can stay."

"Really? Why not?" There is innocence in her voice, but I'm not buying it.

Because I'm going to be in jail for murder.

"I have a big case tomorrow," I lie.

Ellie's brows lift. "You do?"

I release a breath through my nose. "I do."

Connor's eyes move between us for a second, and then he decides to take the wheel of the bus currently backing over me. "You said you weren't in court until next week."

"I got an email saying they're moving it up." My tone is

curt, and I hope I injected enough warning.

"Interesting," Ellie adds before bringing her glass to her lips.

"Well, you know, I should actually get going now. Beat the traffic home and get a jump on things. I would hate for my client to be let down."

Connor's hand darts out, gripping my wrist. "Can you wait five minutes? Ellie and I wanted to talk to you both."

I already know what they're going to talk to us about and have no idea why I'm being forced to stay, but I nod and relax back into my seat. I may want to kick their asses right now, but my happiness for them doesn't overshadow that.

"What's wrong?" Declan's voice immediately turns into concern.

"Nothing," Connor says.

Ever the protector, Declan shifts forward, and his eyes bounce from Connor to Ellie. "Are you okay? Hadley?"

"We're fine, *Mom*." Connor rolls his eyes. "It's nothing bad. In fact, it's great news. We're getting married."

My smile is automatic and tears burn the backs of my eyes. I'm so happy for her. "Married? You're getting married? Seriously?"

Ellie nods, her own eyes brimming with moisture. "*And* we're pregnant."

"I knew that part, but I didn't know he proposed!" I scream and rush toward Ellie. My arms wrap around her as I hold on tight. Could this be any better for them? No, it can't.

Ellie is going to marry Connor, and it's all so damn perfect.

"When?" I ask as I pull back.

"Umm, we're thinking about two months from now. You know ... before I start showing."

I grin and nod. At least now I don't have to worry about

being the size of a house at the reception.

"Wow, that's soon and a lot of news," Declan says as he stands, pulling his brother toward him in an awkward hug.

"I hope you're happy for us." Connor's voice is firm.

"I'm so happy for you!" I say and then give Declan a look of warning. If he ruins this, I'll beat him with his own arms.

Dec smiles as he pats his shoulder. "Of course I am. My baby brother found a girl who is willing to put up with his stupid ass for the rest of his life."

I release a deep breath and hug Ellie again. I was worried about what he would say. While there is basically a year between each brother as they go down the line, he's always been older at heart and his heart has hardened since he left.

Years ago, Declan was easy with a smile and a laugh. It seems that time has made him less of the boy I knew and more of the man I no longer recognize.

He's always been strong but never with this armor that nothing other than an eight-year-old could penetrate, especially not me.

I was once the exception, now it's as though it's physically painful to look at me.

Ellie releases me and then Connor pulls her to his side. "I've been dying to tell you. But we also wanted you guys at dinner to ask if you'd stand up with us?"

I cover my mouth and nod as tears fall without hesitation. "I would be honored."

Connor and Declan share some weird brother hand clap, and then it's my turn to pounce on Connor.

"I'm so happy for you. So, so, happy it's not even normal," I tell him quietly.

"I am too, Syd. I didn't think I would ever find someone like Ellie. I still don't deserve her."

I smile, loving that he feels that way. Not because he doesn't deserve her, which is the furthest thing from the truth, but because it shows how much he wants to be good for her. "You deserve her, if for no other reason than because you don't believe you do. You've cherished Ellie, protected her, and been the man I've always known you to be, and that's why you both are perfect for each other."

He pulls back to assess me in a strange way. "You deserve happiness too. Even if you and Declan never get your heads out of your asses, you shouldn't give up on being happy."

"I know."

"Do you?"

The question makes my heart sink. "I think I do."

His gaze shifts to where his older brother is deep in conversation with Ellie. "You know, I never wanted to be alone for the rest of my life. I'd resigned myself to it, sure, but I had a different vision. I never knew a love like you and Dec had, and it was something that Jacob, Sean, and I were always jealous of. To meet the person who was your other half when you were just kids. But, Declan, he hardened himself when he walked away from you. He put up a wall so high I'm not sure anyone can scale it. He won't even entertain the idea of wanting what I have now." Connor's lips purse and then he shakes his head. "I'm just saying that some of us can't undo what we've done."

Declan may not want a family, but he isn't going to have a choice in about seven months.

"Good thing I have no intention of becoming a climber," I say, knowing I have rope and an axe, and am preparing to start my ascent, hoping I don't break when I fall.

seven

Married and a baby. Jesus, could he have at least waited a bit? I know he loves Ellie, and it's clear they're great for each other, but it seems so damn fast.

"You can wipe that look off your face," Connor says as he hands me a beer. "No one is asking you to follow in my footsteps."

I take the bottle and raise the neck to his. "Here's to that."

"What?"

"That I won't be following in your footsteps."

He chuckles once and then takes a long pull from the beer. After releasing a deep breath, he goes silent for a few moments. We sit on the porch of the house that holds such a fucking host of memories. Some good, some bad, some I would give anything to forget.

"You know we're nothing like him, right?"

The question causes me to sit straighter. "Who?"

"Dad. We're nothing like him. We're not cruel, heartless—well, you might be heartless, I've yet to figure that out."

"Funny."

Connor shrugs. "I'm just saying that the vow we all made was meant to protect not only us but also the women we might have loved and kids we may have fathered. I have never raised my fists in anger, not even if I drank too much. We are nothing like him."

He can't know that. He might be nothing like him, but I'm not so sure. I get angry. I've wanted to throw someone through a wall, and that scared me more than anything. I never did it, but I've seen rage.

"I'll never take the chance."

"So, you're going to spend the rest of your life alone and pissed off?"

"No," I say quickly. "I'll be rich, happy, uncomplicated, and still worrying about my three brothers and their shitty life choices."

I glance through the window, seeing Sydney and Ellie laughing about something, and my chest tightens. Why does seeing her hurt so fucking much? After all this time, I would've hoped to be over her, but then how do you really get over losing the only thing you ever wanted?

She's beautiful, even more so than she was when we were teenagers. Her hair falls in waves down to the middle of her back, and her blue eyes are even brighter than I remembered. I would give anything to go back in time and have her the way I used to.

Sydney was free in her love. She didn't hold back or make me work for it. She gave it away. I wasn't worthy of it, but God, I took all of it.

"She could forgive you, you know?" Connor says as he notices where my eyes landed.

"No."

"You could also forgive yourself, but we both know that's not going to happen."

"When did you become a fucking shrink?" I toss back at him, wanting to stop this conversation.

He laughs and then drains his beer. "You know, I know you're the older one and supposed to be wiser, but you're the dumb one."

I get to my feet, glaring at my younger brother. "Dumb? I'm dumb? I'm the one who saved your ass over and over again. I'm the one who doesn't have anything in the world I'm worried about losing."

"And you think that makes you better? I'll tell you, Dec, there's nothing in this life like having someone by your side and kids. Nothing. We're not the sins of our past, but we spent eight years living there."

He's unreal. He finds Ellie and suddenly thinks all of us can just go back to a life we were never meant to have? It isn't that easy. Eight years ago, I gave up everything for them. I walked away from Sydney to protect not only my brothers but also her.

I knew I could never stay here. I don't want a farm life or anything like this. Maybe if I hadn't spent time in New York, I could've found a way, but when I went to college, I changed. I saw the world was ripe with possibilities, ones that didn't have shit to do with cows and land. I found that I was smart and could run a business without anyone's fucking help.

I did it all.

There are too many nights I work late. Too many weeks where I'm inundated with fires I need to put out, and I never could have handled any of that if I were with her.

So, walking away from her was the hardest thing I ever did as well as the most selfless.

And I'd do it every time.

Loving her would only bring her pain, and I would cut my fucking arm off before I ever let that happen again.

"You act as though this is all so easy, Connor. Some of us made decisions that night that can't be undone."

"And I think Ellie and I understand that more than most."

I let my head fall back and stare at the night sky. He's right. God, everything has been such a mess, and I'm tired of it. "Do you remember when life was easy?"

"I remember when Mom was alive, but after that ..."

"It definitely wasn't easy."

It's sad to see how one instant can alter the trajectory of a life. I had plans, even at eleven years old. I was going to be just like my dad. I wanted to run this farm, live here and raise a family, have it all, just like my parents.

Then she died, and the dream disappeared.

"Being here, it's fucking horrible. I thought since I've been back a few times that it wouldn't be this hard."

Connor's hand rests on my shoulder. "I know it better than anyone. It isn't easy and you feel like you're crawling out of your skin."

"Does it get easier?" I ask him.

"Yes and no. Some days, I swear I can hear him yelling and can remember the feeling before his fist hit my face. Memories and nightmares lurk in every corner of this place."

I turn my head back to the house, seeing the girls and Hadley dancing around the living room. "But they were never the nightmare."

Connor looks over with a gentle smile. "No, they're the light that shines when you open your eyes and realize you're not in that hell anymore."

"The first time Dad ever hit me, I went to Syd's. She

brought me into her house, put ice on my eye, and gave me some milk with cookies. I remember thinking, this is the girl I want to marry." I laugh once. "I loved her more than anything and I still believe that leaving her was the right thing to do."

"But?" Connor asks.

"But being back here, seeing her, it's going to be agony."

Connor places his beer down and sighs deeply. "You being stubborn is what is agony. Tell her the truth, Dec. Let her know all the stupid shit and the hurt we went through. Don't lie to her anymore and stop pretending that you don't love her and want her."

Wanting her and having her are two totally different things. It's not just about the promise we made, it's about knowing that this isn't the right life for us. She needs someone who is whole and willing to give his heart without reservations and a man who will stay. That man is not me.

"I will never love anyone enough to want to marry them. I will never have the life you have, and there's nothing about it that makes me sad. I like being single. I like not having to worry about anyone or anything. The fucking idea of being strapped with some kid is enough to make me want to hurl myself off a cliff. I will never be a father, and I make damn sure of that because it's the last thing I want. So, I'm happy that it's your dream, brother, because it's my fucking nightmare."

I hear a gasp, and when I look at the door, Sydney is there, having heard every goddamn word of the lie I told.

eight

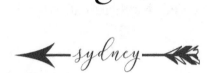

"Syd, wait," Declan says as I'm trying to make my way to the car.

"Why?"

There's no point. He made it abundantly clear that having a wife and kids was a nightmare to him. I'm not stupid enough to misunderstand that.

"The fucking idea of being strapped with some kid is enough to make me want to hurl myself off a cliff."

Well, the cliff is right there buddy, so get ready to jump.

"Because what I said came out wrong."

That pulls me up short. I turn, and he skids to a stop with apprehension clear in his beautiful green eyes. "What came out wrong?"

"The whole thing."

"So, you want to love someone enough to marry them? I mean … clearly, you didn't love me enough, and you let me know as much, but I'm just clarifying for the future women you may meet."

Declan sighs. "I'm never getting married."

"Okay," I say very matter-of-factly. "Did I misunderstand that you wanted kids then?"

"No."

One single word. One word that is so clear and unmistakable that it rocks me to my core.

"No wife. No kids. No Sugarloaf. What exactly am I misunderstanding?"

His hand grips the back of his neck, and he starts to pace. "It wasn't the words or the meaning, it was how it was said. I know you don't understand, but the shit I went through—"

"Absolutely not." I cut him off. "You are not going to use your past against me. I was there. I watched it all go down just as surely as I watched you leave. You came back to my house two months ago and, what? Couldn't help revisiting a woman who gave herself to you a million times? Because that's all I am, right? A memory of the hurt and pain you endured in this town?"

"You were never the hurt and pain."

I shake my head with a half laugh. "No, that was what I got as a consolation prize."

His jaw is set, and I can see him working through it all. I'm forever giving him lectures, but this is going to stop. He is never going to change, and I am always going to want more. How can we be civil? How can we find a middle ground when we're on opposite ends of the spectrum? It's only going to hurt us both and the baby that is going to come into this world.

God, the baby.

My heart aches, and I want to cry.

When did he stop being the kind, sweet guy who would talk about the life we were going to have, including children, and turn into this cynical bastard?

"Hurting you then and now is the last thing I want."

"Then maybe you should keep your mouth shut when I'm around—or, better yet, stay away from me, Declan. I can't handle more heartache."

With that, I get in my car, leaving him behind, and fighting back tears the entire way home.

"Why are you really here, Syd?" my sister, Sierra asks.

My nephews are running around, pretending to shoot each other, as I sit on the deck, staring out at the rolling hills, not even remembering the ride over.

"I needed to get away."

I needed to forget the man who is in the town that has been my home. It's been three days since that dinner, and I haven't seen him since, but I still feel him.

My heart is heavy, my chest is tight, and I have this urge to go to him, tell him everything, and pray we can at least be friends, but I know better. He doesn't want me, and he definitely doesn't want a child.

"Because Declan is there?"

She knows me too well. "It's hard being anywhere in his vicinity."

"I can imagine. If I had to be in the same town as Alex and not be his wife, I don't know if I could do it."

She and Alex are the poster children for the perfect marriage. They met in college, she made him work ridiculously hard to prove his worth, and they married once they were sure they could last. I would've married Declan at eighteen.

"He doesn't want me, just like every other guy." She takes my hand and then slaps me on the back of the head with her free one. "*Oww*, what the hell was that for?"

"For being an idiot. If you came here for me to coddle you and tell you how Dad was stupid and he really did love us and all that shit, then you have lost your mind. Declan isn't like every guy because none of them are the same. And he is nothing like the sperm donor."

Sierra is older than I am, and when our father left, it was different for her. Where I was crushed, feeling abandoned and unloved, she really didn't care. To her, Dad wasn't good enough for us. Any man who chose to leave could just move on. I didn't feel that way.

I resented my mother for pushing him away for a while. I thought that, if she didn't fight with him all the time, he would've stayed. I was young, stupid, and naïve.

Sierra, though, she never shed a tear over him leaving. Where I've cried enough to fill another pond.

"When did you join team Declan?"

"Never. I've been team anything. I know that you both were stupid and young. Yeah, it would've been great if things worked out, but you were kids!"

"We were in our twenties! I loved him, Sierra. I loved him, and I still fucking love him!"

"Mouth!" She hisses as she looks for the kids.

"Sorry."

She shifts in her seat and then squeezes my hand. "He left you, and it broke your heart, but look at what you've done with your life. You're smart, successful, and you run two businesses in that damn town."

I know she's right, but there's a part of me that is still hollow. It's like the old tree on our farm that's still standing. The outside trunk looks tall and secure, but the inside is empty.

Except for the life that's growing.

"I'm pregnant," I blurt out.

Sierra's jaw drops, eyes not blinking for a few seconds, and I wait. "You're pregnant?"

"Yup."

"But ... you don't even ... I mean ... are you dating someone?"

I shake my head and then look down at my feet. "No, it's Declan's."

I hear the air push from her lips. "Declan? Wow. Okay. How? When?"

Seems she can only manage one word at a time.

"When he came home a few months ago, we saw each other at the pond. It just ... happened."

"That fucking pond."

My eyes find my sister's, and I nod. "That pond."

"We should fill it in."

"Doesn't do much good now."

Sierra bobs her head slowly. "Did you tell him?"

And there's the crux of it all. "No, I saw him, heard him say some things, and left."

She leans back in her chair, looking a little less combative and a lot more sympathetic than before. "What did he say?"

Tears form in my eyes as I relay the conversation that I can't stop hearing in my head.

"I will never be a father, and I make damn sure of that because it's the last thing I want."

Only that isn't what happened. He didn't make sure of anything when we had sex. He didn't wear a condom, and apparently, the .01% chance of my birth control failing decided that was it's night.

"He might feel different once he knows," she offers after a few minutes of digesting what I said.

"I don't care if he does or doesn't. I won't ever let my kid know what it feels like to be unwanted and unloved."

"So you're not going to tell him?"

My head falls back, and I look at the ceiling. "I wish I could do that, but I can't. Not to mention, it'll be pretty hard to keep him from noticing my giant pregnant belly."

She laughs without humor. "No shit."

"You're the only person I've told."

She pulls her long brown hair back and then over her shoulder, the nervous gesture she's had since we were kids. Then she squares her shoulders a bit. "Okay, and then what is your plan?"

Sierra usually gives me the best advice and has always been the person I go to when things are just too much for me. She has a way of telling me the truth or forcing me to see it myself, which is what I need from her more than ever.

"I'm going to go to the doctor to verify the pregnancy, make sure everything is okay, and then I'll tell him."

"And after that?"

After that? Who the fuck knows. Maybe I'll have an epiphany, but at this point, I have no plan.

"I don't know."

"What do you want?"

My eyes fill with tears, and I hate the weakness they bring. What I want isn't even possible. I wanted to be married to Declan and for this to be the thing we'd always dreamed of. That isn't what this is, though.

Instead, I'm having a baby out of wedlock, with a man who doesn't want the baby or me, and that man believes I'm dating someone else.

Yeah, I'm a walking episode of Jerry Springer. Well, maybe not that dramatic, but I feel close enough.

My sister waits as I wipe at my cheeks, removing the errant beads of moisture that fell. "I want him to fight for me, which will never happen."

Sierra's lips form into a frown and then she sighs. "Then maybe you should finally leave him behind."

"And how exactly do I do that?"

"Maybe it's time to sell the farm and leave Sugarloaf like you almost did five years ago."

nine

I'm sitting in my car, staring at the tiny thing on this photo that is supposed to be a baby. It doesn't look like one, that's for sure, but the doctor assured me that it is, in fact, a baby. Or it will be once it makes its debut into the world.

I'm really pregnant, which has been confirmed by a medical professional, and I have his or her first version of a selfie in my hand.

In all my life, I never thought I'd be a single mother. I don't know why, but I figured since I don't really have sex that often that it wasn't something I had to worry about. Also, because I've been living my life in slow motion. I didn't see it until Sierra pointed it out, but now it's so clear to me that I've been waiting for Declan to return. Five years ago, a great law firm approached me and offered me a shot at making partner. It wasn't a sure thing, I would have had to earn it, but the opportunity was there. It would have meant more money, bigger cases, and the chance to make changes in a meaningful way. I turned it down.

I grappled with selling the farm and the memories it holds. I couldn't imagine leaving and going where he couldn't find me.

I was a fool.

But I'm not anymore. I don't have the luxury to be one now that I'm going to be someone's mother.

God help us all.

I grab my phone and call Ellie. While I have no plans to tell anyone other than Sierra that I'm pregnant, I miss my friend.

She answers on the first ring.

"Hey! How are you?"

"I'm fine. You?"

I hear rustling through the line. "I'm just grading papers and dealing with the insanity of building a house ... oh, and also planning a wedding."

"Don't forget you're also pregnant," I tack on for good measure.

"And then there's that."

"Are you having a big wedding?"

Ellie sighs. "No, just family and close friends. I wanted to elope, but Connor wants the ceremony, and he wants Hadley to be part of it all too."

Hadley has very clear ideas on what her parents' wedding should be like. That kid is the best thing that's ever happened in most of our lives. She's full of wit and love, and she has no problem dispensing either.

"She let me know a few weeks ago that she wants a big wedding in the castle that Connor should build her," I inform her. "Of course this was before you were even engaged, but the kid was making plans."

Ellie chuckles. "She also informed me that she will not be a flower girl because she's not a baby."

"Well, she is eight now."

"Going on thirty. Hey, what are you up to tonight?"

I go quiet. No way am I falling for another one of Ellie's attempts to force Declan and I together. "No."

"No?"

"No. I'm not going to meet you where your fiancé and his brother will happen to be, forcing us to be coupled up again. No."

Ellie lets out a loud gasp. "Me? I would never do that to you."

"Liar."

"Okay, maybe," she amends. "I only did that because we wanted to talk to you guys together. I'm sorry for forcing it. After what I heard he said, I promise I won't do it again."

And I believe her. Ellie is the kindest person I've ever met. She wouldn't deliberately hurt me.

"Thank you."

"Syd," she hesitates and then begins, "Did he … I mean … are you okay?"

No, I'm not, but I'm really good at pretending.

"Yeah, it was, but I'm fine. It's nothing I didn't already know, right?" I try to brush it off because, really, I can't talk to her about this.

Ellie is quiet for a second. "Okay, if you say so. I know this situation is a bit messy, but you're my best friend. If you want to talk, even about my soon-to-be brother-in-law, I'm always here for you. I won't betray your trust—not even to Connor."

I smile even though she can't see it. Ellie came into my life when I thought it was her who needed me, only it turned out that we needed each other.

I thought I had it all together, only it turns out that I've gotten really good at hiding my feelings and pain. Working, volunteering, running all kinds of town activities was my way of pretending everything was fine—I was fine.

But I wasn't. That much is clear considering it took him showing up just once to alter my entire life. Now it's time to face it and finally find some closure if it's at all possible. However, I won't drag Ellie into the middle of it.

"I wouldn't ask you to lie to Connor."

"What would I have to lie about?" She catches the misstep.

I speak quickly to cover it up. "Nothing, I'm just saying that I wouldn't ask you to keep things from him."

"Where are you?" She changes topics.

One would think she's a lawyer with how well she's managing this conversation. "Am I under interrogation?"

"Should you be?"

"I'm thinking that you missed your calling to become a lawyer."

Ellie laughs. "I deal with teenagers lying about homework, their study habits, not texting during class, and God only knows what else, so ... yeah, I'm good at the sidestep bullshit. Now, out with it."

I don't want to lie to Ellie. I also know that I can't tell her this. There are secrets that we can expect people to keep and those we can't. My asking her not to tell her husband and brother-in-law about my pregnancy is the latter.

"There's nothing wrong, Ells. I did call for a reason, though. I was hoping we could have dinner or lunch soon?"

I hear the resignation in her sigh. She knows I'm not going to tell her whatever is going on. "Of course."

"Good. How about tomorrow?"

"Your place or mine?"

There's not a chance in hell I'm going to her place. "Mine."

She laughs. "I figured."

At my place, I won't run into a dark-haired, green-eyed man who either pisses me off or ends up getting me naked.

Avoidance is the only option.

I pull up my drive, feeling lost.

I'm not sure how I feel about that. This is my home. The place where my roots are planted and I should be secure—and now I don't. The ground has shifted, leaving me unsteady. Sierra's suggestion that I leave Sugarloaf hangs heavy on my mind.

Since she said it, I can't stop wondering if she's right. The timing might be right now.

This baby forced me to think about what it is that has kept me here. My mother left, and this was her family's farm. My sister left and didn't think twice about it. So, why am I fighting so hard to hold on?

Once I'm out of the car, I wrap my arms around my middle, pulling the sweater tighter, and make my way toward the back barn. It isn't cold, but I feel chilled to my marrow.

"Syd," Declan calls out from behind me, forcing me to stop.

It's becoming really hard to avoid the man when he keeps showing up.

I turn. "You know, this is the opposite of staying away, right?"

His lips turn to a smirk that I have always loved. He has the best facial expressions. I've seen them all, memorized them, brought them back to the forefront when something reminded me of him.

This one was always my favorite. It said so much with the quirk of his lip and the devilish gleam in his eyes about how he knew the mischief he was causing was irritating, but had to do it anyway. His face always gave him away—at least to me.

"I wanted to clarify what happened the other night."

"I think you said everything, Dec."

He moves closer, and I steel myself. If he touches me, my resolve may break, so I remember his words. The way he said them without any room for confusion. He doesn't want a wife or a baby or anything that would tie him to another person.

"Yes, but I hurt you."

I take a step back. "It's not the first time."

And then his beautiful green eyes turn sorrowful, and my heart aches. He still makes me feel things I know are stupid. I should be immune to sadness since he's caused me enough of it, and I should be completely over him by now.

"Hopefully it was the last." The sincerity in his voice makes me want to fling myself into his arms, but I don't.

I stay rooted to my spot and just nod. "I hope so too, but I doubt it."

"And here I thought you were the forgiving one."

I shrug. "I was once."

"But I broke her."

"No, you left her."

His hands run through his dark hair, and he lets out a low groan. "Again, we can't seem to have a conversation where I don't feel like a fucking asshole."

I bite back a remark about a shoe that fits. I don't want to fight with him, not now anyway. I'm too raw from seeing our baby, too worried about the future, and too confused about whether I can handle the decisions I need to make.

"Do you want to walk with me? I have to check on a few

things."

The tension seems to release from his shoulders, and he nods. "I'd like that."

We start to move toward the big barn on the back of the property that houses Jimmy's office. I have no idea if he's here or back in the fields, but he's usually doing various paperwork and placing orders around this time of day.

Jimmy is the best thing on this farm, and he might be the strongest reason I've never sold.

"How are you?" Declan asks after a few minutes of amiable silence.

"I'm fine. You?"

"I'm in Sugarloaf."

I snort once. "Yes, that is true. It wasn't always so bad, you know."

Declan's eyes meet mine, a million memories pass between us in that look. "No ... it wasn't, but it's not the same anymore."

I try to slow my rapid pulse and temper my scathing remarks. Sugarloaf has remained mostly the same, it's him who is different. "Nothing stays the same."

"No, and some things change in ways we don't prepare ourselves for." His voice is soft and full of understanding.

"Yeah, but change is good, right?"

Declan lifts one shoulder and then cracks his neck. "I think change is inevitable, but who the fuck knows? I came back here, and some of it is the same as it was eight years ago, some of it, or maybe just the people are nothing like I remembered."

"Eight years is a long time," I say, and then feel like a fool. Eight years is how long I've been living in the past.

"Yeah, it is."

"Declan?"

"Yeah?"

"Did you ever really love me? Was what we shared just some fairy tale that two broken kids told themselves?"

He shakes his head and reaches out to grab my wrist. "What we had was real."

My stomach flips, and I swallow back the words I want to ask. It won't do us any good to keep going around and around. We both need to forge forward and stop going backward.

I struggle to keep my breathing even because his hands are hot against my skin, and I swear I sense him in my bones. Declan has somehow branded me, forcing my body, soul, and heart to know him as though we are one.

He drops his grip and I find the words that need to be said. "I loved you too. I want you to know that. I have never really stopped loving you, even though I hear you loud and clear on what you want."

"I will always love you, Syd."

Just not enough.

But I can't change that, and there is a very real future coming. The baby is what matters, and I need to make my plans. "And I want you to be happy. I want both of us to be. I think you and I need to stop drudging up the past and rehashing it like anything will change. That's the only way we're going to survive being near each other. Do you think that's possible?"

Declan falls quiet, his gaze on the ground, and places his hands in his pockets as we start to walk again. "I still think we need to talk about what happened a couple of months ago."

I swallow hard, not wanting to relive any of it. "There's nothing to say, Dec. It was … I don't know, years of pent-up feelings that all boiled over. Closure?"

"When I left you … when we were … when …"

"When what?" I force the words from my lips.

"Before it all fell apart."

"Please stop saying things like that," I say. "Please stop acting like we fell apart. It's insulting and unfair. It wasn't mutual. It wasn't like time and distance made us drift onto different courses. We were in *love*, Declan. I loved you. You swore you loved me and wanted to *marry* me. We weren't kids—well, we were, but we were old enough to be honest. When you make it out like we just … fell apart, it's a lie, and we both know it."

"So much for not drudging up the past."

"I didn't bring it up. You did, and I'm asking you to at least be honest about it."

"Fine. When I walked away from you. When I ripped both our hearts from our chests and ran them the fuck over with a steamroller. Is that better, Bean?"

My heart races even faster as the nickname that he and Jimmy gave me so many years ago falls from his lips.

"It's at least honest."

Years of holding it together in court and with victims is the only reason I don't burst into tears. I shove my own emotions down, keeping myself almost numb to it all. I loved this man with everything I was, and in some part of my heart, I still do.

"And now what? Now that I've said it, what does it change?" Declan looks to me for an answer I can't give.

"I don't know."

"I don't want to keep doing this," he admits with a hint of defeat. "I don't want to go around and around with you. You and I used to be so … easy."

I release a deep sigh through my nose. "We were."

He steps closer. "We could be again."

There's a part of me that wants exactly that. The friendship we shared was strong, and if we can get back to that, surely we can agree on some sort of life for our child. Declan may not want kids, but I don't believe he would abandon him or her.

Then again, I don't know this new Declan.

"You want to be friends? What would that look like?"

"It could be whatever we want it to be. There are no rules, but you're right on letting go and starting over. Being back here is hard. I feel my father and the past on my shoulders, and I can't do it, Bean. I need for us to be okay. Can we find a way to coexist in Sugarloaf and at least be friends?"

God, I want to say yes. I want to throw myself in his arms and hug the best friend I lost, but him asking this, answers every question I was debating since leaving Sierra.

This will never end for me. Six months of Declan showing up or us running into each other is inevitable. You can't hide from someone in a town like Sugarloaf, and I could never hide from Declan even if I tried.

He may believe that we can put everything aside and be friends, but I know that isn't something I could do. In my heart, I know that I need to be either all in or all out with him. There is no middle ground or half-measures.

"I don't know if we can."

"Why?"

"Because I'm leaving Sugarloaf."

ten

"You're what?" I ask, my throat going dry and thick with emotion.

"I'm going to sell the farm. It's too much for me, and I want to move closer to my mom and Sierra."

I can't explain the feelings that are churning inside me or why it would even bother me if she left. Sydney doesn't need to stay here, and yet, the idea of her selling this farm has my chest tight.

She belongs here. She was made here—*we* were made here.

Every touch. Every memory. Every glance and kiss were all forged here, and now ... she'll leave?

I know I don't have a right to feel anything. I walked away. I gave her up and have to live with that choice, but it's fucking killing me to think of anyone else in this house.

"When?" It's the only question I allow myself to ask.

"As soon as I can. It was something I was going to do years ago, but I didn't. Now, it's the right time. I'm going to talk to Jimmy, and then, I don't know, I guess I'll get things in motion."

"What about your family legacy?"

That is what has always kept her rooted here. That she would one day be able to pass this to her children. It isn't just land, it is her heritage, which Sydney always valued. She wants her children to know that they came from somewhere.

Throughout her life, she struggled with her father's absence, and this farm gave her a place to hold.

I understood it even when she didn't, which is why I don't understand how she can let it go.

"My family isn't in Sugarloaf anymore. What legacy am I living?"

"You can't leave, this is your home."

Her lip quirks up, and she laughs softly. "You did. You walked out of this town, where your family farmed for as long as mine has, and you didn't blink an eye. Why is it hard for you to understand that I would want to leave this place, where I'm basically alone, and move so I'm closer to my sister, who can be there for me."

"Why now?"

She looks away and sighs. "There have been some … changes in my life, and it's the right thing to do. Honestly, Dec, it's a good thing for me."

What I wouldn't give to go back in time and fix everything. I run my hands through my hair, trying to think of what to say. "Are you sure?"

She nods. "It's time to let it go, don't you think?"

I want to scream, grab her in my arms, and kiss her until neither of us can let go. But if she wants to leave, I have no right to stop her. I lost that privilege years ago, and I'd be the biggest asshole who lived if I told her she should stay when I have no intention of doing the same.

Sydney and I can't ever be.

Still, I'm here to make amends. I want us to find a way through the hurt and anger and maybe unearth a little understanding.

"Let me help you," I say before I know what I'm doing.

"Help me? How?"

The wheels start turning quickly. I don't know how exactly to help her, so I start to pace, thinking of a plan. I snap my fingers once I have an idea. "I have a friend who is a real estate investor. He is going to help with selling my family farm once we're through the two-year purgatory. Milo is a genius who knows the market and the best way to posture a property to get the top dollar for it. If your legacy isn't to live here, you can at least make as much money as possible."

"My goal is to sell it quickly," Sydney says and then bites her lower lip.

I push down the urge to run my finger across her mouth and pull that lip out of its restraints before I kiss her. I shove my hands into my pockets to avoid doing just that. "I can help, Syd."

She eyes me curiously and then releases a sigh through her nose. "This goes against my plan to avoid you at all costs."

Avoiding her when she's this close is like telling my lungs not to breathe. I can try for a bit, but eventually, the need is too strong to resist.

"And I thought you wanted to be civil." I try for a casual tone, hoping I pull it off.

"Yes, well, we don't seem to manage civility very well."

"No, I guess we don't, but this could be the jumping point of our new friendship."

Sydney kicks a rock, sending it flying down the dirt drive.

"It's sad, isn't it?"

"What is?"

"That we've been reduced to this. Two people who used to say anything to one another are now struggling to speak. There wasn't a topic that was off-limits, and I used to know you as well as I knew myself," Sydney says, still not looking at me.

Only, I don't need to see her face to know what'll be there. Her blue eyes will dull a bit, like they do when she's sad, and she will be biting the inside of her cheek. Still, I wait because I want her to see me.

After a few seconds of her avoiding me, I step closer and use my finger to tilt her chin up, forcing her to stop looking at the ground.

Our gazes lock, and I swear it's as if I'm thrown back in time. She still has this beautiful innocence that cuts through me, reminding me of the way I fell in love with her without a chance of stopping it.

I may not want to get married or have kids, but my heart and soul have always belonged to one person, and it never will be anyone else's.

"I think we might still know each other that way."

She shakes her head. "I don't know you anymore. I don't know this man who doesn't want to love or can't love. That wasn't who you were."

"It's who I had to become."

The truth of it all is this is probably who I always should've been. Loving Sydney was a mistake because she's always deserved so much more than I could give. The accident took a part of me and having to hold it in for all these years, letting it eat away at me, has forced me to become hardened.

"Why?"

I look at her, my heart pounding as I try to tell her without saying it. "A single moment can define a lifetime. My father taught me that lesson, and I couldn't stay here and hurt you."

There isn't much more I can say because none of it was fair. It was horrible, and I destroyed what could've been a very different life. Now, though, with this new hope for a piece of her—just a piece—I know that I need to tell her everything about the past.

"And the decision you made in that moment defined my life."

"I was letting you go."

She laughs once and steps back. "You knew me better than that. You knew my heart was always and forever going to be yours."

"I didn't deserve it."

"Maybe not, but"—she shrugs—"it was yours, and I guess the worst part is ... that it still is."

My throat is closing as I stare at her, wanting to confess my heart is hers too. If I were a better man, I'd fall to my knees, beg her to forgive me, and promise her whatever she wants. But she's leaving. She wants to sell the farm and move on to a life that I will never be a part of. While what I said to Connor was harsh, it was the truth. I don't want a wife and kids.

She does.

It would be cruel to take another thing away from her.

Sydney watches me before she gives me a sad smile. "I'll take your help on selling the farm. I'd like to be out of here as soon as possible."

She turns and heads toward the barn, and I let her go—like always.

"Uncle Declan!" I hear Hadley's voice on the other side of the door to my box of a home.

An RV would've been better than this.

I get off the bed, which is pretty much my only sitting option, and swing the door open.

Her long brown hair is up on the top of her head, and she's grinning like I'm the best person in the world.

"What's up, Monster?"

"I'm not a monster."

"No?" I look over at the clock. "Who else bangs on the door at seven in the morning?"

"Your favorite niece." Hadley bats her eyelashes and tucks her hands under her chin.

My brother is in for one hell of a time with this one. "You're trouble."

She smiles. "Daddy asked if you could come to the house, he said you would want to eat and then we could go down to the creek and fish. I've never been fishing. He said that you love to fish and you caught the biggest one ever. Did you? Do you fish good?"

Hadley talks so fast I'm not sure what she's asking or what I'm supposed to answer first. "Uh."

"When you go, do you have your own pole? I want a pole. Can you come fishing with us, Uncle Declan?"

My eyes are wide as I stare at this tiny human with equal parts of absolute terror and awe. "I'm pretty sure I have to go fishing. Since you've never been, and I'm much better than your dad at it, I'll get to teach you how to do it."

She beams. "I knew you'd come!" Hadley grabs my hand, pulling me from the tiny house. "Come on! We have to eat and then I have to brush my teeth and *then* we can go!"

I grab my sweatshirt as she drags me out of the tiny house

and toward the main one. I'm not that far away from it since I needed Wi-Fi in order to still work and not completely fuck my company, but we get there in record time since she's basically running.

"Knew she was the best option," Connor says with a smirk.

"Nice. Use the kid to get what you want."

Connor doesn't even look apologetic. "She's irresistible, I go with the sure thing."

"Fishing?"

He shrugs. "It's been a long time since I've been down to that end of the property, and I figure we might as well check things out while I show my superiority over my oldest and dumbest brother."

"Whatever. You want to wager?"

"Sure, loser has to spend tomorrow on the tractor bush hogging the big field."

"You're on."

I don't need to think about it because Connor is a shitty fisher. He talks too much, can't stand still, and has no idea which lure or bait to use. Every time my brother and I went out, he came home empty-handed. This is like taking candy from a baby.

We shake on it, and Hadley bounds back in the room. "Eat and then fish!"

Connor chuckles and follows his daughter into the kitchen. He walks over to Ellie, wrapping his arm around her as she stands at the stove with the spatula in her hand. It's a tender moment that makes my gut flip. Her hand rests on his forearm, and he places a soft kiss to the side of her head.

I turn to look at Hadley, who eyes me with suspicion. "What are you thinking?" I ask, knowing Arrowood blood runs in her veins and that means trouble.

"Why do you look sad?"

"Sad?"

She nods and wraps her arms around my legs, hugging me with all her might. "Don't be sad, Uncle Declan. I love you."

I smile because, who the hell could ever not love this kid? I don't know how the man who raised her until Connor found them didn't think she was the most precious thing in the world. Hadley has been the gift that this family never knew to ask for.

"I love you, too." I pull her up in my arms and then swing her around. "But that doesn't mean I won't spin you until you puke!"

She laughs as she flies around in my arms, her joy is infectious.

"All right, no puking before ten, please," Ellie says, her hand on my shoulder.

"Busted," I say conspiratorially to Hadley.

I put her to rights and then sit at the table.

"What time will you guys be back?" Ellie asks, setting out a plate of bacon and another of pancakes.

"Later in the afternoon. I need to be victorious," Connor informs her.

Ellie eyes him curiously. "Why?"

"Because I'm going to school my brother and have a day off."

I scoff. "Please."

"I don't even want to know."

Ellie sits and we all start to eat.

I can't remember the last time I had anything this normal. Maybe when my mother was alive? She would make breakfast every Sunday and force us to sit as a family. I hated it as a kid and then as soon as it was gone and we no longer had her, I wished for those days again.

"What are your plans today, Ellie?" I ask.

She bites a piece of bacon and smiles warmly. "I'm going to see Sydney. We have to go dress shopping, drop by the florist, and do a few other things. I wanted to go earlier, but she sent a message that she wasn't feeling so great and asked if we could push it back. So, you all get breakfast."

"She seemed fine yesterday," I say, not able to move past her saying Syd wasn't well. "Do you want me to call her or go over there?"

Ellie's brows knit together. "No, I'm sure she's fine. She didn't cancel or anything."

Connor sits in his seat with a grin.

I'm going to kick his ass. "I'm just making sure Ellie doesn't run the risk of catching whatever Syd has," I try to excuse my slip up there.

"Sure you were."

I rub my middle finger along the side of my nose and Connor laughs.

The rest of the meal passes with Hadley urging us to eat faster so we can go fishing. Ellie, who is a goddess and didn't want us to forget to eat lunch later, hands us a basket filled with drinks and food. After kissing both Hadley and Connor, she calls my name, stopping me from following them.

"Yes?"

"Is everything okay? I know that you being back here is hard, and I just … I worry."

I smile at my soon-to-be sister-in-law. "I'm good."

"Really? Sydney mentioned that you and her are going to try to be friends and, well, it's noble and great, but you guys have history."

I nod. "We do, but I can't be in this town and avoid her. I thought this would be a good compromise."

Not to mention I'm fighting the urge to go to her constantly. At least now, I have a reason. If we're friends, we can see each other, and I plan to do exactly that.

"Be careful with her, Dec. You both want very different things, and I worry that both of you will end up hurt." She raises her hand when I open my mouth. "No, I don't want to say anything else and I promise to stay out of it, but I love you both. You're family, and Syd is like a sister to me."

"Yo! Loser! Are you planning to go shopping or are you coming fishing?" Connor yells as he swings Hadley up into his arms.

Ellie sighs and then rolls her eyes. "You go, I'm sorry and I hope you don't think I overstepped."

I lean in and kiss her cheek. "I think we're all very lucky you're a part of our lives."

She blushes and then shoos me away. I rush toward the barn, and Connor calls out, "I think we should take the quads."

I let out a throaty laugh. "I haven't ridden a quad since we were kids."

"You think you suddenly forgot how in eight years?"

"No, and I'll race you there."

He looks down at Hadley. "If I didn't have my daughter on my lap, I would take you up on that and kick your ass with a smile."

Cocky asshole. "You forget who beats you at everything."

"I beg to differ."

"Name one thing."

"Women."

I cover Hadley's eyes with my hand and flip him off with my other. "You wish."

"I'm engaged, and you're …"

"Going to kill you."

He laughs and tosses me the keys to the quad. "You'd have

to catch me first."

We get to the creek, wind blowing and slightly cold, but there is a rush that I haven't felt in so long humming in my veins. There were things about the country I loved. The clean air, trees, the night sky, and the fact that being outdoors was always preferable.

When I'm home, this is not my reality.

I work.

I work and work and work more in my office, stopping only to eat and drag my ass back to my apartment.

But I've been content, so I've let this part of myself go.

Seems the next six months will remind me of everything I used to love.

Once Hadley is set up with her pole and we all have our areas on the creek, Connor makes his way over.

"You really made her day by coming," he says with a hint of appreciation in his voice.

"She's my niece, and it's my job to win my spot as the favorite."

"You mean before Sean gets here and spoils her, knocking you down a peg?"

I nod. "Exactly."

Sean is the sweet guy. Kids love him, girls fawn at his feet, and there's not a woman alive he can't charm. There's no doubt in my mind he'll be Hadley's favorite.

"How is work going?" Connor asks.

"It's fine, I'll have to go into the city next week. There are a few meetings I can't miss, and I need to see a guy for Sydney."

He throws his line out. "What about Syd?"

"I figure she'll tell everyone, but she's selling the farm."

The pole dropping from his hands tells me that's a no. "She'll never sell her farm."

"Well, she is."

"What the fuck did you do, Declan?" His voice is low and my name comes through his teeth.

Of course, it must be my fucking fault. Everything is my fault if you ask them. I step back, instantly angry and frustrated that he jumped to that conclusion. "Couldn't be her decision, right? It has to be something I did?"

Connor grabs his pole and throws his line back out. "I didn't say that, but … this is Syd. This is her home. She wouldn't leave here on a whim."

"She said she wants to be closer to Sierra and her family."

He shakes his head and then rubs his forehead. "This doesn't make sense."

"I said the same."

"And now you're helping her?"

"I'm not sure," I admit. "I don't know if this is what she really wants, but the offer was out of my mouth before I could stop it."

He laughs. "Of course it was. You love her. You've always loved her, and you're back in the town where it was all about you and Syd."

"What does that mean?"

My youngest brother snorts and then stares at me like I'm an idiot. "It means that you can't help yourself when it comes to Sydney. It means that you being around her makes you do dumb shit, like going to her pond and screwing her a couple of months ago." He keeps going when I open my mouth. "Yeah, I know all about that."

"She's not mine anymore."

"No, but neither of you seem to get that. I know you're my

older brother and you know everything, but you're an idiot. That woman is the best thing you had in your life."

"And you know damn well why I had to let her go."

He looks over at Hadley, who is grinning as she twirls the rod. "I know, but while you may not want a wife and kids, you want Sydney."

"Well, I think we both know that, in life, you don't always get what you want."

"No, but we can have something." Connor casts his line out and then continues, "We aren't destined to suffer forever. It's a choice you're making."

Maybe he's right. I made a lot of choices over the last few years that I wish I could go back and change, but maybe my being back here isn't about changing things, but making it right.

"What do you think of telling Sydney about what happened with the accident?"

Connor blinks a few times and then shrugs. "You mean the whole story?"

"Yes, I think maybe … maybe it could make things better. Maybe she'd understand why I left, and we can be friends."

"I don't know, I mean, I'm sure Ellie wouldn't care. Syd is her best friend, but I don't think it would hurt. If you're never going to give in to the obvious feelings you both have, might as well give her some closure."

"I have never denied that I love her."

He releases a heavy sigh. "No, but you won't do anything about it either. You love her, but you won't try again? You love her, but you won't fight for her? You let her go, but you're holding on."

"How am I holding on?" I say with a bit more anger than I wanted.

Connor laughs once. "You showed up two months ago and

went to talk, mauled the girl, and came back with grass stains. Love her or don't, Declan. You can't have both. Do I want you guys to be friends? Sure. Do I think it's possible? Not a fucking chance. You love Sydney with more than your heart. If Ellie and I couldn't be together, I wouldn't be able to see her. Hell, she was married, and I couldn't handle it. I had her *one* night. One. You had Sydney for years. Tell me that the thought of her with some other guy doesn't make you crazy."

I can't.

Hell, I can't even imagine it.

"How does this change anything?"

He shakes his head and then grips my shoulder. "That, brother, is what you need to figure out."

eleven

My office is a mess—like my life. It's late Friday evening, and while my assistant, Devney, is leaving to go on a date, I'm stuck here trying to go over a deposition.

It's so sexy being me.

"You're sure you don't want me to stay?" Devney asks as she walks into my office.

"No, it's totally fine."

She gives me a knowing look that says it isn't fine, but I'm not going to force her to stay. Devney has been my assistant for the last two years, and she's a godsend. This office is always running in perfect harmony because she doesn't allow anyone slack, including me. I thank God that when she came back from college, she chose to stay here. She's been a great friend, and an exemplary employee.

"I can tell Oliver I need to cancel."

Her boyfriend takes her on a date once a month, no matter what, and that's tonight. I stand quickly. "Absolutely not! You will go on your date and be happy, damn it."

She rolls her eyes. "You're a mess."

"No shit."

She doesn't even know the half of it.

Devney turns and then stops. "Hey, are you feeling okay?"

"Yes, why?"

"You just seem … off. Is it because Declan is back?"

I flop back into my chair and huff. "Why does everyone assume it's because of him? Am I that transparent?"

Devney is best friends with Sean Arrowood, and since he and Declan are the closest in age, we all ended up hanging out a lot in high school. While Devney and I are nothing alike, we've always gotten along.

"Not transparent." She smiles softly. "But I can't imagine it's easy for you, Syd. You loved him for a long time, and Sean asked how you were holding up when I spoke to him earlier."

Great, I'm the family topic of conversation. "Declan and I have our issues that are what they are. I'm not off because of him." I'm off because I'm pregnant.

There's a knock at the door of the office and her brows furrow. "That's weird."

"Are we expecting anyone?"

"No, but …"

I get to my feet again, and we both walk to the door. My office is known as being not just a place for great legal advice but also a safe haven for people. My sister used to joke that my law firm was more of a shelter than anything else because I don't turn anyone away if I can help it. There are many women who suffer in relationships and don't feel there's an out—I'm the out.

When I pull it open, I almost burst out laughing. It's a stray all right, but not anyone in need.

"Declan."

He grins. "Sydney." His eyes move to the person beside me, and he smiles so wide it could break his face. "Devney! Get the fuck out of here! You work here? How did I not know that?"

She rushes toward him, arms wrapping around his neck as he pulls her tight. "Yes, you big idiot! I've been here for a few years, but you would have known that if you'd made time to see me since you've been back." Devney slaps his chest as he puts her down.

"I'm sorry."

"I'm not surprised."

Declan pulls her to his side and kisses the top of her head. "I missed that level of honesty."

She pushes out of his arms, turns to face him, and plants her hands right on her hips. Oh, he's in for it now. "Really? So, you'd like me to be honest about how you suck and need to get your cute butt out of here?"

"What did I do now?"

"You"—she pokes her finger into his chest—"were a jerk."

Declan looks to me, but I raise my hands. I happen to agree with my spitfire of a friend. He is a big jerk.

"I'm going to assume you're talking about Syd?"

"Were you a jerk to more women in this town that I should know about?"

I smirk, and he purses his lips. "No, but did she tell you that I'm helping her to sell the farm? I can't be that big of a jerk."

Oh, dear fucking God, can the man ruin anything else for me?

I let out a long breath and wait because the tables are about to turn as soon as Devney does. Sure enough, her body starts to spin, and then her eyes are on me. "You're what?"

"I hadn't told anyone yet," I say to him through gritted teeth.

"Don't look at him. Look at me. You're selling your farm?"

"Yes."

"To buy another farm in Sugarloaf?"

I shake my head. "I was going to talk to you about it this week. It's time, Devney. It's time for me to move on."

I see the hurt in her brown eyes, but she doesn't comment further. "I see."

"Nothing is final yet."

I really didn't want to have this talk now. I planned to tell each of my friends very carefully, and since Ellie and Devney are my two closest friends, I wanted them to hear it from me. Moving wasn't a decision I came to lightly, and I want them to understand.

She looks to Declan and then back to me. "You'll talk to me later?"

I nod. "Of course." Her phone pings, and we both know that's Oliver letting her know he's here. Each date night, it's the same routine. "Go. Come by my house tomorrow."

Devney laughs. "You can bet your ass I will."

With that, she gives me a quick hug and then kisses Declan on the cheek. When she's gone, I head back toward my office, planning to leave him in the lobby. I have nothing to say to him that isn't curse words or threats of bodily harm.

"Sydney, I didn't know ..."

I turn with a giant huff. "Didn't know that I wouldn't have told my friends yet? I have a lot of ducks to get in a row before I move. This town may not have meant anything to you, but it's been my world. I wanted to make sure that I was one hundred percent sure before telling them."

"I see that now. I'm truly sorry."

I'm not even angry, just upset. I hate disappointing my friends.

"It's fine. What brings you by, Dec?"

His lips part, but he closes them before starting to move around the room. "I came because I got back from New York City a few minutes ago. I met with a few people and wanted to tell you what I found out."

"Okay."

I motion to the seat in front of my desk and then take my own chair. The desk between us allows me to relax a bit. He can't touch me or make me feel weak. When I'm here, I'm in charge.

"Milo Huxley is a good friend of mine, he is a real estate investor and would like to come see the property. Based on what I've told him, he feels he can help, and might even purchase it himself if he sees an opportunity."

This is what I wanted. I've told myself dozens of times over the last week that I was ready to sell my farm and move on. I talked at great length with Jimmy, who seemed almost relieved that I was considering it.

But now, I'm not so sure.

There's an ache in my chest as I think about someone else living there, sitting in the tree swing out back, or going near the pond that holds memories I will never forget.

"When?" I choke the word out.

"He lives in London, but he's in New York for the next few days to see his daughter. He'd like to come out as early as the day after tomorrow."

My stomach flips. "Two days?"

"If you're not busy."

I'm not busy other than my normal farm-life thing and finding a way to explain this to my friends.

I have things that are bigger than my sadness to consider. My life isn't going to be the same, and I can't pretend that staying here is the right thing.

A support system is what I need, and that's my mother and sister.

Declan has made it abundantly clear that he won't be that for me—or anyone—and a child is not something he wants.

So, if this friend of his can help me, then I'm not going to be a fool and pass it up.

"No, I'm not busy. That's fine."

He smiles and nods once. "All right. I'll set it up."

Declan stands, and I do the same. He looks as though he wants to say something, but doesn't.

When he gets to the door, I call out. "Dec?"

"Yeah?"

I'm having your baby.

I want this to be better.

I love you still.

I wish I didn't.

Those aren't the words that will be said. "Thank you."

His eyes lock onto mine. "There's not much I wouldn't do for you, Sydney."

Not much except the only thing I've ever wanted.

"So, you're selling the farm?" Devney asks as we sit at my table.

"I am."

Ellie enters the room, taking in the two of us. "What did I miss?"

Devney sighs and looks up. "Syd is moving."

"Moving?" Ellie yells and then takes a seat. "What do you mean you're moving?"

The two of them are going to grill me, and I came prepared with two sleeves of cookies. I put a mug in front of each of them and the cookies in the middle. I have another package in case I need reinforcements.

"It's time for me to move on," I say matter-of-factly. There's nothing either of them can say to change my mind at this point. "I'm going to sell and move closer to Sierra and my mother."

Ellie's hand reaches out to mine. "Is this because of what happened a few months ago?"

"What happened?" Devney sits straighter.

I didn't tell anyone other than Ellie about that because it was embarrassing. Once Devney knows, there will be no escaping the million questions and accusations as to the real reason I'm getting out of Dodge. She knows me too well.

She probably already assumes it's because of Declan, but once she knows what happened, she won't have any doubt.

Might as well get it out now. "I slept with Declan, thought I could be pregnant, and now that he's back, I can't seem to get away from him. I can't escape him, not even with selling my farm. He's just … here. I can't take it anymore."

"But he's only here for a few months," Ellie says. "He's made it crystal clear he's not staying, so you're going to leave your home and your practice because of a short stint?"

Devney nods. "Seriously, Syd, take a sabbatical for fuck's

sake. Don't sell the one thing that you've fought so hard to hold on to."

God, they have no idea. "You can't begin to understand. Neither of you. Ellie, when you found out that Connor was who he was, what did you want to do? Run, right? You didn't want to stay with him. Hell, you fought him at every turn. Why? Because the Arrowood brothers stick their targets. Every fucking time. They pierce through the heart and you never recover. That happened to me when I was a little girl and that arrow is still embedded in me. I have to get away from him, I have to remove it, move on, go somewhere there's no chance of him getting another shot. And the thing is, he doesn't even want me!"

"Syd …" Ellie says with so much sympathy it actually hurts.

"No, that's the thing. He doesn't want me. He may love me. He may want to be friends, but I can't be friends with him, Ellie. I can't. I can't talk to him and not want to kiss him. I can't look at him and not want to throw myself into his arms. When we slept together, it was like the dam that I had closed broke. All the emotions, the love, the feelings all flooded back, and I'm going to drown," I say as tears form in my eyes. "It's too much. I have to go where I can start over."

Ellie rushes toward me, pulling me into her arms as I start to cry. God, these hormones are crazy.

"This isn't you," Devney says from the side of me. "You don't run away from a fight."

I turn to her and shake my head. "Sometimes fighting isn't the answer."

"When it comes to this, it is. He's what you want. This farm is what you want, don't give up."

She's nuts. She shouldn't talk. "Don't get me started with you and giving up or choosing not to fight."

Sean has loved her and she has loved him since we were

kids, and the only two people who don't seem to have a clue about it are Devney and Sean themselves.

"Me? What the hell do I do?" Devney squeaks.

"Nothing. I'm sorry, I just got worked up."

I'm not going to call her out, and ... maybe it's for the best. Loving an Arrowood and not knowing you love them is way better than knowing and not being loved back.

The two of them grab for a cookie as we all let the moment settle around us. "I can't pretend to know what you're feeling," Ellie says. "My relationship with Connor is nothing like yours and Declan's, but I love you, and selfishly, I want you to stay."

I smile and take her hand in mine. "I love you too, Ells. I really do, and it's not easy for me to leave. I've lived here my whole life. I've only ever known this town and ..." I fight back the emotions bubbling up. It's going to be impossible to drive away from this house, but I can't stay. "Well, it's going to just about kill me, but it's time."

"Will you at least wait until after the wedding? It's only a few weeks away."

"I wouldn't miss it for the world. You don't have to worry about that."

Devney grabs my other hand and squeezes it. "I hate to see you hurt like this. I could kill him for making you leave your home."

"He's not at fault—I am. I've spent my life waiting for a man to come back and fight for something that he never wanted to fight for. Declan made his intentions clear when he left me. He doesn't love me the way I need him to. He doesn't want a family. He wants the life he has, and I want more. It just took me a while to see that."

I hate keeping the bigger reason from my friends, but I won't tell anyone else before I tell Declan. He deserves to know about the baby before my friends do.

"I don't like it, but I understand your choice. When will you leave?" Ellie asks.

I lift one shoulder. "It depends on when I can get the house sold."

twelve

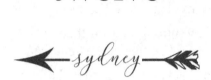

"Sydneybean, I think you're fussing over nothing," Jimmy says as I wipe the counter for the third time.

"I don't know what they're looking for."

"Land, and you have it. A lot of it."

Yes, but I have this house too, and it's worth something. It's where I came down the stairs and found Declan waiting to take me to prom. It's filled with Christmas memories, and the small dent from when Sierra did a handstand and fell, putting a hole in the wall.

Even the bad memories have a voice.

"Still, I don't want anyone to judge the house poorly."

He grabs the coffee mug and takes a long sip, all the while staring at me.

I know he has something he wants to say. "Just spit it out, Jimmy."

He sets his mug down before crossing his arms over his

chest. "You think you're fooling the world, Bean, but you're not fooling this old man. You've got a secret."

Oh, Lord. Not today, please.

"I have many secrets."

"Not with me you don't."

Well, he's wrong there, but I'm not going to argue. The thing is, he does know me. He was always good at seeing through the crap, and I could never get away with lying or telling him half-truths. That said, I'm not ready to tell him either.

"There's something going on that I can't talk about right now, but I promise, I'm fine and when I can tell you, I will."

Jimmy leans back, watching me. "I appreciate the honesty, but that doesn't explain why you're leaving town. This is your home, darling."

"People move."

"Yes, but is that what you really want?"

Would I have stayed here if I weren't pregnant? Yes. I would've, but I am pregnant and not stupid enough to think that raising a baby alone will be easy. I need a support system. So, I'm doing what I have to.

"All I want is for you to be happy, if that means you leave here, then so be it."

I walk over to him and kiss his cheek. "You know, I always wished you could be my daddy."

He pulls me into his arms, chin resting on my head. "I did too, Bean, but the Lord knew we needed each other, so he put us together. Your father didn't deserve you. To leave a child like that is unthinkable. You're the best thing that ever happened to me, and you're not even mine."

We don't talk much about Hal Hastings. No one brings him up because there is not much to say other than he was an ass.

I step back, needing a bit of space. "Do you think he regrets it?"

"He should. If he doesn't, then he's a bigger fool than either of us already know him to be. He punished you and Sierra when you did nothing wrong. How he can stay away from his kids is beyond me, but not to know his grandkids? Well, that's just unforgivable."

For a second, panic grips me, and I wonder if he knows, but then I remember that my sister has two boys. "I keep trying to tell myself it doesn't matter, but it does."

"I don't think any child can not care when a parent doesn't love them. I lost my mother when I was an infant and not having her in my life changed me. But you and Sierra had Hal in your life for years before he left. You'd be lying to yourself if you didn't think that would change you."

I swallow back the fear that bubbles up. This is what I stress over regarding the baby I'm carrying. Wouldn't it be better for him or her to never know Declan than to face knowing he didn't want them?

"But did it make me better?"

He smiles, touching my cheek. "It made you strong."

Funny that a few minutes ago he was saying I was running. "Strong enough to sell the farm."

He chuckles and shakes his head. "I guess you got me there."

The back screen door creaks open, and I jump before seeing dark brown hair and green eyes I would know anywhere appear. "Sorry, I knocked on the front door, but no one answered."

Declan grins when he sees Jimmy. The two of them shared a bond that was deep, and I think Jimmy was as heartbroken as I was when we split up. He lost Declan the same as I did.

"Declan Arrowood, as I live and breathe." Jimmy steps toward him, arms wide.

"I'm so sorry, Jimmy," Declan says, embracing him.

"You were a man." Jimmy's voice is thick with emotion. "Don't apologize for making a choice, son, even if it was the wrong one."

"Not all of us are as smart as you."

Jimmy's deep throaty laugh fills the room. "That's the truth if I've ever heard it."

Declan claps his hand on Jimmy's shoulder. "How are you feeling?"

The two fall into an easy conversation, and I slip out to give them some privacy. I head up to my room, grab my sweater, and then tidy up a bit.

The bed has been in the same place since I was fourteen and still faces the window. I always wanted to be able to see him if he visited at night. I convinced Jimmy that every girl should have a reading area, so we turned the bay window that was there into a nook that had cabinets and a padded bench. It was perfect for Declan to drop down onto.

Does he recall the nights he would sneak into my bedroom and hold me as I cried? I glance out the window, looking at the oak tree that no longer has the long branch he would climb. I cut that down two months after he left me, once I realized he wasn't coming back.

I turn my back to the window and sigh.

It's weird having Declan in my house again. I'm doing what I can not to think about it, but that makes me think even more.

Being near him makes everything so real again. The pain and the love I felt for him wasn't gone, but I could live around it. Now, it's undeniable.

My hand rests on my belly, thinking of the life that grows there. As soon as I sell the house, I'm going to tell him. At least then, I'll be detached from the memories and ready for the next phase of my life. There's no point in staying in Sugarloaf if I won't have a life with him.

It wouldn't be fair to any other man I met. The memories that haunt me are in this home, this town, this room. I need to free myself of it so I can forge ahead.

"You okay?"

I jump at the sound of Declan's voice. "You scared me."

"Sorry about that. Wow, this room is ... incredible."

While some of the room is the same, other things are different. The bedding, draperies, and the ugly striped wallpaper are gone. Now, it's much more me ... a little bit rustic, a little bit glamorous, and a love of style. I look around at the dark gray paint that has pops of yellow and teal to make the space feel bigger. I hung a chandelier over the bed that has crystals shooting prisms everywhere and when the fireplace is on, it's magical. The last thing I did was add a built-in bookcase made of pipe and barn wood to give it a bit of farmhouse.

"Thanks."

"You really did a lot with the house."

"When I got the property, I wanted to update it to match my tastes."

Declan continues to look around. "Well, all of this is beautiful."

My heart warms at his praise. I love this house. I've done everything I could to make it my own and still keep with the original feel of it. It's updated but still has that old farm look.

"Did you and Jimmy have a good talk?"

"We did. He seems happy with the idea of retiring."

I nod. "He's been doing this a long time."

Declan laughs. "You think he'd ever abandon you? He'd cut his arm off before he'd let that happen. You needed him."

My throat grows tighter, and the love I have for Jimmy

swells. I didn't think that I was the reason why. I'm not his daughter, even if he does love me like I am. I thought he liked the farm and needed it to stay busy. Here I had it in my thick head that I was doing him a favor, not the other way around.

"Now I feel like an asshole."

"Why?"

"Because I was keeping the farm for him."

His lazy smile causes my stomach to clench. I really love that one. His eyes crinkle just a bit on the left and his irises seem to darken, making him impossible to resist. Not that I could resist anything about him, but this made it even harder.

"Maybe it's time that you both let it go."

I nod, feeling as if that's exactly what we all need. "And maybe now is the right time, you know?"

Declan nods. "Hopefully, I can help you accomplish that."

"I hope so too." Because in the end, we both have a lot to lose.

thirteen

I would do anything to help her, including helping her put more distance between us, which has been gnawing at me each day since I made her that offer.

I have loved Sydney Hastings since the day I met her, and that has never gone away.

I lift my fingertips, just grazing my knuckles against her cheek. Her eyelids flutter closed, long dark lashes fanning out against her cheekbones, and I cup her face. Her cheek falls into my palm as though it's natural.

God, I want her so much.

Her head is in my hands, and my heart is at her feet. She has no idea how badly I want to be the man she still sees.

Our breathing is heavy and her body leans closer to mine.

My other arm snakes around her without pause and then I lean down, wanting to feel more, be closer.

At the same time, Sydney lifts her head and then our lips

touch.

It's gentle at first, almost as though neither of us meant to do it, and then, I snap.

My arm cinches around her, pulling her tighter to me as her hands grip my face. My tongue slides into her mouth, both of us moan.

I pour everything into the kiss, hoping she feels the anger, love, frustration that it isn't enough to make things different, and the way I wish it could be. The taste of her mouth is like heaven.

"Declan." She groans my name as I push her against the wall.

"You're so beautiful," I tell her, and then my mouth is on hers again.

Sydney's fingers tangle into my hair, keeping me where she wants me, but I wouldn't leave her if an army stormed the house. This is what I need.

Her.

Everything she is makes me feel alive. Our lips move together in the way they always have, as if we're two souls that become one. She's the beat in my heart and for so long, it's been dead.

And then, she turns her head away.

"Stop," she says with so much pain in her voice, it breaks me.

I take a step back, trying to get control over myself. Jesus Christ, I had her shoved against the wall and … I'm a fucking bastard.

"Syd."

"No. Please." Her eyes are pleading as she smooths her clothes. "It was … it's fine. I got carried away."

"What?"

"It was an old memory or a dream I had about you being in here. I apologize."

Now anger takes hold. "I kissed you."

Her eyes widen. "No, I kissed you."

"Sydney, I assure you that I instigated that kiss and I would've kissed you until I had you in the same predicament as the last time if you hadn't stopped it."

She lets out a loud puff of air and then rubs her fingers across her lips. Her gaze lifts to mine and there's a sense of determination and strength in them. "Does this change anything for us?"

I blink a few times. "For us?"

"Are we friends?"

"Of course," I say carefully.

"Do you want to suddenly marry me and become a family?"

My chest tightens, and my throat goes dry. "Syd ..."

"Answer me, Dec."

"No, I don't ..."

She raises her hand. "Then there's nothing to say. We were friends who shared a passionate kiss. We can blame it on a full moon or whatever you want. However, if you want to be friends, that has to be the last time. I can't keep doing this. My feelings for you have always been what they are. I love you, want a life with you, but I can't let myself hope when you're clear there is none. So, I beg you. Love me or let me go because my heart can't take anymore."

And with that, she walks out, leaving me feeling like a complete asshole.

After a second, I collect myself and head downstairs. She's standing at the window, looking lost, and I hate myself.

"Milo should be here soon," I say, wanting to see her eyes

so I can read what's in her head.

However, she doesn't turn to me. Instead, she tucks her blonde hair behind her ear. "What exactly will today entail? Meaning, what should I expect?"

I move toward her, and she steps to the side. "Milo will come and tour the property, and hopefully, he'll give you some insight on what he thinks. He buys and develops property, but he also invests in properties like this one on the side in London mostly, but also here. You'll like Milo, he's a cocky prick, but a great guy."

She nods slowly and then finally looks at me with a smile. "So, he's like you?"

"I'm not sure I'm such a great guy."

Sydney shakes her head. "I think you're just fighting the wrong fight."

"And what fight should I be fighting?"

"That's for you to figure out."

She's the only person who can cut me with a few words or a look. I know I will never be the man she wants, and it would make me the villain if I were to pretend otherwise.

"I guess it is. Either way, Milo will be able to give you some advice that will help if you're still sure you want to sell."

"Oh, I'm sure." She turns back toward the window. "Are you going to leave once you make the introduction?"

"No, I'll walk with you guys."

"Why?"

Because I want to spend whatever time near you that you'll allow.

"Because Milo is my friend, and he's helping me out."

Sydney's eyes narrow. "Are you afraid I'm going to throw myself at him?"

Now I do chuckle. "Milo is happily married."

"All the more reason you don't need to stay around."

One day, she'll stop fighting back on every-damn-thing. Not that I have any hopes of that being today. "Or all the more reason you do."

Her lips pinch. "Whatever."

While a lot has changed, deep down, she's still the same. Her passion and heart are like a siren to me, and I want to answer the call.

Two months ago, I held her in my arms and made love to her. I would've done it again upstairs because I can't stop wanting her. I ache for her. I dream of her—of us—of a life together, even though I know I shouldn't.

Then I wonder if she would give me just the time that I'm back. Then I remember, Sydney doesn't love that way. She's both feet in and no rope anywhere in sight. I would have to jump in with her, knowing I would never need air again because she would be my breath.

And that can't happen.

I can't have her, but I can help her find the surface and not drown her with the weight of my issues.

"He's here," Syd says.

Dread fills me, and I wonder if I'm making a mistake. Maybe I can convince Milo to tell her not to sell, but it's a bit late for that.

Sydney goes and opens the door.

Before she can say anything, he speaks. "Well, no one told me that you are just the most enchanting creature alive." Milo's British accent is extra thick as he takes Sydney's hand and brings it to his lips. "Delighted, love."

She smiles, and a faint blush paints her cheeks. "You must be Milo."

"Yes, I must, and you are the gorgeous woman who has tied this brute of a man up in knots."

"Laying it on a little thick, are we, Milo?"

He shrugs with a grin. "Never."

"Now I see why you didn't want him to be alone with me. He's charming and handsome."

Milo's arm wraps around her, and he pulls her close. "I like her."

"I bet you do. Hands off or I'll call your *wife*."

He leans his head close but doesn't drop his voice. "Isn't it just total fun to poke the bastard? Look, he knows I am desperately in love with my wife, and he's still about ready to rip my arms off. Aren't you, mate?"

I'm going to fucking kill him. We may have been friends for years, but right now, I want to do exactly what he's accusing me of wanting to do.

However, giving Milo any satisfaction is not in my plan. "Not at all, I'll be happy to watch Danielle do it for me."

He grins and then releases Sydney. "Come now, you know she can't resist my charms."

Sydney shakes her head, smiling the entire time. "You two are trouble."

"You have no idea," he replies.

She really doesn't. Milo was the bachelor of the year, living life as he wanted, and then he was knocked on his ass by his now wife. It has been a joy to watch.

"All right, Casanova, let's show you the property so you can give us your expert opinion on this."

"Don't let him fool you, darling, all my opinions are expert." Then he turns to me. "We don't need you, Declan. Sydney and I will walk the property, you can go do ... whatever it is you need to do."

Sydney loops her arm in his and gives me a cheeky smirk. "Yes, do what it is you do."

They walk out the front door, and I ball my hands so tightly I worry I'll crack the skin. I'm going to lose my fucking mind, that's what I'm going to do.

Two fucking hours.

They have been walking around for two hours, and I'm going out of my skull. I have no reason—or right—to be jealous. Milo would never do anything to hurt her or his marriage. I know this, and he knows I know this, and yet, he knows it would still bother me.

The idea of any man with Sydney drives me fucking insane.

Now, I'm walking in circles, waiting for the two of them to show up.

"It's tough waiting around to see if she'll come back in one piece, isn't it?" Jimmy says from behind me.

"Was it like this for you?"

"Always."

"This is why I don't want kids," I say and then look back out the window.

Jimmy grunts. "I didn't have kids, and I still ended up this way. I would bet my life savings that you'll feel the same about Hadley."

I grimace thinking about some boy wanting to touch her or do any of the things I did with Sydney. "I would bet you're right."

He laughs. "Based on the look you had, the idea alone makes you feel a bit sick, huh?"

"Just a bit."

"You know, I felt like that when you left. Part proud and part out of my mind with worry."

Jimmy is the only other thing in this town I missed when I left. He was the father I never had, and I knew that when I gave Sydney up, I was going to lose him too.

"I wanted to reach out ..."

"But you worried I was on her side?"

I nod. "She was yours, I was hers, and when I gave her up ..." I can't finish the sentence because I feel like a fool.

Jimmy wouldn't have turned me out. He would've listened, probably talked some sense into me, and maybe that was why I didn't do it. I didn't need reason and rationale—I needed out. I had to save the people I loved the only way I knew how.

He sits at the table, holding his mug. "Sit, Son."

I do as he asks.

"A man doesn't walk away from the things he loves easily, which is why I think it breaks Sydney's heart so damn much that her father did. She knows that if he loved her as much as he should've, he'd have fought for her. That's why it broke her to pieces when you left because she knew you loved her. She knew it in her bones. That girl would sit up in that window and wait to see if you'd come back."

"I couldn't."

He puts his hand up. "You could've, but you chose not to."

"It feels the same," I admit.

"Maybe so, but you're a grown man now, and you can sling your bullshit wherever you want, but not at me. I throw it back."

I grin and nod. "Understood. My point is that leaving Sydney wasn't easy for me. It wasn't what I wanted, but it was what needed to be done to protect everyone in my life."

"Your father did a number on you boys too, Declan. He

twisted you all up, made you doubt yourselves, and forced you to take on a role that you weren't meant to do. You weren't those boys' father. You are their brother, and he took that from you."

Yes, he did, but I didn't feel like I was being robbed. I was able to do for my brothers what no one else could do for me. I protected them. I gave them a chance by getting out of this town.

As much as the accident stole from us, it gave us a lot too. I started my company, Sean is a professional baseball player, Jacob is an actor, and Connor found all he wanted.

"I did what my mother asked me to on her deathbed."

"And I have no doubt she's proud of you."

I wish I felt the same. If anything, I think my mother is saddened by what we all have become. She would've wanted us to have people in our lives to love and cherish. She believed that family was everything. While we've held up her memory by being loyal to the brotherhood, we haven't lived the way she'd have wanted.

"Now, kissing a girl is a big deal, Declan Arrowood." Mom stands there scowling at me. *"You better not do anything with Sydney until you're much older."*

"Yes, ma'am."

All because my stupid brother couldn't keep his mouth shut. Sydney was crying at school today, and I told her if she didn't quit, I was going to kiss her. I already told her I'd love her forever, and while that stopped her tears for a minute, she started right back up again.

Girls are always crying.

I can't handle it.

"I mean it, you might think you love that girl, but I won't be okay with knowing you aren't treating her right. You're

going to wait until you're both grown and know what adult choices are."

I release a heavy sigh, thinking of how I'm going to pay Sean back for this. She would've never heard us, but he has a big mouth and yelled that I kissed a girl.

Which I didn't ... not yet anyway.

"How long do I have to wait?"

Her eyes widen. "At least until you're thirty!"

"Thirty? But ... that's old!"

"Old enough to know that the only thing in this world that matters is how you love someone else. It's not about kissing and all that. It's about giving your heart to someone and always doing what's best for them. I want you to have that, Declan. To know a love so pure and true that you'd give anything for her. You're too young to know if Sydney is that girl."

That's where she's wrong. "I know it in my heart, Mom. She's the girl I will always love."

She smiles softly and then touches my face. "Then you hold onto that, Declan." Mom places her hand on my chest, right over my heart. "Give her this, and you'll have everything you could ever want. A life without love isn't living, it's just existing and you were destined to live."

I shake my head, saying, "I don't think she'd be happy."

"I said proud, not happy," Jimmy corrects. "I knew your mother, and the one thing she valued most was her family. She wanted you to have what she had."

This is the part I still can't reconcile. "And what did she have, Jimmy? My father couldn't have been perfect with her."

"I don't think anyone has perfect, but you're a fool if you think Michael Arrowood didn't love Elizabeth with his whole entire being. The day that woman died, a part of him went with her, and there was nothing he could do but drink."

What he says is right in some ways, but he could've chosen differently. "He made a choice to drink. He had four boys who lost their mother and were trying to find the strength to breathe. My father died because he didn't care enough about us."

Jimmy nods slowly. "And you chose to leave Sydney much the same way."

"You have it all wrong, Jimmy. I left Sydney because I loved her enough to save her. That is why I can never allow myself back into her life. I love her more than I love anything in the world, regardless of what bullshit I say. I would give anything to be the man she needs, but I'm not. Telling her otherwise would be unfair."

"I think that's up to her, don't you?"

"Not if I know that I would only break her heart in the end. It's better to protect her."

He laughs once. "I think you're protecting yourself."

Maybe he's right, but the one thing I know for sure is that I'm not good enough for her—not anymore.

fourteen

I really have enjoyed my time with Milo. He was meticulous going over all areas of the farm with me. He explained what a potential buyer would want me to fix or what they might ask me about, showed me weaknesses to underplay and strengths to play up, and coached me on what my expectations should be. We also spoke about what I want from the sale and what I was willing to give up in order to get that. It's been a difficult conversation, but I'm glad I had it.

At least now, my eyes are wide open and I know the kind of things to do and look for.

We just walked into the main barn, and there are so many memories in here, I can hardly breathe. All I can think about is that kiss. The way he touched me again, as though there were no other option.

I shove the memory away and remember why letting even a seedling of hope grow will destroy me.

"You've loved him for a long time?" Milo asks as we stand

at the door.

My eyes meet his, and even if I want to lie, I have a feeling he can see right through me. "Too long."

"He's been a good friend and I've learned a lot about him, but you've always been the mystery I couldn't crack."

"Me?"

He grins. "Our wanker of a friend in there is a bit daft when it comes to matters of the heart. He has this ridiculous notion that it's his responsibility to protect the people in his life. While, for my purposes, I appreciate his diligence because he manages my wealth and I pay him to be cautious, when it comes to people, he is a fucking idiot."

I laugh and my hand flies to my mouth. "Yes, I've called him that and worse."

"Deservingly."

This topic is nowhere near what I thought we'd end the tour on though.

"Did he tell you why he left me?"

Milo shakes his head as we walk. "He didn't, and while I would never betray his trust if he had, I would at least tell you that I knew."

"He's lucky to have you as a friend."

His smile is devilish. "Yes, he bloody well is. However, I would like to say that you and I are friends now as well."

"I would like that too."

"Good, and as a friend, I often like to counsel those in need, even though my advice is rarely good. In fact, if you ask my wife, I'm usually quite wrong. Still, I know Declan, and I don't believe that he truly wants what he says he does."

"Which is?"

"To be alone."

My eyes meet his as he stares at me intently. I have no idea what to say. Maybe it's the stupid desire in my heart that wants to rebuke him, but then I think about all he's said and what I heard. He doesn't want what I do.

"I think you're wrong, Milo. Declan isn't alone either, he has his brothers."

His deep chuckle tells me he doesn't believe that. "His brothers who live all over the country? Yes, he has them, love, but they're not the same. He isn't pining over his brothers or having to fight to avoid them and then calling his friend to walk their property. Hell, he didn't even ask me to walk his land, which we all know he wants to sell."

"He called you because he wants me gone. If he can't leave Sugarloaf, then the next best thing is for me to go."

Milo puts his hands behind his back as he looks around, seeming to think on what I said. His arms fall back to his sides, and he watches me before speaking. "Men are simple creatures. I promise that he wants you and his pushing you away has nothing to do with anything other than fear. He's terrified that he won't be able to keep the walls he's built around you up for long. You are a beautiful woman who he's loved most of his life, and now, his excuses to resist you are gone."

I release a shaky breath, wishing this conversation were different. I don't want to think about him or resistance because I have neither. All I have right now is self-preservation, and even that is on shaky ground.

"I appreciate your advice, but my life is going down a path that Declan doesn't want. It's complicated, and we both have issues that neither of us will be able to move past. The sad reality is that he's afraid to let himself love anyone and not even I am enough to change that."

Milo gives me a sad smile. "I hope that maybe you're wrong about that, darling. However, we've been out here for hours and I'm absolutely starving. I'm sure Declan is crawling out of his skin, shall we return and torment him?"

I loop my arm in his. "I would love nothing more."

We make it back to the house, and Declan jumps up, his eyes darting to Milo and then me. Milo leans closer to me and whispers. "I was right about this."

I giggle and then shake my head.

"How did the tour go, Bean?" Jimmy asks.

"Good, I think. Milo had a lot of suggestions to make the property more desirable to the type of buyer I want. He was really kind and I ..." I turn to him. "I really appreciate it. Your insight is invaluable."

He bows just a bit. "It was my pleasure."

"Don't you have a plane to catch back to London tomorrow?" Declan asks with a raised brow.

"Don't be rude to your friend," I chastise him. "Milo drove all the way out here from New York, and I won't let you be a jackass in my house."

Out of the corner of my eye, I catch Milo grinning, but when I turn to him, his smile is gone. "I think he deserves to be punished."

Declan grumbles under his breath.

"I thought you two were friends."

Milo leans in and kisses the top of my head. "That was before I spent three hours making his jealous side a bit testy." He chuckles and then takes a step back. "Settle down, Declan, I was merely enjoying my time with your lovely woman here."

"I am not his woman," I correct.

"Yes, well, semantics. I have to go find my wife before she spends all my money in New York. Remember what I said, love, ask for what you want and don't back down. If a developer comes in, call me, and I'll do what I do best."

"Irritate people?" Declan asks.

He flips him off and then walks out the door, leaving me a

bit stunned.

"He's wonderful," I say with a huge smile.

"He's something."

"Thank you, Dec. You have no idea how much he helped me. I really appreciate you calling him to walk the property."

His anger seems to deflate a little, and he runs his hand through his hair. "Come sit at the table and tell me what he said."

I grab some milk and cookies, setting them out in front of us, and then I take a seat. There is nothing that helps me feel calm quite like this does. Each time I would cry, get hurt, or feel like my world was crumbling, my mother set this out for me. It would just magically be here anytime I needed it.

I dip the cookie into the milk, letting it get soft and soggy, and recount to Declan the areas that Milo was concerned about.

He writes them down, making notes, and offering suggestions as we go.

A sleeve of cookies later, I'm exhausted.

"So, you think any of that is doable?" I ask.

"I think we should look at fixing the big things, but the smaller stuff won't matter to a farmer."

I bite the pad of my thumb. "Maybe, but what if it's a developer that comes in?"

"You want to see condos built here? What would a developer really want with this type of land? Sugarloaf is a farming town and really isn't made for any big industry." Declan leans back in his seat and then takes a long pull of milk. When the glass lowers, he has a milk-mustache, and I try not to laugh.

But I fail.

"No idea."

"Why are you laughing?"

"I'm not."

His eyes narrow. "You're clearly laughing."

I take pity on him and hand him a napkin. "Do you like your mustache?"

Instead of wiping it away, he leans forward. "Do you like a mustache?"

"I don't know, I must ache you later."

Warmth spreads through me as we slipped into the kids we once were. Laughing at ourselves and each other at every turn. There was nothing that could embarrass us, and we loved cheesy jokes.

I'm glad to see something hasn't changed.

He wipes the milk off his face and shifts closer. "I want you to think about it, though, selling this place to a developer."

"Milo thinks I'll make the most money that way."

He scratches the back of his head and shrugs. "Money isn't always everything. You may not want to have the farm anymore, but this place is where you grew up."

It's ironic to me that he's worried about heritage now. He's the one who walked away from his family and would've sold that farm off without hesitating.

"Declan, don't you think that you giving me that advice is ... hypocritical?"

"I didn't love my home."

"Okay, but home is where the people you love are. This farm has meant the world to me because of my family, but they're not here anymore. What do I have left to stay for?"

Please say you. Please say something to make me stay.

He looks at me with deep eyes that are searching mine as I mentally give him the answer. I chant it over and over in my head, waiting for him to say it.

"Nothing, I guess."

"No?" I give him another chance.

Declan releases a shaky breath, but when he answers, there's nothing but steel in his voice. "Nothing worth holding on to at least."

I love him. I always will, but it's clear he won't try. Sure, he wants me—it's undeniable when we're together. It's just not enough. He has to want more.

He has to want it all.

"Okay then. I'm glad we got that settled."

Only I don't feel good or glad or settled. I feel sad and like a part of my soul has just left me.

fifteen

Ugh. This puking thing is for the birds. I thought I was done with the morning sickness thing, but apparently, I am not.

I get up, wash my mouth out, and brush my teeth. Today is the annual Country Tractors and Treat fair in Sugarloaf. It's one of my favorite things we do, but I'm just not feeling it. Tonight is Ellie and Connor's joint bachelor and bachelorette party, and I can't miss that. I figure if I can rest and keep my stomach settled, maybe by tonight I'll be good.

Not that I understand why the hell they want to do this as their send off to being single. A small country concert is not exactly my idea of a good time. At least, not anymore.

Once upon a time, I loved the fair's concert. We would listen to whatever local band or singer they found at the karaoke bar pretend to be the next American Idol, dance, and have fun. I loved how Declan would dance with me, laugh as we made fun of the bad singers, and talk endlessly about our future.

I haven't gone to the concert once since he left. It's not the same anymore, but for my friends, I'll suck it up.

There is a knock on the door, and I head down, not sure who the hell would be at my house now.

When I open the door, I'm greeted by the huge smile of one of my favorite people, who just happens to be in the arms of the man who starred in my dreams last night.

"Good morning, Aunt Syd!"

"Good morning, Miss Hadley!"

"I brought Uncle Declan." She beams.

"I see that."

"Morning, Bean."

I really wish he'd stop calling me that. I'm not his bean anymore. "Dec."

"We're going to the festival today!" Hadley pipes up.

"You are?"

She nods quickly. "Uncle Declan said we're going on a date."

I laugh and lean against the door. "Well, you are a very lucky girl. You know, your uncle loves to buy things and carry them around all day. So, you make sure you take him to every single stand, and don't be afraid to ask for anything you want."

Hadley beams up at him. "You do?"

Declan looks at me with his lips set into a thin line, which disappears when he turns to his niece. "Not every stand, but—"

"Oh, don't let him fool you, princess. He loves to spoil the girls in his life."

Declan clears his throat. "You know, Syd, you're right. I do. And that's why I'm so excited that you're coming with us."

My lips part, and I scramble to think of a way out, but Hadley squeals first.

"You are! I knew it! I knew that was why we were coming. Uncle Declan said he had to come do something here and then we could go, but I was hoping we would be picking you up first. And I was right! Aunt Sydney, it'll be so much fun. We can go see the animals and eat all the food and then they have tractors and all kinds of toys and games. You have to go get dressed so we can go!"

I look down at my attire and quickly put my arms over my chest. I have on a black tank top, my sleeping shorts, and no bra. Great.

"I think Aunt Syd could go just like that."

I glare at him. "Funny."

"Well, what do you say? You want to come to the fair?"

"Of course she does!" Hadley answers for me.

I guess I don't really have a choice. "The child has spoken," I say with a smile.

"She does that a lot."

I giggle and nod. "Yes, she sure does. What was it that really brought you by, though? I know we're all meeting later for the joint party, but I wasn't expecting anyone this early."

"I figured I would stop to put the for sale sign up in the yard, and I wanted to give you the paperwork. You are officially on the market as for sale by owner." Declan lifts the lawn sign that was resting on the other side of the door.

"Oh, wow. I mean, this is great."

He looks back at my chest and then turns away. "Why don't you get dressed while Hadley and I take care of putting the sign up?"

"Sounds like a plan."

I head upstairs to my room, feeling a little dizzy at how quickly my plans for the day have changed. Ten minutes ago, I was going to eat, try not to puke again, and then lie in bed with a book before I had to go to the concert. This sort of screws it all up, but I can't seem to say no to Hadley.

After getting dressed in a pair of leggings and an oversized sweater, I head downstairs. I'm far from glamorous, but at least I'm comfortable.

"Are you ready?" Hadley bounds forward.

"Easy, Monster, give her a second to get off the stairs."

I smile down at her and push her light brown hair back. "I'm ready."

"I want to eat everything they have. I didn't get to go to the fair the last three years. Dad, er, Kevin," she corrects, "didn't let us go, and Mommy didn't want to make him mad, but I could smell the food from my house. If I went all the way to the back fence, I could hear the music, and it was so nice."

This kid never fails to make my heart break just a little. She has the most beautiful spirit of any child I know, and I shudder to think what her life would've been like had Connor not found her.

"Well," Declan says with a tightness in this voice. "I think we might have to stop at every stand, food, and craft, to see what we can find."

I can see the hurt and love he has for her. His lips part a little, and his chest rises and falls heavily. It's hard to see anyone hurt Hadley, but it's clear that Declan cares and will do everything he can to protect her, which is his thing.

The protector.

The one who will deny himself everything if he thinks it's for the greater good.

He's an idiot.

However, today, I don't want to fight. I want to enjoy the time with Hadley and give her happy memories of the fair I grew up attending. She should smile, laugh, and be spoiled by people who love her.

"Where are Connor and Ellie?"

Declan looks around and then shrugs. "I think they had something to do or had to go get something. They'll probably meet up with us later."

Oh, they're doing something, all right. "You gave them some alone time, huh?"

He laughs and shakes his head. "I mean, I wouldn't doubt it, but no, Connor took the truck and had to pick something up."

Whatever that means. "That's good for us then, huh?" I ask Hadley as Declan opens the back door to his Jeep.

"What is?" she asks.

"That we don't have to worry about your mom or dad telling us no." I give her a wink, and she grins back.

"Will Uncle Declan tell us no?"

I drop my voice to a whisper, but I know he can hear us. "I know all the tricks to get what we want from him, you leave it to me."

She buckles herself in and leans back in the seat. "I love you, Aunt Syd."

"I love you most."

Declan's deep voice sounds resigned. "And I'm in so much trouble."

"Yes, yes, you are," I reply, feeling lighter than I have in days.

sixteen

"Can we get another snow cone or maybe a funnel cake?" Hadley asks after we finish with the petting zoo. Well, if you can call it that. Basically, it's a pig from the farm down the road, two goats, and a few cows, which may be from the pasture and not part of the zoo at all.

"I think your stomach might revolt if you keep up at this pace," I suggest.

As much as denying this kid is the last thing I want, I also don't want her sick to her stomach. Since we got here, she's had pizza, a pretzel, a fried Oreo, and a snow cone.

"Okay, then can we go to where all the toys are?"

Declan leans in. "What toys?"

"I have no idea."

"Are you going to clue her in that it's a bunch of crap?"

Not a chance in hell. I'm not breaking her heart. "Nope."

He slides from the bench of the picnic table and extends

his hand to help me up.

"Thank you."

"I may be an asshole, but I'm always a gentleman."

I laugh. Sure, he's not. "Whatever you say."

"Come on, Aunt Sydney!" Hadley grabs my arm, and we start to walk.

It doesn't take long before we're in the throngs of the town people. It's busy, and people stop to wave as I see them. This town has been a huge part of who I am, and I'm going to miss it.

"Sydney!" Mrs. Symonds, the principal at the high school, calls out. "Are you feeling better, dear? I was so upset when I heard you weren't well."

"You were sick?" Declan asks.

My mouth goes dry, and I speak quickly, ignoring him. "I wasn't sick. I was just really tired after being out on a call last night."

She pats my arm. "I'm so glad to hear that. I understand being tired, with running this event and working, it's a lot even for me. I heard that Mr. Grisham fell and broke his leg. Is he all right?"

I nod. "Yeah, just a fracture. I'm sure he'll be all good."

We really need to get some people in this town a hobby. Mrs. Symonds is so incredibly busy, yet she still listens to the police scanner as though it's the radio. She knows everything that goes on in this town. She also knows everyone in this town since she either taught them or was the principal when they were in school.

"And you"— she turns her attention to the tall, sexy, and commanding man at my side—"Declan Arrowood, you have grown up to be a very handsome man and so tall."

He grins, takes her hand in his, and places a kiss against her knuckles. "And you haven't aged a day."

"Clearly, you haven't lost that silver tongue of yours."

"Never."

The mention of his tongue causes my belly to flip. I can feel his lips, taste the mint on his breath, and my body yearns for it.

Mrs. Symonds laughs and then claps her hands together. "It's wonderful seeing you two here together, feels like fifteen years ago when you two would sneak off behind the tents and think no one saw you."

I feel the heat on my cheeks. Declan was always stealing me away, kissing me whenever he could. It was impossible to keep away from him back then, and it seems as if I still suffer from the same affliction.

"That was a long time ago," I say, needing not to go on another stroll down memory lane and end up at the same dead end.

"Yes," Declan agrees. "And a lot has changed."

She tsks. "Of course it has. We all grow and evolve, but there are very few relationships I've seen in my time that were anything like yours."

I blame every damn hormone that's coursing through my pregnant body for the tears that come. I have never been a weepy girl. I've been strong, angry, determined to prove people wrong. Do I cry? Sure, but not like this. I turn my head to hide, but I know he saw.

"There's no one in the world like Sydney."

"I would agree there," she says. "And is that you, Miss Hadley Arrowood?"

She nods. "Hi, Mrs. Symonds."

Of course, she knows who Hadley is.

"Are you having a good time?"

"Uncle Declan is going to buy me a pony!"

"Two of them," I correct her.

He looks heavenward, and I grin. "Don't make promises to a kid."

"*I* didn't. *You* did."

"She doesn't seem to think that," I say with a sing-song tone.

Mrs. Symonds watches the two of us with a wishful gaze. "I always hoped I'd see this again. The two of you smiling at each other. Even before you were a couple, you were friends in a way I've seen only rarely in all my years. Never had two people who just *understood* each other."

I look away, not wanting anything in my eyes to give away the feelings in my heart. I have hoped for us to be this away again too. I waited for so long, and now, we're here, and it's all so ... natural.

Declan and I are just enjoying the day together, no pressure, no talking about the past or being lost in old hurt. I never thought I could let myself feel this again. A friendship, anything less than full-blown love, seemed impossible for us.

But now, I see how wrong I was. At the very core of loving him was a deep friendship.

We've been playing with Hadley, laughing and joking around, and it is like coming home.

A place where things make sense and the world is spinning correctly.

Declan speaks first. "It's something I think we are both grateful for as well."

"Can we please go see the tents now?" Hadley breaks in, her impatience finally winning out.

I've never been more appreciative of this kid than I am now. "Yes. We definitely can, and then we can go see the ponies!"

"Great, I'll go back and get my checkbook," Declan says

with a chuckle.

"You all enjoy yourselves, I have a few vendors to check on," Mrs. Symonds takes a few steps away and turns back. "Oh, and did you hear who the singer is tonight?"

I shake my head. "I didn't."

Her face brightens, and she clasps her hands in front of her chest. "It's Emily Young! The country singer from Tennessee, who toured with Luke and just won a CMA. It's just too much. When I wrote to her, I didn't think it was possible, but then she replied two days ago and, well, I just can't believe we're going to have some real talent tonight."

"That's wonderful!" I say. At least tonight won't be a total shit show and Connor and Ellie can have something special.

"Yes, it really is. All right, you three have fun," Mrs. Symonds says with excitement in her voice.

"We will!" Hadley beams. "Come, Uncle Declan, let's go shopping and then see the ponies!"

He lifts her into his arms and kisses her nose. "All right, Monster, but then let's see if we can find something to drive your Aunt Sydney crazy with."

She laughs while I roll my eyes. The only thing that drives me crazy is the man beside me, and I already know I won't have him.

Once this house sells, I can finally move on and allow Declan and I a chance at finding our futures.

Ellie and Connor went off to get her something to eat while Declan and I were tasked with finding a spot on the lawn.

It seems everyone in the area heard about Emily Young

playing here tonight. Usually, you only find your way to the concert once you're seriously drunk. It's better for the ears.

"You think this is a good spot?" he asks.

"I guess so."

I help him spread out the two blankets we brought and then Declan and I take our seats. "Did you have fun today?"

"I did. It was great spending the day with you and Hadley. She's truly a great kid."

He smiles softly. "She is, and it was nice for us to just be able to be friends again."

"Yeah, I guess we were."

"I felt …" He starts and then stops.

"Yes?" We shift closer to each other as though it's the most natural thing in the world.

Declan's eyes move to my lips and I wonder if he's going to kiss me again. I want it, even though I shouldn't, but there's this sadistic part of me that is always going to crave more. Parts of him are better than nothing, at least that's what my heart is saying.

My head knows that I will never be content without the whole of him.

"It was like old times."

Another shift toward each other. "And what did it feel like?"

"Forgiveness."

My heart is pounding against my chest. I don't know what any of this means, but I pray it means something.

"Well," Connor's voice makes us both freeze. "I guess some things never change."

"I guess not," I say, not moving my gaze from his and backing up.

I swear it was there, the want to say more, but what? It could mean that he finally sees that the feelings we have are worth fighting for or it could mean he's forgiven himself for leaving me and is done.

Declan gets to his feet. "Anyone want a beer?"

What I wouldn't give for one, but I can't drink. "I'm good. I'm thinking I need to avoid adding alcohol tonight."

"I'll go with you," Connor says and then looks at me and Ellie. "I figure you two will want to talk."

"Thank you, babe." Ellie waves as he leaves and then her eyes are on me. "What the hell was that?"

"Keep your voice down," I whisper harshly. "It was nothing. We just ... we had a good day today. It was nice, and we didn't fight or talk about the past or me moving. We had fun with Hadley, and I don't know, maybe it's just a place of understanding."

"Oh, I understand, all right."

I internally groan and look toward where the guys went. Declan is standing at the beer tent, watching me as well.

I feel as though I'm a yo-yo on a string, and it's crazy. I'd been so sure about my life until he came back. Now, it's as though, each time I try to sway one way, I find myself being pulled right back to him.

It's always him, which is why I tried to put up the walls that he scaled so effortlessly.

Maybe it was because they weren't walls so much as mounds. The truth is, I want him to break through and come to me. I want us to ... be something—anything—because I love him.

We may have changed, but my feelings haven't.

This is why I really shouldn't be his friend.

Because I will always want more.

I feel so alone, and I need my best friend. "Ellie, there's so much that I want to say … that I … can't …"

She places her hand on mine. "You don't have to explain anything to me, Syd. I'm not stupid. I know that you love him and he loves you. It's clear to anyone who has eyes, for that matter, but you're leaving, and … he's bullheaded."

And I'm having a baby.

I glance back over to him, but he's turned so I can just make out his profile. He's deep in conversation with Connor, and I wonder if it's anything like this one.

I turn back to Ellie who watches me with kindness. "I know, and one day, my heart will listen to everything my head is saying."

seventeen

My body is tight like a bow. The concert is great. After my tongue lashing from Connor about being a better man regarding Sydney, I pulled back and now I feel like I'm drowning.

I'm standing on the other side of Connor and Ellie, working hard to focus on Emily Young's voice and songs instead of how much prettier Sydney is.

I fail at accomplishing this task.

Instead of being lost in the lyrics of whatever horrible misfortune this country singer is telling, I watch Syd swaying gently to the music. Her blonde hair falls in waves down her back and reminds me of wheat in the wind, moving as though it can't resist.

I want to run my fingers through the silky strands and feel her body against mine, but that would be wrong on so many levels.

Still, I move toward her, and then I hear my brother. "Don't do it, Dec," Connor says quietly as he holds Ellie protectively in front of him.

My heart stops, and I stay in place. I can't do it. He's right. It would undo all the progress we made today.

The lights go down and just a single spotlight stays on Emily. "I'd like to sing a song that you might know. I wrote it when I was head over heels in love with a man who wouldn't make up his mind. Anyone know someone like that?" The crowd hoots and claps. "I thought you might. Anyway, I loved him, and I knew he loved me, but I couldn't handle the pain of him rejecting me each time we got close."

Jesus.

I want to flee, but my feet stay rooted.

Emily laughs softly and then smiles. "Cooper and I got married about two years ago, in case you were wonderin'. So don't give up on the right one, y'all. But don't let him call you darlin' if he ain't going to stick around."

She starts to strum her guitar, and Sydney turns to me. The questions in her eyes as she moves to stand in front of me make me want to rip my heart from my chest because the ache is too great. Sydney doesn't look at anyone else, and my resolve cracks. Every reason I've been clinging to fades away. "Do you want to dance?"

She nods.

I hear my brother make a noise and pretend I didn't. She said yes, and I'm going to cling to that.

Here might be the last time I ever get to hold her in my arms, and I'm going to take it.

"I love this song."

I love you.

"Why is that?" I ask.

Her arms move to my chest, and I wonder if she can feel the pounding of my heart. My nerves are bowstrings, being pulled taut before the arrow is ready to fly. Everything inside of me is strained, but I keep it together.

Sydney and I move, the world falling away as it always does when I am with her. Gone is the hurt of my past, the uncertainty of my present, and the regret of the future ahead. Right now, I have her.

She's here, in my arms, where she's meant to be.

I don't care if the sky lights on fire because she's all I see.

"Listen to her." Sydney's voice is quiet and pensive. "Listen to her talk about him giving up and her asking him to stay."

And I do. I hear the words, and I swear that she's singing to us.

"Don't tell me it's too late," Emily croons.

"I won't give up that easy.

Don't call me darlin' and tell me that you're leavin'.

Don't walk away.

Stop pushing me when you know you want to hold on.

It could be so easy for us, baby.

I've been here, but you don't see me.

Don't let go if you're not ready for me to walk away." The acoustic guitar takes over as her voice drifts off.

"Syd," I say her name as both a plea to let go and hold on.

Her hands grip my shirt tighter. "Don't. Don't let go. Don't push me away."

I see the tears in her eyes. I don't want to push her away. I want to hold her close, kiss her senseless, and love her until she knows it in every fiber of her being that she's everything I want.

I see her. I feel her. I know her in my bones, but I won't be able to be who she needs.

No matter how much I wish it weren't the case, I can't give

her the life she wants with a husband and babies. All I can offer her is a friendship that has an expiration date because once my six-months is up and she has moved, I know I won't allow myself to see her again.

The song ends, and the two of us stop moving, just watching the other.

The spell that was surrounding us seems to break and awareness fills her gaze. Her fingers loosen and drop from where they had been clutching my shirt and she takes a step back.

The loss of her is felt everywhere. My heart doesn't seem to beat as strongly, the cold hits my chest, making it hard to breathe, and the emptiness from her loss leaves me weak.

For those minutes I held her, the world made sense. And now ... I need to leave.

eighteen

"Where did Declan go?" I ask Connor. He said he had to go to the bathroom, but it's been twenty minutes, and I'm beginning to wonder if he decided to just leave.

I grab the blanket and wrap it around myself, feeling the night chill. While I've felt this way since he let me go after the dance, I prefer to blame the weather.

"I don't know, probably to get his head on straight after whatever the hell just happened."

I look at him, trying to decipher the meaning of it. He sounds angry or maybe disappointed.

"What has you upset?"

"Him. I specifically told him to let you be unless he was going to give you what you deserve."

"And what do I deserve, Connor?" Now, I'm pissed. "You have no right."

"The hell I don't." He throws his hands up. "You think I don't love you like a sister? Your friendship with Ellie and your relationship with Hadley is everything to us. My brother promised me that he wouldn't do anything to jeopardize our lives here, and not a week after he shows up, you decide you're fucking moving. I'm not dumb enough to think it's a coincidence."

I take each of his statements and break them down. Connor is acting like a big brother, which is sweet, if not a bit late, and he doesn't have all the information. Also, he needs to stop it. If Declan and I want to make a million mistakes, then that's what we'll do, he can't prevent it.

"I went to him when that song played. I went to him because I needed him. I know your heart is in the right place, and I love you for it, Duckie, but I love him. I always have. The two of us are grown-ups, and we need to figure out how to be around each other without being at one another's throats."

Ellie places her hand on his arm and then shakes her head. "We just don't want to see either of you hurt. It's hard on him being back here and facing the things that have haunted him in his past."

Things like his family and me. I know all this.

Connor pulls Ellie into his arms and then takes a drink.

"Where you guys fighting before?" I ask, remembering them when they went to get a drink.

"No, but we were talking ... forcefully."

Ellie releases a deep sigh. "Can you stop riding him so hard?"

"I'm not riding him," Connor says with exasperation in his voice. "I'm not going to lie to him. If he asks my opinion, I'm going to give it to him."

Declan isn't one to run away from conflict, but I can't imagine it's easy for him to be chastised by his brother. I look out toward the field and see something moving in the direction of where my land is. I don't know why, but I know it's him.

"I'm going to see if he's okay."

Connor puts his hand on my shoulder to stop me. "Syd."

"I know him better than you do, Connor. It'll be fine."

"I just ..."

Ellie grips his wrist. "Let her go. It's late, and we're all tired." Then she turns to me. "Will you call me tomorrow or if you need me?"

"Of course." I lean in and kiss her cheek and then Connor's. "I love you both, but this is our battle to fight. If Declan and I can't figure this out, then we have bigger problems than Duckie giving his opinion a little too freely."

With that, I head over to where I saw someone last. It's dark, but the moon is bright and the stars above are so beautiful. I love the night sky. It's filled with so much wonder and a vast unknown. I fixate on the star I want to make a wish on—like I've done so many other nights—and hope this time it'll come true.

Star light, star bright, first star I see tonight. I wish I may, I wish I might, make my wish come true tonight. I hope that Declan and I can find a way through the future. I hope you can heal him enough to love our child and be the father I know he can be ... if he lets himself.

As I move through the field, the sounds of the countryside fill my ears. There are crickets chirping, and in the distance, an owl hoots. As I move deeper, the creek that runs along our two property lines and the frogs that call the water home add themselves to the symphony.

I love how nature is never silent. I never feel alone when I'm out here.

The music that had been roaring in the background has faded to a muted hum. I don't know where he went, it's hundreds of acres between his farm and mine, and he could be anywhere, but I keep walking.

I take a deep breath and focus, trying to feel more than think.

After another fifteen minutes of letting my heart lead my steps, I see him.

Declan's back is to me, and his chin is down to his chest as though he's praying. I make my way there, knowing this could backfire but also believing in my heart that being alone isn't what he needs right now.

He stiffens, and I continue forward.

"You shouldn't have followed me." His voice is low, and he doesn't turn.

"You shouldn't have left."

I hear the breath release through his nose as I come to a stop beside him.

This place means something to all the brothers. It's where their mother rests.

"Did you make sure this place was taken care of for her?"

I shake my head. While I made it a point to come out and check on the sights, my care was never needed. "No, I never had to. Your father took care of it after you all left."

We both fall silent. There were so many nights I met Declan out here as he dealt with his loss. So many times he wanted the solace of being close to the woman who loved him with her whole heart. She was why he fought for his brothers. The promises he made her as she died were what fueled him to take blow after blow from his father.

As much as the abandonment I felt from my own father hurt, I couldn't imagine what he endured.

To face his father and know it would end in bruises and cruelness no one deserved broke my heart as a kid as much as it breaks my heart as an adult.

I would do anything to go back in time and do something to save him. I kept his secrets after he begged me to. He was so sure they'd take him and his brothers away, separate them, and that would've been more than he could bear. I never knew if I did the right thing, but then, the idea of losing him was enough to make me *want* to stay quiet, and for what?

It broke him, and it destroyed us.

I failed him, and I lost us.

Declan lifts his head to the sky and then finally speaks. "He loved her."

"He did."

His father, for all his faults, never let Elizabeth Arrowood's final resting place crumble. Each time I came, thinking it might be overgrown, it wasn't. The headstone is black with her name etched in white as though time stood still here. No matter how many years passed, this little patch of Arrowood land has been maintained. The grass was always cut, and the flowers were rotated based on the season.

In the eight years of their absence, this was the only place he took care of.

"Did you come out often to check?"

"Yes. I knew that even with you gone, you'd want her cared for."

I close my eyes, remembering how he would drag the push mower from my home to this spot. It's equal distance from both our farms, but he kept it at my barn so his father could never take it from him as a punishment.

We'd walk out here, and it would take him hours to ensure that everything was just right.

"She loved him too," Declan says after a moment.

She loved everyone. There wasn't a soul that Elizabeth met that she didn't find the goodness in. Her heart was ten times too big for her body and was the epitome of what people should strive to be like.

However, nothing came close to the love she had for her boys. No matter what, they came first. She fought through whatever she needed to in order to keep them safe, and everyone admired her for it.

When she fell sick, it was as though the angels wept.

"She would've wanted you to be free, Declan."

"How?"

There's so much beneath that one word. Years of hatred, self-doubt, and sadness for the things he's endured. If I didn't know his pain as well as I know my own, it would be so easy to hate him for breaking my heart.

I've tried over the years to blame him wholly for walking away from me. There was so much effort put into wishing to see only my own struggles, but I always saw that Declan was struggling too. He had to be. Regardless of what we said that day, I knew him, and in my soul, I knew that whatever he was doing, he believed was right.

Not that it eased my broken heart, but it made it so that I could stifle the pain.

Without pause, I reach for his hand.

He laces our fingers together, palms kissing as though it were always meant to be this way. Two souls whose fathers destroyed them, search for comfort in one another. Here, between us, I find the peace I've been without for years.

I could tell him what he wants to hear, but I won't. Not because I don't want to console him, I do, but because I know there is no consolation because the pain is there.

"He's gone, Declan. He's gone, and you're not. There's no answer to your question because the only man who could tell you—can't. And ..." I pause, trying to think of the right way to say it. "And there's nothing he could say that would ever make it okay. What he did to you, Sean, Jacob, and Connor was horrific and wrong and unforgivable. But she wouldn't *want* you to live like this."

He finally meets my gaze, and even though I can't see his eyes through the darkness, I feel him in my core.

This is why I should've stayed away. This deep feeling of being exposed and open to him is what scares me.

Declan squeezes my hand and then leans his head down. Our foreheads touch, and I can do nothing but breathe.

"Why, Syd? Why after all this time?"

My hands lift, resting on his chest, needing the feel of his heartbeat to anchor me to this earth. His question leaves me feeling as though I'm floating.

Only, I don't know what he's asking.

"Why what?"

"Why do you make me feel this way? Why does being near you ..." His hands grip my hips, pulling me closer to him. "Why does it make me feel so lost and so found at the same time?"

Maybe it's the darkness and the dance we shared.

Maybe it's my insane pregnancy hormones.

Maybe it's because I want him more than anything but am too selfish to give him the easy road.

All I want is him. Us. This closeness and understanding.

"Because we're still searching for what we lost." Declan sucks in a breath. "I've been lonely and lost for a long time. I've waited and hoped for you to come back because I've needed you. Now that you have, I feel it even more. You were my best friend. My person. My heart and the other part of my soul." My lip quivers, and I hate myself for saying this, but it's in my heart. I can't hold back anymore. "But you won't give me you back, will you?"

His heavy breathing flows between us, and the silence is

all the confirmation I need. "Not because I don't want you or because you aren't everything I've ever wanted. I can't give myself back to you because you're the sun, stars, and the air I breathe. You're everything, and I can never be more than the shell I am now."

I bring my hands up to his chest, needing him to really hear me just this once. "That's where you're wrong," I say, feeling less brave than my voice sounds. "You just are too afraid to fight for me."

His fingertips brush against my lips. "This is me fighting for you. Go, Sydney. Go before we make a mistake we can't undo."

Tears fill my vision, making his face blur away. They fall, cascading down my cheeks, and the pain of his rejection shreds me. "We could never be a mistake."

Declan wipes the tears from my cheeks and then takes a step back. "You and I both know what our future is. I'll go back to New York, and you're moving closer to your sister. Go, Syd."

And then I do what I should've done when I saw him standing here ... I walk away. Because there's nothing I can do to change his mind, there is no hope for anything between us, and my heart can't possibly endure another shot by an Arrowood.

nineteen

"You have a call," Devney says as her head pops in my doorway.

"From?"

"A really sexy sounding British guy."

Milo.

It's been a week since my house went up for sale. I got an offer and sent it over to Milo to see if I was crazy. It is over asking, but they are a developer and want to split the farm into forty, ten-acre lots and then build big, million-dollar homes that they claim will fit into the small-town appeal of the area.

I'm not really sure how that works since most of the farmhouses here are original. We aren't close to a major big city, so moving out here isn't ideal for commuting. It doesn't seem like a great idea, but what do I know?

"I'll pick it up, please close the door." She nods and then clicks it closed. "Milo?"

"Ahh, I knew I was unforgettable. How are things? Anything naughty or new that you want to share about Declan?" His accent slides over his name.

"No, but if there were, I probably wouldn't tell you."

"Smart girl."

I laugh. "Did you get my email?"

"I did, and I actually have my gorgeous and much-too-good-for-me wife sitting here now. She looked over the offer and had her own ideas as well."

"Oh!" I say excitedly. "Hello, Danielle."

"Hello, Sydney. It's great to sort of meet you. I'm sorry I couldn't go out to your farm when Milo did, but we were in New York visiting our daughter, and I couldn't slip away. Anyway, I heard a lot about you, plus, I've heard bits and pieces from Declan over the years."

He's talked about me to her too?

"Darling, you'll give the girl the wrong idea," Milo chides. "I'm sure Sydney knows that our Declan is a tortured soul who is the worst sort of a miserable bastard who only complains about women." He drops to a low voice and says the rest as though it's through the side of his mouth. "We must give her the wrong idea so she'll want him more."

Danielle huffs. "You're an idiot. She should know that he has thought about her and has at least mentioned her."

"Yes, but *I've* already done that."

I smile as the two of them go back and forth.

"Clearly, not well."

"I'll give you not well." Milo's voice rises just a touch.

"I'm sorry about this," Danielle returns her attention to me. "We tend to be a little stubborn and argumentative."

I laugh softly. "I get it. I hate to push this along, but I have court in about an hour—"

"No, no," Milo steps in. "I went over it, and I understand your hesitation, but really, it won't be your problem once you sell. I know that's probably not what you want to hear, but once you sign, you lose the right to dictate the use of the land."

I sit back in my seat and let that settle over me. I knew all of this, of course. Still, I just hoped it would be a sweet family from Chicago who was tired of the city life and wanted to raise cows and make no money. It's a charmed life—sort of.

"Are you saying I should take the offer?" I ask.

"No."

"Yes."

Milo and Danielle answer the opposite at the same time.

"Sydney," Danielle begins before he can, "I'm from the States, so I feel more qualified to talk about this than Milo. If you sell, this legacy that you spoke of will be cut up and sold off. Now, you can take this offer, which is a good one, and make a lot of money—"

"Which is what you should do," Milo says. "I assure you that no family is going to come in and buy your land at that price. A developer like Dovetail will see a greater profit and pay your asking price."

It all makes sense, but it feels wrong.

A sympathetic sigh comes through the line. "I understand your hesitancy." Danielle's voice is soft. "I know you want to move quickly."

"I need to move. I need to be settled. I can't stay here."

It's best to sell the house, move, and let Declan know about the baby.

"Then give me another few days," Milo suggests. "Let me look into this company a bit deeper. I'll see if I can figure out a way to make this all work out the way you're hoping it will."

"I appreciate this. I really do. This farm has been in my family for almost a century, it's just ... difficult."

I keep trying to picture life not in Sugarloaf, and I fail each time. My sister left and never looked back. My mother said she was completely fine deeding the farm to me when she left and she's fine with me selling it now.

Milo clears his throat. "Give us some time, the one thing I've learned in my pathetic life is that there's always another way. Until then, be sure to drive Declan fucking miserable for ever letting you go. Us brooding, stupid types can't seem to resist a woman who doesn't want us."

Danielle bursts out laughing. "And trust me, he would know."

"Running away again?" Sierra asks before drinking her coffee.

After spending the morning looking at houses, I landed in the coffee shop in her town and called her, hoping for some sisterly advice. Now, I regret my line of thinking.

"No, I came to make sure I was doing the right thing and find somewhere to live."

Sierra places her cup down and then shrugs. "And have you figured out if it is the right thing? Did you tell Declan about the baby yet?"

I shake my head. "I plan to as soon as the house is sold and I know I'm leaving. If I do it before then and he offers me some grand life, I'll back out, I know I will."

"I think that's a smart plan. Declan's sense of right and wrong will win out."

And that's the exact issue. "He'll offer to marry me because he wants to do what he thinks is the honorable thing, not because he loves me."

Her hand touches mine. "I'm sorry."

I sniff and then pull back. "That's the saddest part, Sierra, he does love me. I know he does. He just doesn't think he deserves to be happy."

"Why do you think that?"

"Because he's admitted it. He's told me he wants me, he kisses me like a man who is desperate, but he's so headstrong and won't budge. I don't get it. Why does he think pushing me away is better for me instead of loving me and letting us just be together? I feel like I could accept everything if I *truly* knew he didn't love me."

Sierra leans back in her chair and rubs her bottom lip. "You guys always seemed so steadfast, you know? I think I was more surprised by him leaving than I was when Dad left. It was almost as if nothing made sense."

"No shit."

"Have you asked him?"

"Of course I've asked him."

Sierra smiles softly. "No, I mean point-blank. Why did you end things?"

I sigh heavily, feeling like the weight of the world is on me. "I think I have. I mean ... maybe." I think about it, slowly realizing that we really haven't gotten anywhere. I've asked and he's evaded or when he's wanted to talk, I couldn't handle it. "He told me when we broke up that he didn't love me."

"And we all know that's not true."

"Okay." I can concede on that. I don't believe it either. "He said he was doing what he had to in order to protect me."

I see Sierra's mind working to put the pieces together. I may be a lawyer and good at figuring things out, but Sierra has me beat. She would've been an excellent detective.

"Protect you from what?"

"Himself, I guess. I think he believes a lot of his father lives in him."

She rolls her eyes. "Please, nothing of that asshole is in any of those boys."

"I agree."

"Well, then there's something else. I don't know what it is or why he's not telling you, but I don't believe that, after all the time you were together and planning a life, he suddenly woke up some random day and was like, we're done."

I mull that over and try to see it through different eyes. It wasn't an angle I'd ever looked at before, but maybe something happened that convinced him he needed to walk away from me. I wouldn't believe for one second that he cheated on me—that type of betrayal isn't in that man's blood. Only, it's the only thing I can think of that would push him to such lengths.

Whatever it was, if it was anything at all, I don't understand why he wouldn't just tell me. We had no secrets. My thoughts, my heart, my world was open to him and it was the same way—at least I thought—for him as well. Nothing he could've ever said or done would've changed how I felt for him.

"Does it really matter?" I ask.

"I don't know, but it would to me."

"I guess that's the point. If he loved me, with his whole heart loved me, then why wouldn't he come to me with his issue, if there even is one? Why wouldn't he confide in me and let me help him, like equals?"

Sierra lifts her hands and then lets them fall back to the table. "Far be it for me to try to understand his mind. You would know that better than I would."

Maybe years ago, but not now. I don't really know the Declan of today. He's changed so much and doesn't laugh as freely or love as openly as he used to. It's as though a part of him is closed off.

"I'm just saying that, in the end, none of it makes a difference. I'm selling the farm, moving here, and I'm going to have a baby."

"Yes, but you haven't sold the farm, moved, or told him about the baby yet," Sierra points out. Then my sister gives me her smirk that makes me want to choke her.

"*You* were the one who suggested I sell the farm!"

"And when the hell have you ever listened to me?"

I swear that God made sisters as a punishment for Eve and her stupid apple eating. I never would've considered listing the farm if Sierra hadn't suggested leaving town. "Why are you saying this now?"

Sierra shifts in her seat. "Because I don't want to see you regret it. Yes, it's time to move on, but you love that town, the farm, and your life in Sugarloaf."

"I also am going to be alone, with a baby, no help, a farm, a law practice, and a million other reasons that I need to get out of there for."

"Jimmy would run the farm," she counters.

"Yes, but he wants to retire. He's been doing this for a long time, and it's selfish of me to ask him to stay on. If he left, I'd have to hire someone else and hope to God they do the things we need to sustain the farm. Even then, I don't know that I can do it. I need my family."

"What you really need is Declan."

My head falls back, and I groan. My sister is worse than I am, and I'm pregnant and emotional. Declan isn't going to give me what I want, so there's no point in this conversation. "Living by you might just make me finally snap."

She laughs once. "Please, you snapped a long time ago. Listen, I love you with my whole heart, but no one told you to list the farm the day after I suggested it. I didn't think you'd actually give it up. You're the one who dreamed of raising children there and growing old with the cows. I never did. The idea of moving back to Sugarloaf is enough to make my skin crawl." She shudders as though it does. "I said it because I wanted to see what you'd do." I open my mouth to say something, but she holds her hand up. "Not that I don't love you and want you to be closer. God knows it would be great to have someone else around to help deal with Mom, but the point is that I didn't think you'd actually list it. Threaten it, sure. Maybe talk to a realtor, okay fine, but not do it."

I glare at my sister, and then suddenly, a wash of sadness comes over me. Tears prick my eyes, and I want to crumple into her arms and just lose it.

"Syd?"

"Why is this so hard?"

Sierra doesn't hesitate before she wraps me in her arms and presses my head to her shoulder. "Oh, Syd, it's supposed to be hard. Life is hard and people suck. Things don't go our way, but we muddle through it."

I lift my head, feeling stupid for breaking down. "People leave, Sierra. Men leave us. Look at how many times it has happened. I can't stick around, hoping that he'll be different. They always leave."

"Alex hasn't. I push him, most of the time without even meaning to, and he stays. Each time I think that this is finally it, he proves me wrong."

"He's a unicorn."

She smiles. "Maybe, but if he is, then at least we know they exist. You have a right to be hurt, but you are also judging Declan on the past and, what I believe, is only half the information. I'm not telling you what to do, but at least talk to the man. Let him know you're having his love child and see what he does."

"And if he breaks my heart?"

Sierra tilts her head to the side. "Then I'll chop his nuts off."

twenty

I'm sitting in my living quarters, if I can even call it that, going over emails. My clients have understood about my new schedule, and it's been nice to go at a slightly slower pace. The two other financial advisers in my office have been working all the backend things for me as well.

Four years ago, this wouldn't have been possible. I wasn't able to take time off. I couldn't make my own hours, and I sure as hell wouldn't trust anyone to do what I could do. Now, I'm learning that I was an idiot.

An email comes in from Milo, and I open it immediately.

Declan,

I've done a bit of research regarding the company that submitted an offer on Sydney's farm. It's all on the up and up, but I can sense she's apprehensive.

Have you gotten any signals on which way she's leaning?

The best person in the world,

Milo

I roll my eyes at his sign off and reply.

Jackass,

No, she hasn't mentioned anything to me. Why is she apprehensive?

Man with the biggest dick ever,

Declan

I can't wait to hear this response.
Sure enough, just a few seconds go by and my email pings.

Delusional Dickhead,

Let's not even go there, mate. As for the lovely Sydney, I just know she wasn't fully comfortable. The offer is above asking, and I have advised her to accept it, but she needed time. I can't help but feel as though she's running from something, not that we all don't know what it could be ... you know, YOU.

I believe, as does Danielle, that she wants a family

to take over. Someone who won't divide the property and sell it off in pieces, but live there and love the place as she does.

The Undisputed God Amongst Men

I ignore the ending and desire to spar with him and focus on Sydney. She never mentioned wanting a specific type of buyer. Her goal is to leave Sugarloaf, so I figured that, if she got a good offer, she would take it.

Having a family buy it is a great idea, but it is not really what the current economic climate is doing, buying small dairy farms in the middle of Pennsylvania. No, the people here have been here. It's a generational town. The more likely possibility would've been the neighboring farmers buying off her land to increase their own.

This need to fix this situation starts to build.

I know she's leaving because I'm here, no matter what she says about wanting to be close to her family. There's no reason for her to do that on my account. She'll regret this decision in a few months, and I can't let that happen.

I love her, and all I've ever wanted is for her to be happy and content. Forcing her to move away from her home and life is the exact opposite of what I've spent my life trying to do. It makes the sacrifice I made eight years ago completely worthless.

I can fix this.

I fire off three emails.

The first is to my accountant, instructing him to create an LLC. It'll act as a shell company to hide who I am.

The second is to my investment company, and it outlines my request for them to wire money against my company line of credit into the shell once it's formed. I need a few days to liquidate that type of money.

The third is to Milo.

> I'm buying her farm. I want you to act as my broker. Keep my name out of it, but get the deal done for me.
>
> Declan

I get a response back from Milo immediately.

> And there's a grand gesture if I've ever seen one. Still want to continue lying about how you're not in love with her, want to marry her, and be happy?
>
> Don't worry, I'll get it done.
>
> Milo

Looks like I'm going to have roots in Sugarloaf no matter what my plans are.

This time, it doesn't feel like a prison sentence. It's the right choice, and it's something I can give to her because I have nothing else to give. I know in my heart that Sydney doesn't really want to go. She loves this town, her home, and the farm. I'm only here temporarily, and when I leave, she'll have what matters most to her.

"How long are you out for?" I ask Sean. Earlier this evening, he twisted his knee while attempting to steal second base.

I don't normally watch his games, but Connor and I were stuck at his place while Ellie and Hadley were doing a girls' day with Devney and Sydney. So, we were able to see the whole thing.

As soon as it happened, I called him, even knowing he doesn't have his phone on him during games, but it looked horrible on television. It doesn't help to listen to the announcers give their un-expert opinions on what it all means either.

For hours, Connor and I waited for Sean to finally call back.

"I don't know yet. I have another MRI tomorrow, but so far, they haven't seen anything in the first scans, so that's hopeful."

"I'm sorry, man."

Baseball is Sean's life. It's what keeps him from going crazy. He lives for game days, and I know it'll kill him to have to sit out.

"Whatever. If I have to have surgery or something else, at least it'll work out timing wise to be back ... there."

He already got it worked out to be here during the off-season anyway, so I guess it works out in a fucked-up way.

"It's not as bad as I thought it would be," I admit.

"Well, Syd is there."

"Yes, but that's not why."

Sean laughs. "I love you, Dec, but you're a fucking idiot. I would give anything for a woman like her."

He could have a woman like her. Devney has been his best friend since some asshole pushed him, and she punched the guy. They were in second grade. That was all it took for him to fall in love with her, only he never had the balls to tell her. Instead, they pretend as though there isn't a damn thing between them, and it's fucking insane.

"Sure you wouldn't."

"Don't start with this shit about Devney again. She and I aren't anything more than friends. If I did care about her, I wouldn't be able to give her advice on love and other shit."

He's so delusional. Neither of them has ever had anything serious enough to scare the other. They date, sometimes even for longer than I ever could handle it, but in the end, there's always something wrong with the other person.

It allows them to keep up their bullshit and remain unattached in case the other finds the courage.

"I could give Syd love advice if I knew it would never matter."

"All right, asshole, do this for me." Sean's voice is hard, and I know I'm pissing him off. "Think about Sydney with a guy—any guy—and tell me that you could give her pointers on how to make him happy."

Rage at another man that doesn't exist claws at me. My hands start to sweat and bile begins to rise in my throat. This reaction is exactly why I never think about this shit. She's mine, and I would do anything for her, including spend millions to buy her farm without her knowing. The tightness in my throat makes it hard to breathe, and I hate my brother for making me even entertain the thought.

"Fair enough."

"That's what I thought." He laughs once. "Imagine loving her the way you do and trying to help her work on shit with some idiot. It wouldn't happen. No matter how strong you try to tell yourself that you are."

"I also haven't ever denied loving her. I know what it feels like to have her, to see her eyes on mine and know she loves me. It's a different thing, Sean. I'm not saying you can't put your feelings aside. We all know you're a master at it."

"I'm not a master at it. I just don't want to fight all the time. We had enough of that in our childhood, I'd like to have some damn peace."

"There is no peace here," I say and then pinch the bridge of my nose.

Sean goes quiet for a second. "You could have peace, Dec. The war inside you has nothing to do with Sugarloaf. It has to do with regret. We all thought we'd be like Dad so we purposely did everything opposite. We didn't get married, didn't have kids, didn't allow ourselves to put down roots or start a family. And in the end, for all we know, he died happy. And look at us."

Yeah, look at us. I'm in fucking agony each time I see Sydney.

"Are you unhappy?" I ask.

"I don't know. I love baseball and I have a great life, but … sure, there's room for more. We're moving off this topic." Sean leaves no room for debate. "I'll be back next week for the wedding, and hopefully, I'll have some answers about my knee. So far though, it looks like it's nothing and I'll be back out there for the next series."

"Good, I guess it looked worse than it was."

"Yeah, thank God."

My head is a mess, but the last thing I want is my brother to be unhappy. "Look, I just want to say one more thing. It may be too late for me, but it's not for you to find someone. You're a good guy, and I know that kids and a wife are something you've always wanted."

Sean is quiet for a minute. "And why is it too late for you?"

I glance out toward the field that divides me from what I want most in this world and grip the windowsill. "Because I lost the only person who could ever be worth it, but I'm not good enough for her. She's leaving and I have to let her go."

"And that's where you're a fool. That woman thinks you're more than enough. Maybe it's time you start believing it yourself."

twenty-one

"That's ... that's a great offer, right?" I look at Devney, who's reading the email from Milo over my shoulder.

"It's what you wanted."

This one is the full asking price, which is less than the one I got from the developer, but Milo knows the buyer personally. He sent over the offer, and I'm in shock. The buyer wishes to remain anonymous because the person is influential, but whoever it is, is looking for a quaint home in the country with land for days. Apparently, they want a respite from the city life where their cows can roam and they can work.

"Do you think it's someone famous?" Devney asks.

"I mean, it makes sense."

She beams. "What if it's Emily Young and her husband? She was just here, right? She could've fallen in love with our little town and wants to make her next big hit in Sugarloaf."

It could be. I don't know if Milo knows her personally, but it makes sense. "I don't know, should I care? It's exactly what I wanted. You know? Like, this is the kind of thing I hoped for. Not a builder who would come in and tear up the land and build strip malls or condos."

Devney scratches the side of her head and then moves her lips side to side.

I groan, knowing this won't end until she says her piece. "Spit it out."

"Fine. You could stay. You don't need to sell the farm. I said it before, and I mean it, Declan will be gone in a few months. Why do you need to move?"

"Because it's too hard!"

"What is? He's been fine. You guys aren't fighting and you haven't been holed up inside your house just to avoid him. Hell, if you didn't want to see him, all you would have to do is just ... tell him to go away when you're coming around. I feel like there's something more you don't want to tell me, which is *not* like you."

There is so much more. Sierra didn't help, and now, Devney isn't either. It's all so much weighing on me, and I can't take it. I feel as though I'm breaking apart and no one understands.

"It's too much! I love him, Dev. I love him, and I can't keep walking around where we should be, you know? Like, I see the barn and think about how we made love there. I can't even go to the fucking pond. Everything at that place reminds me of him."

"Why is it so much worse now?" Her voice is tender, and there's a bit of understanding there.

"He's always been everywhere, but now that I've been around him again, I know that when he leaves, I'll have to feel that loss again. All that we could've been will be back in full force, and I won't be able to pretend anymore. I've done it for so long, but I won't be able to go back to that."

She touches her hand to her chest and nods. "I understand. I hate to see you go. I wish I could do something—anything— to make it easier for you. I wish I could go with you, Syd, but ... I can't."

I bounce at the idea. "Why can't you? We could start over."

Her lips part and she exhales. "There are things that I can't leave."

"Like what?"

Devney smiles softly. "My family is here."

I shake my head. It's no big secret that Devney can't stand her family. She and her mother are constantly fighting. She went away to college and I was shocked when she came back. I thought for sure she'd stay out there. "Dev ..."

"Look, I can't go. I have things that are important to me here. And so do you, Sydney. I don't want you to have regrets."

That's what I fear most. I don't think it'll happen right away. I'll be close to my sister and family, and they'll help me through it. I know I won't be alone. It's down the road when the baby is older and wants to know about the farm or Declan that I worry about.

Although, who knows what'll happen when I tell Declan. He may be glad to have me farther away since he's made it clear that children and a life with me isn't what he wants. He can go back to New York and live his life, and I'll take care of everything else.

Then there's the possibility that he'll want to be a part of it. I just don't know what to do, but I have to make choices and then deal with it. If Declan wants to be a part of the baby's life, of course, I'd encourage it. It just doesn't mean I have to stay here. At least in a new place, it won't be the past haunting me.

"Sydney?" Devney breaks through my thoughts.

"Sorry, yeah, I don't either, but I worry I'll regret not doing what I can to preserve the rest of my heart."

Her smile doesn't reach her eyes. "Well, you have a big decision to make, I hope you're happy no matter what you choose. I know all too well how hard it is to live with your choices."

She leaves the room, and I lean back, pushing away from the desk. My hand rests on my belly, and I wonder about the life inside me.

There are so many unknowns. All of then hang on what will happen when I finally tell Declan, which I still have to do. My ultrasound is in less than a week, and it's time for us to face our future, whatever it may be.

All of this is weighing me down, and I'm tired.

I don't know how much longer I'll be able to conceal my pregnancy either. I'm out of the first trimester, which is what all the books say is the dangerous period of a pregnancy. There're no more reasons to avoid telling him.

"I think we should sell the farm and go where we're wanted," I say down at my stomach. "It'll be hard, but we'll have your aunt and grandma close. I can't stay here, as much as I want to." A tear slips down my cheek. "I love your daddy so much, little one. I would give anything for him to choose us, but I don't think he will."

With that thought in mind, I send an email back to Milo, telling him I'm going to accept the offer.

twenty-two

"You look absolutely gorgeous," I tell Ellie as I stand back to look at her. She's truly glowing. The sun is just starting to fall behind the tree line, and Connor is out there waiting for her.

"I can't believe I'm getting married already. It feels like I've been with him forever, and now we're really going to be husband and wife."

I smile at her and hold back the tears. "I'm so happy for you, Els."

"I couldn't have gotten to this point without you. Your friendship is everything to me."

The tear falls, and I pull her into a careful hug. "I love you guys. You both deserve to be happy."

She laughs and then fans at her eyes. "I don't want to cry."

There isn't a doubt in my mind she won't be able to hold back once she sees Connor and the barn.

All the Arrowood brothers are in town and have worked extra hard to pull off a few surprises for Ellie.

"Are you ready?" I ask her.

She nods. "I am."

We head outside to find the sky painted in reds and oranges. Everything is so pretty, and joy fills my heart for my friend. She deserves to marry the perfect man on this perfect day.

Hadley comes running over. "I put the petals down, like you said, and now I'm here because you told me to come back."

She crouches and then cups her daughter's face between her palms. "I love you, Hadley."

"I love you too, Mommy."

"Are you happy?"

Hadley nods. "You look pretty. Are you happy?"

The smile on Ellie's face is wide and full of love and hope for her future. "I am so happy. I love your daddy very much."

"Me too. He's the best. I have the best mommy, daddy, best friend, and now I'm going to have a sister or a brother. Can we go now?"

My hand is over my mouth as more tears fall. Weddings are always emotional for me, but add the fact that it's Ellie's wedding in a barn, there wasn't a chance I wouldn't lose it.

Ellie looks back to me and nods. It's time.

"All right, Hadley. You're going to walk your mommy down the aisle after I go. Okay?"

Hadley stands a little taller and squares her shoulders. "I'm ready."

Yes, they are. They're ready to go on to the next chapter of their lives, as am I.

The music cues, and I make my way into the barn.

The back door is open, offering a picturesque background for the ceremony, and there are lights going from beam to beam all the way across the inside. Flowers are everywhere, white with hints of yellow and Ellie's favorite color: pink. The guys hung paper lanterns all throughout it and it's truly breathtaking. As I walk down the path lined with petals, I smile at guests. Some of Connor's friends from the military, teachers from Ellie's school, Devney and her boyfriend, and then my eyes find the Arrowood brothers.

Connor stands there, hands clasped in front of him, brimming with a nervousness I can't remember ever seeing in him before. When my gaze latches on to the man behind him, the rest just fades away.

There is Declan. In a black suit with his dark brown hair trimmed just a bit shorter than it was the last time I saw him. He watches me make my way toward him, and I wonder if he's thinking the same.

This could've been us.

It should've been us.

My stomach is in knots as I keep my feet going, wishing I was in the white dress and Declan was standing in front of Connor. I would've loved him with everything I am. I do now, but it isn't enough. Declan and I are the tragic love story.

The tears that had ceased when I started walking fill my vision again, but I push them down. I won't cry, not tears of sadness today.

Today is for joy. Today is for Ellie. Today is for goodbyes.

"Dance with me?" Jacob asks me.

"What?"

"Dance with me, Syd." He gets up and walks over, hand extended.

Connor and Ellie just finished their first dance, and now Declan is dancing with her. Jacob stands there, waiting with a sly grin.

"All right," I say and allow him to lead me to the dance floor.

Last time I saw Jacob, his head was shaved for a role he was playing in a movie, and thank God, it's grown back. "You look good."

"So do you."

"Thank you for the compliment."

Jacob leans in and rests his head to the side of mine. "You know, I was always so jealous of Declan."

"Yeah? Why is that?"

"Because he had you." Jacob turns me slightly so we're even farther away from his brother.

"Uh," I stammer. I don't know what the hell that means.

He laughs and then spins me. "Relax, I'm not saying I've been secretly in love with you. I'm saying that he had you. He had ... someone. Connor and I were the lone sheep in the pack. Sean had Devney, and Declan had you. It was good for him."

"Until it wasn't."

He looks toward his family and then back to me. "Maybe. It wasn't easy for him to lose you, Syd. It wasn't easy for any of us, to be honest."

"You didn't have to, Jake. You could've come back at any time, and I would've wept in your arms."

There wasn't a moment I didn't wish at least one of them would stroll back into my life. They chose to stay away, and it broke me a little each day.

"I wish it were that simple," he says, effortlessly turning

me around the dance floor.

"Why did you guys leave?"

Jacob swallows hard and then shakes his head. "It's not my place to talk about it, Syd. I wish it were, but that's up to Declan."

I didn't think he'd tell me. The best I hoped for was for him to confirm there was something for him not to tell me, which he just did.

"Can I cut in?" Declan's deep voice asks from behind.

Jacob looks at me with an understanding smile and then nods. "Of course. She was always yours anyway."

I go to open my mouth, but before I can, Declan is leading me out of the barn and into the night air.

The music is still going on behind us, people dancing, laughing, and enjoying the celebration, but out here, it's just us.

"Declan?"

Instead of answering, he pulls me into his arms, and I can't speak.

He looks so handsome. So very freaking handsome.

His suit forms perfectly to him, giving him an air of authority that makes me weak in the knees. There's a dusting of whiskers along his strong jawline, which adds to the appeal. His eyes are soft and a little somber. Yet, I know he's happy for his brother. Connor has pushed past his fears and loves Ellie with a ferocity that rivals any love story.

Declan's one hand is splayed against my back, holding me tightly to him, while his other hand clasps mine and tucks it between our chests. He moves just enough so we aren't standing still, but I can feel a strong pulse between us.

It feels as though the dance we shared at the concert was just the beginning of the song we're creating the harmony to in this moment. Right now, we're building to something. I can feel it in my bones, and it terrifies me.

Our eyes are on each other's, both asking questions and searching for the answers.

"It's like prom again," I say, needing to break the silence.

He smiles and shakes his head. "I'd like to think we've grown up some."

"Maybe, but I remember feeling this nervousness with you back then too."

That night, I knew I would give myself to him. It was all planned, and we both tried to make it through the night without making a scene. I loved him with my entire heart, and I wanted him to have my body too.

We made love, which was exactly what it was for us—love.

"I remember wanting to throw you over my shoulder and take you to the barn. I had that hay bed made and was desperate for you."

"Well, maybe it's nothing like prom," I say, trying to joke.

"No, I think it's exactly like prom. Only now I know what it feels like to love you, to kiss you, and to hold you in my arms, knowing that nothing else will ever come close to what we share."

I look away, not wanting to hear this.

"Declan ..."

"I know," he says quickly. "I know all of it. I know I hurt you. I know I don't deserve to touch you or breathe the same air as you, but tonight, Sydney, I can't stop it. You're so beautiful. All I could do all day was watch you, wish I were a better man and that I was marrying you tonight." I close my eyes, holding back tears. "You have no idea ..."

"No idea?" I ask with a laugh. "Do you think I wasn't picturing the same thing? Do you know how badly my heart is breaking as I look at you and know that if you'd just trusted me, we could've figured out a way—together."

"You don't—"

"No. You don't, Declan. You don't understand how my soul is calling out for you. I want you. I want you more than anything, and I can never have you."

He shakes his head, still holding me close. "You are the only person who has ever had me."

"Had. I don't want past tense. I want you—all of you. I want the broken parts and the loving parts, the ones that are afraid of me and the ones that will fight for me."

"Those parts that you want?" He breathes heavily, eyes filled with heartbreak. "They're not worthy."

"Okay then," I say, unwilling to keep doing this.

"Okay?"

"Yes."

Declan's arms tighten just a bit. "What are you saying?"

My heart is beating so fast, my stomach doing flips and I let the fight go. "I'm not going to keep pushing you anymore. I can't do it. I can't make you try or see sense. We're both standing here, right now, wanting and needing each other."

"Sydney, it's …"

"No, it's the truth." There is resignation and sadness in each word. He might be battling, but I've already tried. I've failed. I'm waving the white banner and accepting defeat. "I needed you to fight, Declan. I wanted and begged you to fight for me. For us. For the love we share and the life that we could have, but you won't, and I can't make you. I love you, but it's time for me to accept that we won't be." I move my hands to his face. His beautiful face that I can see when I close my eyes. I brush my thumb against his cheek. "I have a lot that I need to say, but not here and not now. Today is for your brother."

"What are you saying?"

My throat is tight as I stare at him. "You don't have to fight anymore, Declan. I see it all now and I'm so sorry that I've pushed you these last few months. I'm sorry I didn't hear you. I thought that if I could make you fight …"

Declan releases me, retreating a few paces, his chest rising and falling. There's anger, hurt, and frustration in his eyes. "I am fighting for you!" He roars before stepping forward and cupping my face between his gentle palms. "I'm fighting with everything I am because I love you." His voice has dropped to almost a whisper. "I would rather cut my own heart out than ever hurt you again. Don't you see that? Do you understand that my not falling to my knees and begging you to just fucking love all the pieces you say you want is to save you? It's not that I don't want you, Sydney. I don't fucking deserve you! I need you more than anything in this world!"

That's where he's wrong. I grab his wrists and push forward. His hands hold my face as he pulls me so we're a breath apart and then he slams our lips together. He kisses me with everything in him, and then, I kiss Declan back. Two planets colliding couldn't hold a candle to the way we connect.

Gone is sanity and reason, all that exists is us.

I hold on to him, afraid he'll let me go, but he doesn't.

Declan pulls me tighter against him, his hands moving down to my neck and then around to my back.

Our tongues move in unison and I drink in all that is him. His power, his strength, and I give him back all of mine.

We are stronger together.

His hands move down, cupping my ass, and I moan into his mouth. I need him more than anything. Once again, he makes me crazy, only this time, it isn't with the need to say goodbye. It's with the hope for something more that is driving the madness.

Yes, I'm moving.

Yes, he's leaving.

But, God, what if ... we can be more?

What if he can see that we could be a family?

We can figure this out and I won't give up or run away.

That's what we're both doing, and I'm too tired to take another step. So, it has to be up to him to stop with me.

"I need you, Declan. I need you, so please don't push me away," I beg and then kiss him again. If his lips are to mine, he can't refuse me.

For a split second, he breaks away, and I want to scream, but then he leans down and scoops me into his arms.

My hand rests against his neck, and he stares down at me. "It's me who needs you."

twenty-three

 *deelan*

This is everything I've been fighting against, but holding her, kissing her, and seeing her smile has fucked me up in the head.

Sydney was supposed to be my forever. As Connor spoke his vows, it was like a part of me broke away. I saw her eyes, the way the tears hovered just on the edge, and it was me who fell.

I could see it all, and then, watched it leave when she walked back down the aisle.

Now, Syd is here, asking for my all, and I'm unable to refuse.

In my arms, I hold all that matters. Looking away from here isn't possible because this could all be a mirage. As soon as I let go, she might disappear, but Sydney is real. She stares right back at me as we enter the small living space.

"This isn't what I pictured?" Her voice is the sweetest sound.

"No?" I ask as I flick the switch to turn the fireplace on and then approach.

My arms wrap around her, holding the only thing in the world that matters. When she said all that, gave in, it was like I snapped. Everything I had feared disappeared because no matter what I've tried to convince myself of, losing her again would be the end.

"Don't let me go," Sydney begs.

I walk back to the bed and put her down. I look at the woman I love, wanting to say all the things I'm feeling. Give her the truth that I'm the buyer of the house, the night I left, and all the fucked-up dreams I have about the future.

For some reason, she believes in me.

She sees the man I can be instead of the man I am. To her, I'm not broken, a failure, or unworthy.

I would give anything for that to be true. "You have no idea how beautiful you are. How much I want you."

She leans up, pressing her hand to my lips. "When we talk, we say things we can't take back."

I rub my thumb against her cheek. "Then let me show you all I want to say."

I vow, right here, to love her with everything I am so that tomorrow maybe she'll hate me a little less. Maybe she'll feel all that I wish we could be.

"Declan, I should—"

It's my turn to stop her from speaking, pressing my lips to hers. Once I feel the fight drain from her, I murmur against her lips. "No talking, Sydney. Just let me love you."

A soft, sweet cry escapes her lips, and she nods. Her fingers trace lines down my cheeks, and I kiss her more reverently this time. It isn't to silence her. It's because I've gone so long without this, and I want to drown in her touch, rejoice in her love, and stay here where I don't belong.

Her head falls back, and I trail wet kisses down the column of her neck. The last time we were together, it was frantic and hurried. I was out of my mind with desire, and we were like teenagers.

Tonight, I want to brand her into my soul.

Nothing about this time will be hurried.

I slowly pull the thin straps of her dress off her shoulders, moving my lips in the direction they fall.

"Declan." She sighs my name and tangles her fingers in my hair. "I need you."

"You have me," I tell her and mean it. I'm hers. I won't pull away, not until the sun comes back up and we no longer have the dark to conceal all that's wrong and hopefully we can find a way back to the light.

I unzip the back of her dress and pull it down. She undoes each button on my shirt, watching me with her bottom lip between her teeth. Syd pushes the dress shirt away, a coy smile now playing on her lips.

She's absolutely gorgeous. She's wearing a lace bra that causes my throat to go dry.

Then she reaches up, removes a few pins from her blonde hair, and lets it fall around her, framing her face, and I freeze. I don't know that I can breathe. Everything about this moment is too much. I know I've said I would let her go, but I don't think I can.

Sydney is the answer to questions I seek and I'm not strong enough to ask anymore.

I'm done with keeping my distance.

I've fought against my better judgment, and yet, here we are again. My heart has always been hers, and if we can make it through tonight, after I tell her everything, then maybe I can stop fighting the wrong thing.

"I don't ..." I try to speak. To tell her how fucking magnificent she is and what I want, but the words don't come.

Sydney stares at me as a blush paints her cheeks.

"What?" I ask, not sure I want to know the answer.

"This is exactly like prom."

Maybe, but I don't want it to be like that. I want to give her pleasure, show her how much I fucking love her. I want the memory of this night to hold onto forever. Ellie may have been the center of everyone else's attention today, but all I saw was Sydney.

I chuckle softly and run the pad of my finger down her chest. "But I'm not a boy now."

"No, you're not."

"And I won't fumble through what to do to you," I assure her.

"I don't doubt that. But we're on a farm, were dressed up, and about to repeat what we did that night."

Her body trembles slightly as I move my finger back up, this time grazing her nipple. I lean in, my tongue lavishing the scrap of silk, and her head falls back. "Did I do that on prom night?"

"No," she murmurs.

I grab and pull until she falls back onto the bed with a soft laugh.

Sydney's gaze looks to the window that takes up the entire wall and the view around us is truly beautiful. I wake to sunlight and fall asleep to stars.

"It's like we're outside," Sydney muses.

"No one can see in, though." I made sure that the one-way glass is completely private. Last thing I wanted was Hadley strolling out to the tiny house and finding me ... in a compromising position.

"So they can't see us do this?" she asks as she slinks her

hand into my pants, wrapping her fingers around my dick, pumping up and down a few times.

"No, and thank god they can't see us do this either."

We kiss for what feels like eternity. Her hands roam my back, arms, and chest, touching everywhere she can reach.

My lips trail down the slope of her neck and then to her ear. "I'm going to do a lot more, Bean. I'm going to give you so much pleasure you won't be able to think straight. I'm going to make love to you until we both collapse, and then, I'm going to do it again."

She pushes onto her elbows, eyes taunting as she tilts her head just slightly to the side. "That's a lot of talk for a man who said he didn't want to speak."

God, I love her.

I move in, watching her breathing accelerate and her eyes fill with desire. There's no rush, and I take my time, going inch by inch in agonizing slowness.

When our lips are almost touching and the heat of her breath is on my mouth, I wait. Her panting fills the small space, and I revel in the fact that it's me who's making this woman desperate. "I can think of another way I'd like to use my mouth, can you?"

"Yes."

"Good."

And then I kiss her.

Our tongues duel, both vying for control, but she won't get me to relinquish it. Sydney has always wanted the upper hand, but not now. Not when I need her this much. I want to conquer her, own her in every way.

We both lift up so I can remove her bra. "I love you in lace."

"I love you naked," she replies.

I smile, loving how the warmth of the fireplace illuminates her perfect skin.

Instead of replying, I lean down and take her nipple into my mouth, sucking and then rolling my tongue over it. Sydney moans, and I cup them so I can suck, lick, and caress both at the same time.

I pin her arms above her head. "Keep them there," I command.

Then I slide down her body, kissing my way down. She sucks in a breath when I get to her stomach, and I grin. She knows exactly where I'm going.

I push down her lace panties, and then it's my turn to catch my breath. Here she is, laid out like a fucking feast for me. The sight will be burned into my brain. I bring my lips down to her center and slide her legs over my shoulders.

My tongue moves against her as she makes incoherent noises. I taste her, licking at her clit, as she grips the pillows, not moving her arms. I continue to drive her crazy as the heels of her feet dig into my back.

"I'm close." Her voice is breathless, and I increase the pressure of my tongue. I can feel the strain in her body as her legs clench around my head. I suck, flick harder, and then repeat it until a loud cry releases from her body.

I keep going, drawing out every ounce of pleasure I can.

The tightness in her body releases, and I make my way back up, pulling my pants down as I watch her lust-heavy eyelids flutter open.

"That definitely didn't happen on prom night."

"No, I wasn't very sure how to do that. Not until at least the fourth time." I laugh and lean down to kiss her. Sydney's hands fall to my boxer-briefs, and she pushes them down over my hips.

Then there is nothing between us, just like I want it to be.

"I liked us when we were inexperienced."

"You did?"

She nods and brushes the hair off my forehead. "We learned together. We grew as a couple, and it was beautiful."

"You're still beautiful."

She shakes her head and moves her hand down my chest. "I don't mean that way. Although, I'm glad you still think I'm pretty. I mean it in the way that we found each other."

"And is now that way?" I ask, hating the question the minute it leaves my lips.

"Now, it's ... different. We're both different."

I wish it weren't the truth, but it is. We've both been through things in the last eight years that we can't pretend never happened. I can't undo the past, but I can give her what we both want—a future.

"Maybe we are, but I need you more than anything. You make me someone else—someone better."

Sydney lifts up so our lips touch. "Make love to me."

"Do we need ..." I look over for a condom, but Sydney pulls my face back to hers.

"Not tonight."

"You're sure?"

Her eyes flash with something and then she nods. "It's fine. I promise."

Good because I don't want anything between us. I feel the heat of her as I push inside, her body enveloping me, pulling me deep.

I've never felt such pleasure before. Maybe it's because of everything that happened today, but this time feels like heaven.

Sydney's eyes stay on mine as I bury myself to the hilt. My entire body feels as though it's being turned inside out.

I don't move, needing to hold on to the sensation for as long as I can.

She clenches around me, and I groan, unable to hold back any longer. I slide in and out, both of us panting with exertion. It's so good. I can't tell where I begin and she ends. It's just us—two people who fit together perfectly.

I love her. I need her more than I can ever explain.

The idea of letting her go again is incomprehensible, and I'll do anything to keep her.

"Declan." She moans my name as her fingers dig into my back. "I can't hold on."

"Let go, Bean. Let go, I have you—always."

Her head falls back, neck arching and nails scraping down my arms. I slip my hand between our bodies and rub her clit. Sydney's breathing grows faster.

"Look at me, Syd."

When she does, there is so much love in her gaze that it has my lungs struggling to find air. She gives it freely, and I take it like the greedy bastard I am. Whenever I felt low, she filled me up, and I didn't realize how much I needed it until now.

Her eyes shut as another orgasm takes over her, and I follow right behind.

Panting and sated, I roll over to the side, pulling her into my arms, not caring about anything else. I need to hold her, breathe in her lavender and vanilla scent that feels like home.

As we both come down, her hand rests on my chest, and I press my lips to her forehead.

When I look back at her, a tear falls down her cheek. Worry fills me. Fuck. I hurt her … or maybe she already regrets this. "Syd?"

"I'm sorry," she says quickly.

"Why are you crying? Did I do something? Did I hurt

you?"

She sits up, pulling my dress shirt on. "No, no, it's just that ... I'm sorry I didn't say this before."

"Say what?"

Another tear falls, and she wraps the shirt tighter. "I'm pregnant."

twenty-four

I wait, and he stares at me. "Already? We just ... and how ..."

I wipe away the tear that rests on my cheek. "Not from just now ... from the last time. When we were at the pond."

"You're ... *months* pregnant?"

Guilt hits me, and I nod. "Four months. Well, closer to five now."

"But you're not even—"

"Showing?" I finish for him. "I know, but I am starting to show, I have a small bump here." I move my hand to where it looks like I'm bloated.

Declan stares and his mouth opens and closes a few times. "That's ... the baby?"

"Yes."

When I asked the doctor a few weeks ago, she said it was

very normal not to show until the middle of the second trimester if you're skinny and have never had a baby before.

Declan rubs his hand down his face and then blinks a few times. "Were you ever going to tell me?"

"Of course I was."

"When?"

The anger is clear in his voice. "Today. Tomorrow. I don't know. I wanted things to be settled for me."

"Settled?"

My lip trembles, and I fight back the fear that builds with each second. I didn't think things would go this way. I thought, we'd have sex and then he'd push me away. After I was broken and alone, I would tell him and we could part ways.

But then he held me.

He loved me.

He gave me more than I could've ever wanted, and I couldn't hold it in.

He kissed my stomach, and I thought, right then, I would sob.

When we were both done and he pulled me close, I couldn't hold it in any longer.

We're going to have a baby, and if we could share what we just had, then maybe we can have more.

Now, he looks as though I've just betrayed him. "Yes, I wanted to have the house sold so that when you rejected us, I had a plan."

"So this is why you were moving?"

I close my eyes and feel the tear break free. "Yes."

"And what about me?"

I open them again to look at him. "What about you? What about *you*, Dec? You made it abundantly clear that you didn't want me or a baby. You practically screamed it and mocked your brother. I was right there, I heard it. I stood there, already pregnant and terrified, and listened to you talk about throwing yourself off a cliff. What did you want me to think?"

He huffs and runs his hands through his hair. "I didn't know."

"No, but then I made comments and said small things to gauge where you were at, and still, you were clear about not wanting a life with me. You were so hard-pressed to tell me over and over how there would never be an us."

I feel stupid and ashamed, but I did what I felt was right for me and the baby.

"And you thought that meant the baby?"

"I would've never held this child from you. Never. I want you to love him or her. I want you to be a part of their life, but you were the one who said you wanted no part of a life like that."

"Fucking hell, Sydney, this is our baby! I ... I wouldn't leave you to raise the child without help."

Without help. Two words that I have dreaded hearing from him.

"Tell me what your version of help is." Declan says he won't leave me alone to raise a child, and I believe him, but now I want more. I want it all.

"I don't know," he says, sliding from the bed. Declan throws on a pair of sweatpants and then starts to pace the very small space. "I need a minute."

"I'm sorry I didn't tell you."

He shakes his head. "What is it you want, since you've planned this out?"

There's a bitterness to his voice that puts me on edge. Gone is the sweet, caring lover that held me. "I didn't really plan this. I just knew that I needed to get myself situated."

"By moving."

"Yes," I admit. "I wanted to be near my mother and Sierra."

"And what was my role?"

I pull my lip into my mouth and fight back the tears. "I wasn't sure what you'd want. I know you wouldn't abandon us or not fulfill your obligations."

Declan scoffs. "I would, of course, help financially."

He's angry and he has every right to be, but it stings. I have to remember that I've had plenty of time to absorb this and ... well, he hasn't. Not only that, we just had a very special moment.

I step closer, keeping my voice even. "Yes, I assumed you would. But what about love, Declan? What about being a father? What about spending time with them? Loving him or her? Giving the baby a family?"

"What the fuck do I know about a family?" he yells and then turns away and releases a deep breath. "I'm ... I'm not the guy you think I am."

"And what guy is that?"

When he turns back to me, I don't see anger in his eyes, I see fear. He's absolutely fucking terrified. "The one who can be a father. I don't know the first thing about what a father does. All I know is anger, fists, and being not good enough."

"And what about how you raised your brothers? What about the man who took those fists so another didn't have to?"

"That is what you want around a kid? A guy who can take a beating?"

God, he doesn't see it. It's so maddening. "You." I step to him. "You are a good man. You're loving, honest, and would do anything for someone you love."

"Like leave them? Abandon them? That's what I did to you," he tosses back.

My heart is pounding, but I try to push aside my own feelings so I can focus on him. I've had almost five months to come to terms with all of this while he's only just been dropped into the water with me.

Still, I want to rail at him, throw something at his head, and knock some damn sense into him.

This feels like another excuse. Yes, he left me. Yes, he says it was to protect me, but he's never explained it. There's a reason and I'm not going anywhere without knowing what it is.

"Why did you leave me all those years ago?"

"What?"

"Why did you walk away? What was it that night that made you go?"

I put my armor over my heart and refuse to let anything penetrate it. Not until I have the truth.

"You know why."

I push back. "Tell me again."

"Because I didn't fucking love you!"

"Liar."

"Don't call me a liar."

"Don't lie to me!" I yell back. "You didn't love me? Bullshit! If you didn't, then it would've meant nothing when you saw me a few months ago. You wouldn't have sought me out at the pond. You wouldn't have tried to make things okay between us. And ..." My breathing is coming in short bursts as the emotions tangle and crash inside me. "You wouldn't have *told* people you love me! I know you love me, you chicken shit! I know it in my goddamn bones."

"It doesn't change anything!" His hands are shaking as he reaches toward me, only to pull them back at the last second. "It doesn't matter that I loved you then or now, I had to leave. I had no choice. I did what was best for all of us. None of us know if I have more of my father in me than we want to believe."

"You won't hurt me."

"You don't know that."

"I do. Why did you leave?" I push him again.

This might be the only chance I have. Right now, he's not thinking and the walls he so carefully constructed can't hold it for too much longer. I need to tear them down and get to the heart of it.

"I told you why."

"The truth, Declan."

He shakes his head and tries to move back, but there's nowhere to go. "It doesn't matter."

"I think it does. I think something happened, and you and your brothers decided to leave. I think it had to do with your dad, and whatever it was, it was so bad that you felt you couldn't tell me, so you walked away instead. Am I right?"

His eyes meet mine with his jaw clenched tight. "Syd."

"There's something you're not telling me, and I'm not letting this go. What happened with your brothers? What are you protecting them from?"

The only thing that would ever cause Declan to walk away had to be something with his brothers. How I couldn't see it sooner is beyond me, but now that I do, it's crystal clear.

Declan steps forward, hands still trembling.

I move to him, knowing he's battling with wanting to tell me, but there's a deep-seated need to protect those he loves.

"Choose me, Declan," I beg softly. "Choose us and just tell me what made you walk away eight years ago."

"Let this go."

"Why did you leave me? Why did you give up everything? Why didn't you choose me then?"

"Fucking hell, Sydney! I can't do this!"

I can see the agony, but I can't back down. As much as I want to, I can't. So, I step closer to him until there's almost no space between us. "Why? Why did you let me go? Why did you lie to me? Why?"

"Because my father killed someone and we were all there!" His breathing is labored, and I take a step back.

"What?" I clutch my stomach, feeling like I might be sick.

"That's why I left you. My father took Sean's car and drove drunk. He ran two people off the road, killing them instantly. We were there. The four of us saw it, watched in fucking horror as they flipped and he drove off."

I shake my head in denial. "You're not making sense."

Declan lets out a half laugh and then pinches the bridge of his nose. "We were there, Bean. We watched him kill those people and then drive off, but it gets so much worse."

The way his voice breaks at the end causes my chest to ache. I sit on the bed, the fight leaving my body as I brace myself for a different kind of answer.

"Tell me."

He leans against the counter, looking worn and tired. "We confronted my father, demanding that he turn himself in, but he laughed and said he would tell the cops he was home all night and that it was one of us. Syd, he was driving Sean's car, but we couldn't be sure if anyone actually saw our dad behind the wheel. We didn't have a choice. We had nothing and he had all the cards."

"Declan—"

"No, let me finish. You want to know all of it? Well, here it is. The people in that car, they were Ellie's parents."

I gasp, and my hand flies to my mouth. "No."

"Yes. My father killed Ellie's parents. So, you ask why I left you? That's why. My father was a murderer, my brother's car was the one that it could've all been tied back to, and I loved you so fucking much that I knew the only way to keep you free from all of it was to walk away."

I can see the tremors raking through his body, but for the first time since I met Declan Arrowood, I don't know what to do.

I've seen him at his breaking point, but this is past that.

I'm afraid for Declan.

Of what this has done to him.

All these years, he's held this inside himself and pushed away people he thought he loved, and he's done it all because of sins that weren't his own.

My heart breaks for him.

And then I think of Ellie and how impossible this must've been for her. The night she showed up at my house, broken and inconsolable, saying things that I didn't understand at the time but make so much sense now. Still, she forgave Connor.

Hell, she just married him.

I look to Declan, wondering why he's still punishing himself. "You didn't kill those people. Sean, Jacob, and Connor didn't either. Your father did, and you spent eight years of your life protecting your brothers. You don't have to do that any longer." The words come out softly, as though I'm dealing with a small, wounded child, which is what he partially is. "You don't have to save me anymore, Dec. I'm right here. I'm fine."

"Because I didn't come back for you. Don't you see? If I had, then what would we be?"

"Together." I breathe the word.

He shakes his head. "No, this doesn't change things. Now you know exactly what this family is capable of. Ellie may have forgiven Connor and the rest of us, but I haven't."

And there lies the heart of the issue. Nothing has changed. We are still here, even with our entire lives altered. We're having a baby, he's told me everything, and he still won't give himself the chance to be happy.

He will always be the baby's father. I will always care for him and hope that they can have a relationship, but it's where my heart has to break free. For the sake of our child.

I get to my feet, removing his shirt and reaching for my dress, slipping it back on. I can't stay here another minute. I need some time to think, process, and get a grip on all that's happened.

"Where are you going?" Declan asks from behind me.

"Home."

"So you push me to talk and then you leave? What about everything I said?"

"I heard it all, and I am so sorry that you've suffered. I would've been there for you eight years ago, but I understand that you did what you thought was best. However, now I have to do the same. I need to think, as do you. There are a lot of decisions to be made for the both of us and we're both far too emotional to do it now. You need to get it through your thick skull that we're having a baby, I'm not breakable, and I don't need you to protect me, I need you to choose me." I look to the bed where I felt whole again in his arms. "You made love to me. You showed me, made me feel every ounce of your love. It was so beautiful that I cried. There is no way you can tell me that wasn't real or that you don't want me. But if you can't, then … that's on you."

He rubs his teeth over his lips and then sighs. "I won't deny that I love you. Everything was supposed to be different tonight! Goddamn it, Sydney! I … I had let you in and now I find out this. I can't do it all in one night. I can't give you back what you want *and* wrap my mind around being a father."

"I *know* that you love me, and you say you can't be what I want you to be, but all I've ever wanted is you—the good, the bad, and the broken parts of you. But, Declan"—I step toward him, feeling naked and exposed as tears fall down my cheeks—"we are *having* a baby. One who needs to be loved with your whole heart, even if you can't find the courage to do that for me."

He gets to his feet, moving toward me, but I step back. Tears are his kryptonite in general, but my tears ... they destroy him.

"I don't know what you want—or, I do, but there's no way I can erase the past."

I move toward him and settle my open palm over his racing heart. "I'm not asking you to, but you have to make a choice. Your past is muddy and filled with pain, but you have something in the future. A beautiful possibility and a woman who, despite everything, still loves you with her whole heart. In two days, I have an ultrasound appointment in Conyngham. I'll text you the details. I hope you'll be there to see our baby and choose the future."

I lean up and press my lips to his as he stands ramrod straight. My hand is on the doorknob when his voice fills the space around us.

"You talk about letting go of the past, but you're running too. You're selling the farm and moving away even knowing that you're pregnant. You kept this from me, and now what am I supposed to do?"Bottom of Form

My fingers squeeze tight around the cool metal in my hand, and I draw in a fortifying breath. When I turn to look at him, I hold myself strong and say the only two words I can think of. "Chase me."

twenty-five

"Where the hell have you been?" Connor asks as I come to a stop in the doorway of the barn, debating if I can even walk back into the reception.

"Lost."

"Lost?" His head tilts to the side as though I'm an idiot—and I am.

I'm a total fucking idiot.

I knew better than to ask her to dance. The minute I touched her skin, I was gone. It was hard enough to walk away from her after we danced at the concert, but tonight ... it was impossible. I have fought against going to her so many times, and I just couldn't do it anymore.

Now, I've really gone and fucked it up.

"I was with Sydney."

"I figured. We all knew it was coming."

I look at my youngest brother and feel a thread of anger. "Did you know?"

"Know what?"

"Know about Sydney ..."

Connor's brows furrow, and he looks at me from side to side. "Did you hit your head? You said you were lost, maybe you're coming down with something?"

I step closer to him, my voice low and tense. "Tell me if you knew and you've been hiding it from me."

Connor releases a heavy sigh and takes a step back. "As much as I love kicking your ass, today is my wedding day, and my wife probably won't appreciate it. I don't know what the hell is going on with you and Sydney, but she came running in here, kissed Ellie and me, said she was sorry but she wasn't feeling well, and then she left. I came out here to see where you were because I figured you fucked up something, but I find you rambling and ready to rip someone's head off. What the hell happened?"

It's none of his business, and it's clear he doesn't know about the baby. I have no idea if Ellie, Devney, or anyone else does, but I can't say the words right now.

She kept it from me for so long. Months of her planning to run away and, what? Pretend? Did she think I wouldn't figure it out? The small bump she has now is only going to grow, and I still have a little over two months here.

"Nothing."

Connor grabs my arm as I try to move around him. "No, Dec, I'm sorry, it's not nothing. You have always been the adult, but I'm your brother, not your son. My wedding present from you can be the big fat check you wrote and also you telling me what has you both running away again."

"I love her."

"We all know this."

"I love her, and I told her about Ellie's parents."

Connor grips the back of his neck and nods. "You told her everything?"

"After ... we ... tonight, she was relentless. She wouldn't give up, and I just kind of snapped and told her."

Connor sighs heavily and then shrugs. "I'm glad you did. Although, you probably should've done it differently. Since, I'm sure you weren't tactful."

"No, I wasn't. But I don't know if telling her was right."

"It's time that we stopped acting as though we did something wrong. Yeah, we made some bad choices, but Dad is the one who was to blame. Look at her." Connor juts his chin toward Ellie, who is standing inside the barn. "I don't deserve her. Not for one fucking second am I good enough to walk in the same universe as she does. She's beautiful, kind, and has given me more than my worthless ass could ever want. But she loves me. She loves you and Sean and even Jacob, God knows why. She lost everything because of that night, and yet, there she stands as my wife. If Ellie could forgive us, then so can Syd and everyone else we've pushed away."

It isn't that simple, but there is a lot of wisdom in his words. I only wish that we weren't moving so fast. I'm not ready to be a father, and I had just finally been ready to move forward with her. We all know I don't deserve Sydney, but I never have.

Everything is so fucking complicated. My instinct is to run after her, but I'm so messed up in the head that I know I won't say the right thing. I'll end up pushing her further or making her see that I'm not worth her tears, and I need to fix that first.

All in two days.

She's the only thing that I've ever wanted, and she's giving me a gift—a child. I wish she had told me sooner. I would've ... I don't know, been there. Then tonight would've been different for us in so many ways. Instead, after I told her I loved her and was willing to try, she dropped a bomb on me.

Now I've gone and fucked it all up.

"What if she doesn't forgive me for how I was tonight?" I ask him even though he has no idea that there's so much more than what he assumes.

"Then you don't know Sydney at all, brother."

He's right. She's already forgiven me because she knows me. I just need time to get everything together. Then I can prove to her how I feel instead of giving her words she won't believe. Sydney will take me back, and I'm going to make sure I never disappoint her again.

"When did you get so smart?"

Connor laughs, clapping me on the back. "When I learned that some things are worth fighting for."

"What's worth fighting for?" Sean asks as he joins the two of us.

"Sydney," Connor responds.

"What about Syd?" Jacob asks as he makes his way toward us.

"This is great, all three of you at once," I say with sarcasm thick in my voice. I love my brothers individually, but when we're together, it usually ends with someone bleeding or bruised.

Jacob nudges my shoulder and glances around. "Is no one going to clue me in?"

"I just got here," Sean responds. "I heard this asshole"—he lifts his thumb toward Connor—"say something about fighting for something. And guess what they were discussing?"

Connor smiles as though this is hilarious. "I was just informing our idiot brother that he needs to get his head out of his ass."

Yeah, but he doesn't know the whole of it. "It's easy for you all when you're on the outside looking in," I try to defend.

Sean shrugs. "Maybe so, but you've been back here for a while now and you've yet to accomplish it."

"Oh, he accomplished something," Connor adds unhelpfully.

"Wait," Jacob draws out the word. "Where the hell have you been?"

I glare at Connor. Him and his big freaking mouth. "I've been here."

"Where? I haven't seen you or Syd since you asked to cut in."

Jacob just became my least favorite brother.

Sean glances at Connor who raises his hands up. "Don't ask me. It's up to Declan to tell you that he and Sydney went back to his tiny house and screwed each other's brains out and then he let her leave. I mean, it would be really rude of me to tell you that."

"I hate you all and if it weren't your wedding, I'd beat you."

Jacob laughs while shaking his head. "Man, you really are an idiot."

"I know this," I admit. The three of them watch me. "What?"

Connor rubs his jaw. "It's just that you've always been the one who was so sure of your decisions."

When it comes to Sydney, I don't ever feel sure. It's as though we're on two different levels and I've never been equal to her. She's better than me in every way. Now, it's all so damn complicated. We're going to have a kid, which I never thought was going to happen for me.

If I give in, let myself love her, and it doesn't work out … I won't recover. For so long, I've fought against ever seeing a future other than my job. Now, all of it has changed.

"I don't know that I've ever been sure, Connor. I've just

made the choice and lived with it."

Sean huffs. "Except where Syd is concerned. Look, Dec, we're not stupid kids anymore. All of us have been living in the past."

"What made her leave after your interlude?" Jacob asks, eying me more closely.

"I told her everything."

"Everything?" Sean asks.

Connor rests his hand on Sean's shoulder. "Yes, the accident, how it happened, and why we all left town. It was the right thing to do. No matter what, it affected all of us, including Syd."

I look at my brother, thankful to have him as a part of my family.

"So, she didn't take it well?" Jacob's voice is full of curiosity.

I sigh. "More like I didn't handle it well."

The three of them all chuckle. "There's a shock," Sean digs at me.

"There's more, but, I can't get into it now."

Today is for Connor, and I've already taken up too much of it. "Besides, Ellie is shooting daggers at us as we all stand out here."

"Everyone smile," Jacob says as he lifts his hand to wave. The three of us all mimic him.

Connor speaks through his smile. "I'm a dead man."

"You sure are," Sean agrees.

"We look like fools," I say. The four of us are waving and smiling as though we're at a damn parade.

Ellie shakes her head and walks to another guest. Then the three of them turn back to me. Connor speaking first. "We may look like fools, but you're acting like one. Go to her tomorrow and fix it."

And then he walks back to his wife, kisses her temple and a pang of jealousy so strong nearly drops me to my knees.

I want that. Right there. I want it all.

This bed smells like her. The entire place does.

I roll over, press my face in the pillow, and inhale. The lavender and vanilla cling to the fabric, and I sit up. I can't take this.

Today is the day I'll go to her and tell her I want a future with her. I'm going to battle the demons that plague me about being a father, and I'm going to figure it out.

I roll over and grab my phone for the tenth time, checking to see if she's called or texted.

Nothing.

It's useless to lie around when I need to deal with my mess of a life. I fire up my laptop and find an email from Milo.

Declan,

She accepted the deal last week and was fine with the original closing date, but I got an email from her late last night saying she wants to expedite the sale and close by the end of the week or she would take the other offer. The paperwork is being sent by courier to your office to be signed by tomorrow.

What in the bloody fucking hell did you do to her?

Milo

Fuck.

She's running. I screwed up last night by not telling her how I really felt, and now she thinks I didn't choose her. Well, I have news for her. I'm not going to let her run off with my kid. I'm not going to allow her to make these choices without me, not when I love her like this.

When the dust settles, we will figure it all out—together.

Last night wasn't some fluke. It was long overdue and high time I got my head out of my ass.

I get a cup of coffee and throw some clothes into a bag, I need to get into the city, sign the papers so she doesn't sell the farm to some other random company and get back here.

I dial Milo, and he answers on the first ring.

"Seriously, what the fuck did you do?"

"I told her I loved her."

He laughs. "It's about bloody time."

"And then she told me she's pregnant."

Silence falls. "You know I don't want to ask the follow-up question."

Now, it's my turn to laugh. I bet he doesn't. "It's mine. We slept together a few months back, and well, I guess we all know what she was running from. But, I was a fool when I showed up and hurt her. I felt guilty that she was leaving because I came back into her life."

Milo lets out a long breath through the line. "So, naturally you decided to buy her farm?"

"She doesn't want to sell, and I love her. I want her to raise our kid wherever she wants, and if it means I jump through hoops to make this closing happen, then so be it. When will the papers be there?"

"Tomorrow. I need to call her as soon as we disconnect and let her know you agreed to move up the closing."

"Good."

"Are you sure about this, Declan? I know you have good intentions, but I don't know if she'll see it that way and it's a lot of cash."

I can see why he thinks that, but I see it as doing exactly what she asked me to do ... chase her.

Only this time, I'm going to catch her and I won't be letting go.

"I'm sure. I'll be in the office in a few hours. I need to sign them and then get back out to Sugarloaf."

"Do you have the cash already?"

"Yes, I had the money borrowed against my company."

Milo clears his throat. "If you only knew how fucking stupid you are for ever letting her go in the first place."

I laugh once and toss my bag in my car. "Oh, I know, but I'm not stupid anymore."

I hang up the phone and hear the ping of a text.

Sydney: Here is the information for the appointment tomorrow at two o'clock. I've given them your name as the father and let them know you may be attending, so there should be no issues with you going in. I want you to know that only Sierra knows about the baby. I don't know if you told anyone, but I didn't. I haven't lied to anyone, but I thought you should know before anyone else. As for the other night, I had hoped, so much so, that you'd see how much I love you. I don't know what else I can do, but if you choose not to come, then I'll have my answer.

Oh, she'll have her answer, and then she'll have to make her own choice as well.

twenty-six

My leg is bouncing as I sit in the office waiting room, waiting. Not just for my appointment, but for Declan.

I haven't heard from him in two days, and my heart is in my stomach at the idea that he's not coming.

I check my phone again for any missed calls, of which there are none, and then send a text to Ellie.

Me: Hey, have you seen Declan?

Ellie: He left yesterday to go into New York.

The breath pushes from my lungs as though I've been punched. He left?

Me: You're sure?

Ellie: Yes, he stopped by the house to let Connor and I know he was going to be gone for a bit.

He left me. He ... he went to New York. I knew it was stupid to get my hopes up, but I did. I thought that maybe he'd hear what I said and give us a chance. I'm such a fool.

Time and time again, he has shown me what he wants, and I keep trying to believe otherwise. Why do I never learn?

"Ms. Hastings?" A nurse calls my name.

"Yes." I stand and shove my phone into my bag.

I may feel like falling to the ground and crying, but I won't. Today is the day I get to see my baby. I'll hear his or her heartbeat and, hopefully, find out if it's a girl or boy. I may be alone, but I'm strong enough to do this.

"Right this way," she says and extends her arm. "I'm Jenna, and I'll be with you through the ultrasound. I need you to go in here and get changed. Once you're ready, go through that door."

I nod, knowing I can't speak yet. I may feel determined, but I'm shattered at the same time. This is not the Declan I know. He wouldn't do this to me. He wouldn't abandon a child either.

I'm livid, and I will never forgive him for this.

Letting another deep breath out through my mouth, I close my eyes and try to push all of it from my heart.

But it hurts.

It hurts so much that it's hard to breathe.

How can I love him while he's so willing to break my heart like this? Why can I not let him go like he's done to me?

Another tear slides down my face as I stand in this empty room and strip down. I focus on the mundane things like folding my clothing neatly. I slip the robe on and shiver. I feel cold, numb, angry, and disappointed.

I gave him a final chance to choose me, and there is no clearer answer than him not showing up today.

I step through the door and force a smile onto my lips.

"Are you ready to see your baby?" Jenna asks as I hop onto the table.

"Yeah, will we find out the sex?"

"If you want me to, I definitely can try. Sometimes they don't cooperate."

I smile and fight back the urge to say: then they'd be like their dad. "I understand."

She goes over what she'll be looking for and how the appointment should proceed. "Do you have any other questions?"

"I think I'm good. I'm just ready to see him or her."

Jenna touches my arm. "Are we waiting for anyone?"

I look at the door and then shake my head. "No. I'm doing this on my own."

"All right." Her voice is soft and understanding.

I settle a blanket over my legs and then lie back while she dims the lights. After a second, she takes a seat on the rolling stool next to the bed and gently tugs the gown up to expose my belly.

"Your bump is just starting to pop."

"I've been lucky, I guess."

"With my first, I didn't start to show until about twenty-three weeks. People just assumed I was eating a lot." She lets out a light laugh and then holds up the ultrasound wand. "I'm going to start now, if you need me to stop or anything, just let me know."

"Thank you."

Jenna puts some goopy stuff on my stomach, uses the ultrasound wand to smear it around, and then she presses the small device firmly against my lower abdomen.

The whooshing sound fills the room, and I turn my head to look at the machine, wondering what the hell that is.

"That's the baby's heartbeat."

"It sounds so fast," I muse.

"Yeah, it's much faster than an adult heartbeat. It sounds healthy, though." She tilts the wand, pushing it around. "That's the heart there. If you look closely, you can see the four chambers."

Tears fall because my baby has a heart ... and it beats ... and has all its chambers. I stare at the screen, not really sure of what the hell I'm seeing, but Jenna's easy smile makes me feel better.

Then I see a face. A little face, but it's clear as day. There are two eyes, a nose, and a mouth. The baby moves a bit, and the profile is so clear. My hand moves to my lips, and I suck in a breath as more tears fall.

"How can I love him or her already?" I ask.

She smiles and moves the wand around again. "Because you're a mom."

"Let me just look around and take some measurements," Jenna's voice changes just slightly as she starts clicking keys and nodding to herself.

I think I see an arm, but the kid could be an octopus for all I know with how many times things move, but Jenna seems to be sure of what she's seeing. She clicks about some more, tilting her head and drifting closer to the screen while she looks at something.

"Is everything okay?" I ask, feeling nervous suddenly.

"I'm just measuring, that's all." Jenna smiles and then goes back. "You're just about twenty weeks, right?"

I nod. "Yes. You know, I had some cramping the last two weeks, but Dr. Madison said it was completely normal."

"Yes, cramping is normal while your uterus is stretching."

Jenna seems focused, so I force myself to focus on staying calm. If there's something wrong, they'll tell me. I can't freak out just because I think there's some change in the room.

Yet, my instincts won't allow me to do that.

My throat is tight, and there's a gnawing feeling in my gut that has nothing to do with the baby.

"Jenna," I whisper because speaking too loudly seems like bad luck. "Is everything okay?"

"I'm just going to grab the radiologist and have her take a look at something. I don't want you to be alarmed, which I know is impossible, but know that everything is okay. I just can't seem to see something, and I want a second person to give it a try, okay?"

I nod because what else can I do? I'm lying on this bed—alone. My head rests on the pillow, and I begin to count. I count because it's mindless and requires no effort. I get up to one thousand and thirty-five before Jenna and two other women enter.

One of them being Dr. Madison.

"Everything is not okay, is it?"

Dr. Madison comes to the side of the bed and rests a reassuring hand on my shoulder. "We don't know if what Jenna is seeing is right. I didn't want you to be alone, so I'm just here for support."

If she feels that she needed to stand here and hold my hand, I have no comfort because it's bad.

"What's wrong with my baby?" I ask as another volley of tears slide down my face.

"Nothing is wrong with the baby, we just see something here," the other doctor says while pointing to the screen. "This is your placenta, and there's a shadow that shouldn't be there. The baby is measuring a bit small, and I'd like to have you sent for another type of ultrasound that will give me a better view of what's going on."

I shake my head, trying to push the tears back. "I don't understand."

Natasha squeezes my hand. "I want to send you to Lehigh Valley for a test. I'll call ahead to the team there."

"Do I need to be scared?"

"Not at this point. The baby is okay, the heart, lungs, and everything is fine. We think it's better to air on the side of caution when we find anything abnormal on an ultrasound. Does that make sense?" Her smile is soft, and her words are probably meant to be reassuring, but all I hear is "abnormal."

Here I thought this was going to be a great day. Declan would've come, we would've seen our baby, found out the sex, and then maybe started to plan differently.

Instead, I got the notification from Milo that the buyer agreed to move up the closing date, Declan is in New York instead of here with me, and now this.

They help me up to a sitting position because I'm shaking too hard to do it myself. I've never felt as vulnerable as I do now.

"Do you have anyone who can drive you?"

I shake my head. "No, I can drive."

"I'd rather you didn't. You're upset, so we'll call for a ride, okay?"

I want to argue, but there's really no other options. No one other than Sierra and Declan know. I can't tell Ellie, not with her being pregnant. I could call Devney, but I can't even think straight.

"I'll call my sister and have her meet me there so she can drive me back," I tell Natasha, who nods.

"I'm going to head over there in about an hour."

An hour of waiting, wondering, and searching the internet for whatever the possibilities are and how serious this could actually be. I can't lose this baby.

Not when it might be the only thing I ever have of his that won't leave me.

The test is done. I've only thrown up once since I got here, and I'm now resting in a room. The only comforts I have are that Sierra is on her way and the sound of the baby's heartbeat is echoing in the room.

At least I know he or she is in there. Living. Heart beating. I still don't know what they're looking for, but the two radiologists were very sure they found whatever it was that alerted my doctor.

There's a soft knock on the door and then Natasha peeks her head in. "Hey."

"Please don't keep this from me. Whatever it is, I need to know. I'm freaking the fuck out."

She sits on the side of the bed and takes my hand. "I don't want you to freak out. During the first ultrasound, we found the baby was just a bit smaller than we'd like to see with how far along you are. It's not a huge thing considering all babies grow and develop at slightly different rates, but when we don't see an appropriate amount of growth between ultrasounds, we check for other possible signs as to why."

I nod, holding back the urge to be sick again. Tremors wrack my body as I edge closer to the end of my control. "Just say it."

"It's called chorioangioma, which is a tumor on your placenta. Sometimes, this happens and they're small and not an issue, but yours is very large, and ... I'm concerned. With the baby's decreased size and the location on the placenta being close to the umbilical cord, we need to discuss options."

The floor drops out beneath me, and I might pass out. I have a tumor, and it could be hurting the baby? "What about the baby?" I ask frantically.

This baby that I never planned for is the only thing that matters. They have to help it. We need to do whatever we can so he or she can grow. Everything is going wrong, and I need to stop it.

"Relax, Sydney." She tries to soothe me. "I know this is a lot to take in, and I have several colleagues weighing in on this, one at Children's in Philly. There are options, and once they can assess your condition, and you, they will give you the best course. However, I want you to go immediately. Do you need to call anyone?"

"No, Sierra should be here soon."

I called her immediately, freaking out and sobbing, and she said she was on her way. It should take her about three hours, but I've been here for almost two now. I pray she gets here fast. I need someone to hold my hand and tell me this will be okay.

"Good, do you need to call Declan? I'm assuming he's ..."

I shake my head. "He is, but Declan didn't show up or call, so I'm not really inclined to call him until I have more information."

My hand drops to my stomach where the baby is.

"Okay, then. Do you have any other questions?"

There's just one. "Do you know if it's a girl or a boy?"

Natasha's eyes go soft, and she smiles. "It's a boy."

I hold it together until she walks out of the room, but as soon as the door closes, I fall apart and tears stream down my face until I fall asleep.

twenty-seven

"Today? You want to operate *today*?" I ask the doctor, who I just met a few hours ago.

"Right now, where everything is located, it's imperative that we don't wait. I worry about blood flow to the baby, which could lead to other complications. This is a very rare condition, Ms. Hastings. The size of your tumor is the concern. The last thing we want is for it to get bigger. I know it's scary, but I wouldn't rush into this if I thought there was another option."

"Right. No. I ... I get it."

"Syd," Sierra's voice sounds strangled as she grips my hand. "If they think ..."

I know what she's saying, and she's right. If they weren't concerned, I wouldn't have been transported immediately to Philadelphia.

I don't know that I've ever cried so much. In the hospital, in the ambulance, now here, it's just constant tears. I've cried for the baby, for myself, for the fact that Declan isn't here with me. I need him here. This is his baby too, and he's in New York.

I'm angry at all of this.

"Can you explain everything again?" I ask.

He nods and goes over how they came to the diagnosis, what that means for the baby and me, and then what they consider to be the safest course of action. I'm a planner by nature. I have to know that there's some kind of contingencies as well. No matter how many times he assures me that it's relatively safe, this is still scary, and it's surgery while I'm pregnant. This is all happening so fast.

He finishes talking and waits for me to say something.

Anything.

But I don't know that I heard a word he said. It was almost as though I was looking at the entire scene from a distance.

"Sydney?" Sierra pushes me to say something.

"I just ... I'm scared," I admit. "I don't want to lose the baby. It's too ... soon ... too ... we're not ready. I was just supposed to have an ultrasound. This wasn't supposed to happen." I start to cry again. "I want to go home and just start over."

Sierra wraps her arms around me and holds me tight. "I know you're scared, but you're so strong. You're going to do fine, and they have a great team here."

She's right that this is one of the best places to be, and Natasha has already assured me of that ten times. She was adamant that I go to the absolute top-of-the-line hospital.

It's a small silver lining as my entire world seemingly crumbles around me.

But then I think of my son. The little life inside me that needs me to make the right choice. He is who will suffer from my fear.

"When will you do the surgery?" I ask, wiping the remaining tears away.

"In the next few hours. I'd normally do this procedure with local anesthesia and more of a twilight, but I see in your chart you've had some adverse reactions?"

I nod. "Yes, the last two times it took a lot of effort to get me to go under and I woke up both times."

He writes something down. "I'm going to confer with our anesthesiologist, but I'd like to have you fully under where we can work quickly and not have that situation arise. However, it is completely up to you. This does put us at a little bit of a higher risk, but I think it's a better choice."

"Okay. I would prefer that as well. My ... my nerves and I ... I can't." My voice is barely a whisper, and the words felt like they tore through me.

"Don't worry, we'll talk it over and come back with the options again, okay?"

"Thank you."

Sierra rubs my back, and the doctor leaves the room.

"I need my phone," I say, suddenly frantic. I have two hours, and I need to get a lawyer here to write up something for me.

Sierra sits up and grabs it from her pocket. "Are you call-ing Declan?"

"No, can you give me a few minutes though?"

She looks torn, but after a second, she agrees and heads out. I call my friend from law school who has a practice in Philly. The line rings and rings, and the whole time, I'm shak-ing and it's as though the walls are closing in.

I have to protect the baby. I need to have this done as soon as possible.

It rings and no one answers.

There has to be someone else. If anything happens to me ...

I call another number, but they don't answer either.

Shit. What the hell do I do?

I rack my brain to remember anything about wills and medical directives. Sierra knocks and then peeks her head in. "Can I come in?"

I nod. I'm going to have to do this the best way I can and pray no one contests anything. My sister will honor my wishes, I have to believe that, but I'm not sure if my mom will.

I look up at my older sister and her lip quivers. "I'm so sorry, Sydney. I ... did you decide to call Declan?"

I shake my head. "No, I don't know if I should or if I can. I'm so broken right now I don't know that I can talk to him."

She pushes the hair back off my face like she did what I was little. "You're not broken."

My chest is so tight it hurts to breathe. "I told him about the baby. I told him I loved him, and I told him he had to choose. He didn't pick me, Sierra. Instead of coming to the ultrasound today, he left."

"Left?"

"He went back to New York. He didn't even tell me!" I yell, my emotions overtaking me. "He left me and the baby, and ... now, God, I can't." I curl in on myself, thinking of all the things I need to do. I should've been more prepared. All this time, I knew better. Thank God, I have a will, but now I need to do this. I have to be as prepared as I can be. "I want to name him, in case ..." I confess.

"Sydney, no."

"No, please don't say anything. I want him to have a name. I want this baby to know that I loved him no matter what. I *need* to name him."

Sierra seems to understand and then waits. I think of what Declan would say if he knew he had a son. So many years ago, we played the name game, and there's only one name for this baby. I close my eyes, imagining what he might look like. I hope he has the Arrowood eyes, green with little flecks of gold and a dark black rim around the outside, making the green brighter. I imagine him to have puffy cheeks like I had when I was a baby, and then I give him a smile that would make me weep.

I want the name to be something, to mean something, and I also want it to remind my son of who he is no matter who is in his life.

"Can you get me a piece of paper?"

My sister looks confused and then walks over to her purse and grabs a notepad. "I carry it around in case the boys need it."

I open the notebook and find a picture of the boys holding who I assume is Sierra's hands. The sun is a bright yellow and there are clouds above them. They're all smiling, and the ache in my chest grows.

She's their mom.

They love her.

I might never have drawings of a boy holding my hand. I might never know the joys of motherhood. However, if something happens to me, I know that my sister will love him like her own.

From what the doctor explained, I am the one at greatest risk, so I have to make sure my wishes are clear and that they will be carried out.

I, Sydney Hastings, of sound mind and body, write this as a letter to supplement my last will and testament. This will act as my medical directive. I grant all medical decisions if I am incapacitated to my sister, Sierra Cassi. These are my wishes to be followed out by her.

If I should die, I want my son to be named Deacon Hastings-Arrowood. His father is Declan Arrowood, and my hope is that he will assume parental responsibilities, but if he should choose not to, then custody is to be awarded to Sierra and Alexander Cassi.

If I do not pass, I would like to remain on life support until the time that my child can be safely delivered. Once that passes, I would like to be removed from all machines and allowed to pass on.

If the decision of life comes down to either my unborn child or me, the decision should be to save the child.

I look back to my sister. "Can you go get the doctor and a nurse please?"

"Sure, but why?"

"Just, please do it."

She will never understand this, and I need to be sure it's legal.

A doctor I don't know and the nurse who is assigned to me enters "Is everything okay?" The nurse asks.

"Yes, I've written a medical directive that I need witnessed by you both. Please read it first, and then I will read it aloud and sign it. You both will need to sign as well."

My sister gasps. "What? *No!* Stop thinking like this."

I hand the note to the doctor first, and a look of understanding passes between us before he turns his attention to my directive and I turn to my sister. "I am thinking like a mother, Sierra. I am thinking like a person who knows exactly what I want. You may not decide the way I have, but before I go in there, you need to know what I want and that I'm making the decisions you will never want to make on my behalf. It's because I love you that I'm doing this."

My sister drops into the chair at the side of my bed and lets her head fall to the mattress as she cries. What I'm asking of her is incredibly hard and unfair, but Sierra would save me instead of this child, I know it, which is why I needed to say it.

I have to know that the baby Declan and I made will survive. It's the only option in my heart.

The doctor nods and hands it to the nurse to read. When she's done, she gives it back to me.

I read it aloud.

Tears stream down my face as my sister sobs harder with each word. Sierra has always been the strong one, but not even she can withstand this heartache. Both of us fear the worst, but I'm prepared for whatever. I've lived. I've loved. I've been broken and mended. I want my son to be what people remember of me.

"I need the pen, please," I say as I finish. The doctor hands it to me. "Thank you."

"You know the likely outcome is that you will all be fine, right?" he says.

"Yes, but the lawyer in me needs to know that, no matter what, all will be good."

Sierra sits up and stares at me with bloodshot eyes. "Please, don't fucking die."

I smile at her because, even through the pain, she makes me feel hope. "I won't."

"Then all this is just a formality," Sierra says as I sign the paper.

The witnesses do the same, and when they turn to leave, the nurse's eyes are wet as her lips attempt to lift but never quite make it.

She climbs onto the bed beside me, like we did as kids when we felt sad or alone. When I felt worthless, Sierra was the only other person besides Declan who could help me find value in myself.

"It's going to be fine," she tells me.

"I know."

"All that was just … pomp and circumstance."

"Yup."

Sierra lifts her head. "The baby will be fine."

"I know he will." No matter what, I believe my son will be okay. Declan has a great capacity for love, and I believe in my heart he'll do the right thing. If he doesn't, my sister is the best person I know.

I want to ask her to do all kinds of things like tell him about me. I hope they relay the stories of how much I loved him and how I was willing to die just so he could survive. I want him to know that his mother placed him above all else. I close my eyes, press my hand to my belly, and tell him what's in my heart.

Whether you know it or not, you came from love. Your father may not make the best choices when he's scared, but I loved him when you were made. He's always been a good guy, does the best he can, but sometimes he's stupid, so please forgive him. His life hasn't been easy, and he's made a habit of punishing himself when he feels the slightest bit of happiness. Even if he didn't choose me, he will never turn you away. I know this in my heart because you will be the best part of him.

You see, you were never planned, but you're the prayer I never thought would be answered. I will never regret one moment of the time I've had loving you. How could I? You are proof that true love exists. You are the miracle that I didn't know I needed. I hope that this is all for naught. That in a few hours, I'll be awake and telling you that Mommy did it. I just need you to know that, if I don't, you are so loved, Deacon.

The doctor enters, goes over the operation again and informs me it'll be general anesthesia.

I wipe my tears, and Sierra watches me with troubled eyes. "You have to fight, Sydney. For him. For Declan. For me and Mom and everyone else who loves you more than anything. Please promise me."

She doesn't have to worry about that. I won't ever give up. "I promise."

twenty-eight

I call Sydney again, but she doesn't answer, and I don't blame her. For the last two days, everything that could've gone wrong, has. The paperwork that was supposed to arrive that day didn't come until this morning. Then there was an accident on the highway that shut it down, preventing me from getting back to Sugarloaf in time.

My fucking phone died, and I didn't have a charger in the car because I wasn't supposed to have to stay overnight. Now, I'm on my way to her house prepared to grovel, beg, and pray she forgives me.

I get there, and her car isn't parked in the drive.

Shit.

I call Ellie, hoping she knows. "Hey, have you heard from Syd?"

"I did earlier. She asked me if I knew where you were."

Dread fills my limbs, and I stand here, hand on the door

handle. "What did you tell her?"

"That you left."

Fuck. I close my eyes and slam my hand on the hood of the car. "Do you know where she is now?"

"No, is everything okay?"

"I don't know. If you hear from her let me know."

There's no way she should still be at her appointment, but maybe …

I rush into the car and make the twenty-minute drive, all the while waiting and hoping she'll call me back. This is such a nightmare. I've screwed up at every turn and I'm going to grovel for her forgiveness. I could've had Milo push the closing back. I could've stopped at some store on the way and bought a damn charger. All these things just seemed to have slowed me down. Now, I see what a fool I am.

Nothing should've been less important than letting her know I was going to her.

I grip the wheel and then pull into the parking lot.

Thankfully, her car is in the parking lot. Relief fills me as I enter the office. There's a nurse standing at the desk.

"Hi, I'm here for Sydney Hastings. I'm late, but I see her car here. I'm Declan Arrowood," I say quickly, not taking a breath. "I'm the … the father."

The nurse gives me a soft smile and then tucks her hair behind her ear. "I'm sorry, Mr. Arrowood, I see you listed here as to be allowed access into her appointment, but unfortunately, she's not in the office."

That doesn't make any sense.

"But? Her car"—I look out of the big windows and point—"it's right there. Did she have the appointment? Did someone else come?"

Sydney wouldn't just leave her car.

"I can't give you any other information than to tell you she's not here."

"Then where is she?"

"Again, I can't give you any other information."

"Can I talk to the doctor?"

The nurse looks away and then dials a number. "Dr. Madison, there's a Mr. Declan Arrowood here inquiring about Ms. Hastings. Would you be able to speak with him?" A pause. "Yes. Okay." She gives me a look that borders on irritated and disappointed but then points to the door. "I'll bring you back to see the doctor."

"Thank you." And I truly mean it. Maybe the doctor can tell me something that she can't.

When the door opens, I see a familiar face and thank God for miracles. "Natasha."

She walks forward, a slightly older version of the girl I've known for a very long time. She's still short, long brown hair, and a smile that tells you she's still mischievous, even in her very serious profession.

"Declan, it's good to see you." She pulls me into a hug.

"Where is Syd? Her car is here, and I've been calling her nonstop."

She puts her hand up. "She gave us the approval to allow you into her appointments, but I can't disclose her medical information. I just reread the letter she granted, and I can't tell you anything about the appointment without her present."

"I'm not asking for that, I'm just asking if you know where she is."

She lets out a noise that's a sigh and a grumble. "I know that, and as your *friend*, I would love to be able to give you that answer, but since she's also my *patient*, I really can't."

I shake my head, irritated that she's talking in circles. What the hell does one have to do with the other? "I've had a horrible day and all I want to do is to try to plead my case and get her to forgive me. I wanted to be here. I was doing everything I could, but the highway was shut down and then my phone died, and then I didn't want to stop to buy a charger because it would have just wasted more time. I just ... please, I'm begging you as a friend, where is our other friend?"

My heart is pounding in my chest. I have never hated myself as much as I do now. I should've been here. I never should've left any of this to chance.

She looks up with her teeth between her lips. "All I can say is that you might want to call Sierra."

I'm out of my seat before she can say anything else. "Thank you."

I rush out of the office, back into my car. I have no clue how to get in touch with Sierra, but I'm sure Jimmy does. I'll beg anyone to get it.

I'm heading back toward Sugarloaf, my mind all over the place as to why Sierra would know where she is and why her car was there when my phone rings.

Sydney.

Thank God.

"Syd?" I say quickly. There's a pause, and I go on, needing to say it all. "Syd, I'm so sorry. I was on my way and something happened on route 80 and then my phone died. I swear, I was coming to the appointment. I just left there, and I'm ... God, I can't say anything other than I'm sorry. This will be the last time I disappoint you. I love you, Bean. So fucking much and ... please, forgive me."

There's nothing on the other line and panic builds. Jesus, I really fucked up.

Then a sniffle.

"Syd?"

"Declan, it's Sierra."

My heart starts pounding, and my mouth goes dry. "Sierra, where is Sydney?"

Her breathing is loud through the line. "We're in Philadelphia. I think, I don't know ... I wasn't supposed to call you, but ..."

"Tell me where you are," I say pulling the car off the side of the road. "Please, I need to explain to her."

"There's a problem, and I think you should come."

"What problem?"

"With Sydney. They just took her back into surgery ..."

My heart stops and time goes still. "She's in surgery? Did she lose the baby? Is that what happened?" Tears fill my eyes as the vision of the life I was going to give her disappears. "The baby?" I just barely choke out.

"Oh God," she rushes to say. "No, it's not the baby, it's her. They found something and—just come here and I'll tell you everything. Hopefully, she'll be out of surgery when you get here."

She gives me the information to the hospital and where to go. "I'm on my way now, I'll call this phone when I get there."

Once I hang up the phone, I send a prayer that I get there and everything is okay, then I drive as though I've already lost everything.

"Sierra," I say as I enter the small waiting room.

"Declan!"

She's on her feet and rushing to me a moment later. I catch her and she starts to cry again. I've known her pretty much my entire life and I don't think I've ever seen her this distraught.

Her fingers grip the back of my shirt as she holds on.

"It's okay, just ... tell me what's going on," I urge us both into chairs.

She draws a deep breath and starts to speak. "I got a call that they found something in the ultrasound today, she was hysterical, and Syd doesn't get hysterical, you know? I got to the hospital where they did a different type of ultrasound, and it was all very confusing. Needless to say, it wasn't good, and they transferred her here where they decided to operate."

"But she's pregnant."

"Yes, and they say they can do this, but, Dec, she was terrified. I'm freaking the fuck out. She made me take this letter." Sierra digs in her purse and hands it to me. "I can't do this. I can't pick."

"Pick? Pick what?"

I open the letter up and start to read. My hands are shaking and I have to focus to stay calm. "No," I say the word when I read her requests. She can't ask this. To save the baby over her. "The baby isn't even here. No. This is crazy. There can be another baby, but there is no other Sydney."

The words fall from my lips as dread fills my heart. She can't ask this. No, more than that, she can't die.

Sierra rests her hand on my arm. "She said she needed to make her wishes known so I wouldn't have to decide. I'm sick to my stomach, and I just keep reassuring myself that this is the planner in Sydney. The girl who needs to have all her ducks in a row."

I can't think about her dying. There's no way because I just got her back. I just decided we were going to make it work and love again. So, she is not going to die. There are no ducks to be in a row.

"Did the doctor say anything about the risks?" I ask.

"Yes. There's a chance that either she or the baby could go

into distress. It's surgery, while pregnant, but they said it just couldn't wait. The tumor is sitting in an area that could hurt the baby. She was devastated, Dec. I've never seen her so broken. Well, I have, but it was when ..."

When I broke her heart. She doesn't have to say it, I know it all too well. It's also probably the last time I felt this out of control. Everything feels like it's falling apart all over again. I want to scream and throw something. "Why didn't she call me?"

Sierra looks down and then back up. "You hurt her."

"I was coming."

"She didn't know that. Ellie told her you left, and ..."

"You all assumed that meant for good." My track record would prove that to be the case. Now, I could lose her or both of them. I read the letter again, seeing the name. "It's a boy?"

She nods. "She wants to name him Deacon. I'm assuming that, even as much as you hurt her, she still has faith in you."

I run my hand over my face and then rest my elbows on my knees before I look over to her. "Faith I don't deserve."

"Maybe not, but isn't that what faith is?"

I look to Sierra, feeling this overwhelming sense of grief. "I hurt her when I was doing everything I could to make her happy."

Her head tilts to the side. "What exactly were you doing?"

"I bought the farm."

Her eyes widen, and her lips part in surprise. "Our farm?"

"Yes. I knew she didn't really want to sell it, so I figured I would buy it, hold it for her, and she could have it back when she realized it was a mistake."

She leans back in her chair and smiles at me. "You bought our farm."

"A lot of good it did me. I missed the appointment today

because I …" I fall silent, hating that I will have to admit this. I was such a fool, and now, I have to wait to tell her how I feel.

"Because you?" Sierra prompts.

"Because I didn't fight for her. I let her walk away that night, and I spent the next two days securing the house instead of making sure she knew I loved her and the baby."

Sierra rubs my back and then sighs. "You know, my sister has loved you for as long as I can remember. She was broken after you left, but she could never fully let you go, no matter how hard I pushed. Sydney doesn't know what her heart would look like without you holding a piece of it. Love like that doesn't disappear."

I hope to God that's true. "I've never stopped loving her."

"I think she knows that, in her heart at least."

I shake my head, wishing I could make sure she knew that in her mind too. I failed her in so many ways. I should've done so many things differently, and as soon as she wakes up, I plan to tell her all of that.

I think about the child we're about to have, and how I will do better for him.

I look back at Sierra. "We're having a boy."

She smiles softly. "Yeah. You guys are."

"She's going to be fine." There is no other option. They will both pull out of this and then I'll find a way to explain it to Sydney. The two of us will work it out and be a family.

"Sydney isn't a quitter."

"No, she's not."

She has to be okay. They both do.

Just then a doctor enters, and Sierra gets to her feet. We both watch for any sign from him, and when his eyes drop to the floor, my heart does as well.

twenty-nine

There are moments in my life that I have felt helpless, but this brings a whole other meaning to that word. When my mother died, I thought my world would end. When my father caused the accident that changed my life, I knew nothing would be the same.

Hearing the doctor try to explain what is happening with Sydney has broken me.

"I don't understand," Sierra says as she clutches my arm, tears falling down her face.

"The surgery went well, and the tumor has been removed, but we're having a hard time waking her from anesthesia. I'm not sure what is going on, but we're running tests to see what is causing her to stay under."

My breathing is short, trying to keep myself together and comprehend what the hell is happening. "So, she's alive?" I ask.

"Yes, she's alive and breathing on her own, but she isn't

waking or responding."

"Were there any complications during the surgery?" I push for more clarification. "Can't she just wake up? Is this normal?"

The doctor shakes his head. "No, it's not normal, and we didn't encounter anything we didn't expect. She lost a little more blood than I would've liked, but nothing I was concerned over."

"What about the baby?" My voice is strained, even to my own ears.

"The baby was monitored the entire time, and he's doing great. Heart rate is still strong. I don't want you to panic," he says quickly. "It could be nothing, but we are keeping an eye on her anyway, and like I said, we are going to run some additional tests to make sure she isn't having a reaction to the anesthesia. Know that we're doing everything we can, and we'll continue to keep her in ICU just so she has continuous care."

"Can we see her?" Sierra's voice cracks.

"Just one at a time."

I turn to Sierra, and she wipes her face. "You should go first, I have to call … family and … go see her, Dec."

This can't be happening. I can't lose her now. I just got her back. She'll wake up, she just needs a reason to do it. I follow the doctor back to the room, not saying a word, wishing that, when I walk in there, she'll be glaring at me and I can fall to my knees and beg her to understand.

I'll tell her everything, prove to her that I love her and explain that I wasn't away because I left her but because I wanted to give her something she cherished.

All of this will be cleared up, I know it. It has to because no god is cruel enough to take away the only thing I have left.

Sure, I have my brothers, but they aren't Sydney.

They aren't my reason for living.

The glass door to her room slides to the left, and time stops.

All the lies about this not being real prove true.

There she is.

Lying there, unmoving with her eyes closed as monitors beep all around her.

My Sydney, the girl who had more life in her tiny body than a thousand people, is still. Her laughter and smart comments aren't filling the air.

Instead, it's silent.

Eerily quiet.

And I want to die.

I want her back. I want to be able to beg her to forgive me, promise to let myself love her, and give her the faith that I've failed to show her.

And then, I do something I haven't done since I lost my mother ... I cry. Tears fall down my cheeks as the despair grips me in a way I have never felt before this moment.

Please, God, don't do this. Please give me another chance to make this right. Don't take everything I never knew I needed. Let me ... please.

I move forward, dread making my feet feel like they're lead balloons. My heart is beating fast, and I can't speak as I make my way to the side of her bed and take her hand in mine.

Tears fall freely down my cheeks, but I don't brush them aside. I let them slice down my face, right through to my heart.

"Can she ... is she?" I try to form a question, but the words are garbled and halting as they catch in my throat.

"She's alive and breathing on her own, we're not sure if she can hear, but she's not responding at this point. I'll give you some time before we take her down for another test. Maybe hearing your voice will help." The doctor pushes the door open and leaves.

I'm not sure what to do. Nothing feels right, and there's an emptiness inside me.

I push her blonde hair back from her face. "Syd, you have to wake up." She doesn't move. "See, I can't live in a world where you don't exist, and I can't handle losing you, so I need you to wake up. I know what I'm asking is selfish, and you have no reason to care if I'm in agony without you, but I need you, Bean." I sit in the chair, my hand wraps around hers. "I should've come after you that night. I should've run to you and begged you to forgive me for being a coward. If I had told you about it all—my plans, my fears, my heart—then maybe you would be awake right now. I love you, Sydney. I love you more than I can ever express. You need to wake up so I can tell you all of this though. I want to make it up to you and our son." My throat tightens, my voice cracks and another sob breaks free.

Our son.

He's inside her right now while she sleeps. Does he know his mother loves him more than her own life? Does he know how perfect she is and how lucky he is to have her? Will he be what keeps her fighting?

My thumb rubs against the top of her hand, and I wait for anything. "I bought your farm. I would buy a hundred of them if it meant you'd be happy. So many things I did wrong, Syd. Please, Bean, open your eyes and let me make them up to you."

There's a knock on the glass door before it opens, and the doctor steps back in. "Her sister is asking to come in, but you both can't be in here while we wait for the results from the tests."

My hand tightens around hers, and I push back the urge to rage against the injustice of it all.

"Okay."

"I'll come back to the waiting room and get you both once we have her settled."

I stand, unable to release her hand. Two nurses enter and start to adjust wires and tubes. I still don't move. I can't let her go.

I can't make my hands move.

I watch her, willing her to open her eyes and stop this. "Please," my voice is barely a whisper but sounds like a scream in the room.

Everyone stops moving and then the nurse rests her hand on top of mine. I look up at her face, which is warm and kind. The nurse is maybe in her late fifties and reminds me of my mother in some way. She doesn't offer me anything other than comfort and something to ground myself to.

"I can't let her go," I admit.

She squeezes just a bit. "We will be with her and watching."

"She's my world." Only she doesn't know it.

The nurse smiles softly and nods. "I understand. Let us take care of her."

She pulls my hand off Sydney's, and I feel her loss in my soul. I have to let her go, and pray it isn't forever.

"Declan." Connor's voice causes my eyes to fly open, and I get to my feet.

"What are you doing here?"

He shakes his head like I'm an idiot for asking. "We came as soon as Sierra called."

It's been six hours. Six hours and just as many tests to try to figure out why Sydney is nonresponsive. They have no answers that tell what is going on, just that she's not waking up.

She has brain activity, her blood sugar is normal, and there's no indication of a stroke, but still, she sleeps.

"Right. Sorry. Of course. It's just …"

"No change."

"None." I take a few breaths through my nose, trying to calm myself. I can't fall apart now. I have to be strong, sure, and believe that Sydney will be fine. Whatever is happening can be fixed.

"Syd will wake up."

I nod because it's true. "People don't just slip into comas, right? Not when there's nothing pointing to why it could be happening. They wake up when they're ready. For all I know, this is her way of punishing me." I laugh humorlessly. "It's working too, so she can feel good about this."

"She's not that cruel."

"Isn't she, though? She didn't tell me about the baby until two days ago. Then she finds out there's something wrong and she has a fucking tumor, but she doesn't tell me." Anger and frustration start to build. "I find out *while she's in surgery*, and she didn't even know why I didn't make it to the appointment."

"Which was?" Connor asks.

"I was busy buying her damn farm, which she pushed the sale up for. It was either it sold that day or she was pulling it and going to another buyer."

Connor smirks. "So you're pissed at her?"

"I'm pissed—no, I'm fucking livid. I can't lose her! I need her to wake up. I need her to live. She wrote this fucking direction sheet that says if it's her or the baby, we have to save him. I can't …"

Connor steps forward, pulling me into his arms. My youngest brother, who I've been more like a father to than anything, comforts me. I slam my hand on his back, and he does the same. He grips my shoulders, pulling me back, and then sets his jaw. "It won't come to that."

"I wasted so much time." I step back and walk to the window. "All these years, I've been so sure that staying away was the right thing. I thought I was giving her a chance at a life I couldn't provide. Now, I want to erase it all. I would give up everything to have time with her. I just want a second chance to make it all right."

He sits in the chair beside me. "A true second shot will split the first arrow and create a solid path."

"A lot of good that advice is now. I know the path I want, it's clear and solid, but it might have an ending."

Connor laughs without humor. "I feel like Mom was telling us things we needed to hear, but we weren't smart enough to actually listen."

"I'm terrified I'm going to lose her." I confess my deepest fear.

His hand squeezes my shoulder. "Don't give up hope, Declan. Sydney needs to believe she has something to fight for. Be that for her."

I'll be everything she needs.

thirty

"I

t's been twenty-four hours. I need you to hear me,
Bean. Wake up. Open your blue eyes and let me see
you." I try to urge her to wake again. I can't sleep. I
can't eat. All I do is alternate with Sierra or Ellie by her bedside. Mostly, they can't get me out of here though.

"Declan," Ellie says softly as she stands at the glass door.
"Please take a break."

"I'll rest when she's awake."

She comes in the room farther and watches me. "Connor
and I have to head home. I'm going to get you some clean
clothes and bring them back tomorrow."

"That's fine."

She sighs heavily, looking at me and then to Syd. "You're
making him crazy," Ellie whispers, but it's loud enough I can
hear. "He hasn't shaved, showered, or done much of anything
but pester you. Let him out of his misery, Syd. He loves you,
and I promise that you can kill him if he hurts you again. We

have enough land between the two of us to hide a body."

I huff with a smile, thinking of how much she'd love that.

Ellie turns to me. "Call me if anything changes?"

"I will."

She comes to my side and kisses my cheek. "At the least try to eat something. You're no good to her if you're worn down."

I don't say anything because food is the last thing I care about.

More hours pass, but nothing changes. All I can do is sit, waiting for any movement that doesn't come. I watch, thinking maybe her eyelids will flutter. Maybe her fingers will twitch, but they don't. I beg, plead, and bargain with her, but she doesn't move.

I lean back in the chair, defeat filling my body and leaving my limbs heavy. The doctor explained to Sierra and me this morning that they're going to run another battery of tests because this is definitely abnormal.

Something is wrong, and they have no idea where to start.

Everything about this situation, from the time I got to New York all the way until this moment, has been surreal and abnormal. I need the universe to get its act together and straighten up before I lose my mind because I don't know if I can take much more.

My brothers call, but I don't answer, there's nothing to say, and I can't explain the situation again.

I close my eyes for just a second as the heaviness weighs me down. I'm exhausted, but I can't give up.

"Will you love me forever?"

"Forever and always," I reply as Sydney gives me a sly smile and dips her toes into the pond.

"Good answer."

In just a few weeks, we'll both head off to college. It's been a summer that neither of us will forget. After as much bad shit as I've endured, each moment with her is heaven. Sydney is the best thing in the world.

"What about you?" I ask her back.

Syd shrugs with a gleam in her eyes. *"Depends on if you deserve it."*

I clutch my chest, falling back to the ground. *"You wound me."*

She rushes over, her hands covering my mock wound as she kisses me. *"Never. I would save you."*

"You already have saved me."

"Yeah?"

More than she can ever know. Just her smile makes it easier to breathe. Her touch soothes the bruises and pain inflicted by my father's hands, and her love reminds me that there is good in the world.

"Everyday."

Syd lies beside me, both of us now facing the summer sky. Her fingers entwine with mine. It's a simple touch, but it feels like everything.

"Do you think we'll get married?"

I turn to look at her. *"I know we will."*

"Have kids?"

"If that's what you want ..."

Syd's blue eyes meet mine. *"I want to have kids with you. Two boys and a girl."*

"Are you placing an order?" I laugh.

"No, just letting you know what to expect. I want our oldest to be Deacon."

I roll my eyes at the name. "Why not just name him Declan then?"

"Because you're the only Declan my heart can ever love. I want his name to be close to yours because he'll be strong and handsome like his father. Our second son can be named anything you want."

"Gee." I laugh. "Thanks for that. And what if we have a girl?"

Syd moves her head so that it's resting on my shoulder. "Bean."

Now I wonder if she's had too much sun. "You want to name our daughter Bean? You hate that I call you that."

The name has evolved as we have. When we were kids, she was jumping all the time and always bouncing around, so Jimmy called her a jumping bean. It bugged her, so naturally, I called her it as a way to torture her like eight-year-old boys do. Then, when she was about twelve, she was taller than most of the girls and flat, so Sean was being a dick and told her she looked like a string bean. Eventually, she just became my bean. Always changing, growing into something more beautiful than the last thing, and it stuck.

Still, she hates it.

"But you love it."

"Well, I love you."

She lifts her chin just a bit, a devilish smirk playing on her lips. "And you'll love our bean."

A noise causes me to jerk awake, and the dream fades away when I see that she isn't smiling at me. A nurse walks in, a soft smile on her face when she sees I'm up. It's the same one from last night. Sophie is her name.

"How's our patient doing? Any changes?"

"No. Was I out for a while?"

She nods. "I came and checked on her about two hours ago, and you were asleep. You must be exhausted."

Shit. What if she moved? What if I missed something? I shift closer to her, touching her face, but she doesn't stir.

"I'm tired, but I'm more worried."

"I understand that. We're doing everything we can."

Everything except figuring out why the hell she isn't waking up. I'm doing my best to stay patient, but with each hour that passes, my hope dwindles. If we knew what it was ... if we could fix it ... then I would feel better. This crushing helplessness is what's killing me.

"If she would just wake up ..."

"Well, I've been a nurse a long time, and it's always a mystery to me, these things." She checks the bags of fluids and then the monitors. "The body sometimes doesn't respond when the heart and mind do. Keep talking to her," she urges. "Let her soul hear everything you want to say, and see if she can't get her body to respond. I'll be back in an hour." Sophie pats my shoulder and then leaves us alone.

I've talked for what feels like an eternity, but there's still so much I have left to say, so I move onto the edge of her bed. She's so beautiful. Even like this, she takes my breath away. I lift my hand and run my fingers along her jaw, her soft skin reminding me of just how fragile she is. I brush my thumb across her lips and have to fight back the tears that threaten to overwhelm me.

"It's been almost twenty years since I've cried," I tell her. "Nothing has meant enough to me to cause them to fall. I haven't allowed myself to love anything enough, and yet, here I am, wanting to break down and lose my mind. The idea of losing you, Sydney ... it's too much. You and Deacon are all I want to be worthy of." I recall the dream I had, her smile, her voice, the happiness at the idea of building a family with me. "I dreamed we were kids again, lying on the grass, talking about having a life. We deserve another chance, Syd. Even if you turn me away when you wake up, I'll keep coming back. I'll do whatever I have to do to prove that you're my choice. You're what I want. You asked me to chase you, and I'll follow you to the ends of the earth if that's what it takes."

My heart is pounding as I bare myself to her, hoping that somehow, she hears it and fights to come back to me.

"You need to shower," Connor shoves a bag of clothes at me and points in the direction of the hotel. "You're not doing anyone any good refusing to eat, shower, or leave her bedside unless Sierra or Ellie want to visit."

We're standing outside the hospital after he dragged me out to get some fresh air—not that I wanted or needed it.

"Fuck you," I snap at him. "You haven't been watching Ellie lie there for three days not responding, moving, or answering your pleas and praying to God for her to just open her eyes!"

"No, I haven't been, but you're not going to change things by running yourself into the ground. When's the last time you slept?"

I glare and huff. "I don't know."

"Ate something?"

I move away from him, needing to work off my anger. "Let this go, Connor."

"That's what I thought. Sydney is going to wake up, and it would be preferable if she didn't gag when she smells you. Take a fucking shower, shave, eat a meal, and come back when you look like yourself. This"—he points at my face—"isn't okay."

Anger that was simmering beneath the surface starts to boil. "How easy for you to judge me!"

"I'm not judging you, I'm helping you!"

"Helping? How? By ordering me away from her? What if she wakes up? What if she looks for me, and I'm not there like I haven't been for the past eight years. She's all that fucking matters!"

Connor lifts his hands and purses his lips. "And that's great. I'm glad you finally figured all this out, but the fact remains that you need to get your shit together. Now, go to the hotel and clean yourself up."

My breathing is heavy as I ball my fists. "I'm not leaving her."

"Well, we're not letting you back in that room."

I move toward him, and Connor straightens his back. "You're angry? Good. You'll need that to get through this, Dec. You feel helpless, and it's not something any of us like to feel, but you won't hit me, no matter how much I bait you. Do you know why?"

I step back as my senses return. "Because I'm nothing like him."

"Exactly. If you need to get it out, I'm happy to spar with you and let you work off your steam. It's been a long time since I've kicked your ass."

He's never kicked my ass, but I don't correct him. Truth is, I'm too fucking tired to. The last few days have been the longest of my life.

No change in Sydney. The baby is still okay, but they are putting her on another form of medication and running another scan. Her brain activity is reading as normal, which has the doctors baffled, and I'm losing my grip.

"I can't do this, Connor."

He puts his hand on my shoulder and squeezes. "Let's

walk."

We head toward the hotel, which is right across the street from the hospital. We got two rooms there so people could stay overnight if they wanted. Sierra is heading back home tonight, and Ellie is staying. The two of them are alternating, and Connor is driving them each day. I'm the only one who won't leave.

I can't.

I have to be here.

As we walk slowly, Connor stays quiet as I form what to say in my head. "I've always taken care of everything."

"Yeah, you have."

"I can't fix this."

He bobs his head as we keep going. "I know the feeling well. You want to make her happy and do what you can to give her security, but this is out of your hands. I've been there, brother, I know what you're feeling. You'd do anything, wouldn't you?"

I would steal the breath from my body and give it to her. "Anything."

"Then be the man she has always believed you are. The one we all know you are. Put the past behind you."

I already have in some ways. However, I have some mistakes I need to atone for, leaving Syd being the biggest. I will never run the risk of losing her again. When she wakes up—which will happen—I will prove it to her.

"Connor," I say carefully, needing to say this. "If this goes badly."

"It won't."

"If it does ..."

Connor grips the back of his neck and releases a heavy breath. "Then you have three brothers who will hold you together."

I hope that's enough because I know I will fucking shatter.

thirty-one

"We're starting to worry about how shallow her breathing has gotten," Dr. Voigt explains.

Sydney has been in a coma for six days.

Days that I don't even remember passing. I sit here, holding her hand, telling her stories, and pretending I'm holding it together.

Today, her mother is here. "And what does that mean?" she asks, unable to stop her tears from falling.

"It means that we may have to intubate her. We're watching, and if there are any signs of distress, we just want you to be aware."

Jane stumbles into my arms, her tears fall rapidly as I hold her tight. I close my eyes, using all the strength I have left to be strong.

I hold her mother, letting her soak my shirt as she fears the same thing I do.

Things aren't getting better.

She's getting worse.

"And the baby?" I ask. Deacon was Sydney's one concern, and if—when—she wakes, I want to be able to give her the most up-to-date information I can.

The doctor clears his throat. "She's receiving nutrients and vitamins to ensure the baby is fine. We have the fetal monitors on, and her OB team is following her very closely. As far as we can tell, the surgery to remove the tumor was the right move for the baby. But, we'll do another ultrasound to measure against the previous one to see if he's grown. I know this is a lot, and it's frustrating that we don't have answers, but we are doing everything we can."

Jane leans back, wiping her face, and sniffles. "Thank you, Doctor."

He gives a stiff nod and then leaves.

She walks over to the other side of the bed and tucks Sydney's hair behind her ear. "I can't watch her wither away like this. She's a strong girl who never backs down. I feel so helpless."

I move to the opposite side. "I know. I do too."

Jane's eyes meet mine. "You know, when you left her, I thought she would crumple and die. You were ... well, she loved you without reserve. No matter what, her faith in you was unwavering, even when I didn't think you deserved it."

"I didn't deserve it. I proved that by not being here when she needed me." Shame washes through my words.

"You're here now, Declan. You're standing at her side. You've been here continuously. Others have abandoned her, but you didn't." There is a long pause, and then she says, "Sierra told me that you bought the farm."

"I did."

"You're a good man."

I look down at Sydney and brush my fingers against her cheek before looking back at Jane. "I've made mistakes, but I love her. I'd like your blessing to marry her when she wakes up."

Jane smiles. "I gave it to you once before, why should I do it again?"

I square my shoulders and don't waver. "Because this time, I plan to actually ask her."

"Good. Be sure you do, and if that doesn't rouse her, then I don't know what will."

But it doesn't, and more time passes while her breathing grows shallower.

"We're getting closer to needing to move forward with intubating," Dr. Voigt informs us. "She has moments of respiratory stability, but more often, she's struggling, and her oxygen levels are starting to become concerning."

This can't be happening. "Are we losing her?" I ask him.

"At this point, we are just trying to make it easier for her to breathe. The more she struggles, the lower her blood oxygen becomes, and we want to avoid any damage that could cause."

I run my hand down my face, and Jane's eyes well up with tears. "And we still have no idea why she's in a coma?"

He shakes his head. "No. None of the tests show anything to suggest why she hasn't woken since the surgery."

I look to where she sleeps and pinch the bridge of my nose. I'm losing her. "Can I have a few minutes?" I ask them both.

Jane nods. "I have to call Sierra."

They walk out, and I make my way to her bed. I'm done

being patient, if we can even call it that. She has to wake up now. "No more, Sydney," I say with authority. "Our son needs you. He needs you to push through this and open your eyes." My face is close to hers, watching for anything to tell me she hears me. "Deacon is inside you, and he needs his mother to take care of him. You can't leave him to me or your sister. You can't just ... give up. You can't do this to everyone who loves you and needs you."

Tears fall down my cheeks. I love her so much, and I'm breaking apart. I can feel her drifting away. It's as though, in just the last hour, I've been able to watch the woman before me fade. It isn't real, or at least that's what I've been telling myself, but yet, I feel it in my bones.

Sydney won't come back from this, and I can't handle it.

I grip her hands, lacing my fingers in hers. "Don't leave me, Sydney. Please don't fucking leave me. I need to make this up to you. I want years to prove that I love you and that I can be what you need. You are all I want in this world, and I don't want you to give up." My head falls to the bed, resting on her hands. "Don't give up, baby. Please, fight for me." I stand, taking her face in my hands and leaning in to kiss her. She's warm, soft, and completely absent. I don't feel her with me. "I love you, Sydney."

I release her, my heart feeling like a boulder in my chest. I take a step back, needing to get out of this room.

I can't watch her fall deeper into the abyss.

I feel helpless, devastated, and so fucking alone.

My feet keep moving as my eyes stay on her, wanting to be near her but needing to pull away.

Each breath is labored, burning my soul as I retreat.

I can't survive losing her. I don't know how I ever let her go before. It's killing me. Everything inside me is raging, clawing through my chest, desperate to get out.

I open the door, Jane's eyes meet mine, and then I turn.

I can't be here.

I have to … move.

My heart is thumping so hard I can hear nothing other than my pulse. I don't know how to exist in a world without her. Even when I didn't have her—she was here. She was already making the world a better place, just by drawing in air.

I walk, not seeing the people, hearing their words, or marking the halls I traverse. I'm just lost because I'm losing her.

I see the life we could've had. The life on the farm, heading into the city a few times a month but working beside her. The children we could have, running around, chasing their friends, and laughing. Sydney with her long blonde hair, torturing me with her sweet kisses and beautiful smiles.

We would run away to the pond for alone time when the kids were busy.

That future fades away before my eyes.

I'm standing in the hospital chapel.

I don't even know how I got here …

"So, is this my punishment?" I ask the empty room or God or whoever is listening. "Do I have to atone for what my father did? Is this my penance? To live alone in a world without her? Have I not suffered enough?" My voice is full of rage. "Were all the years being beaten down, watching people I love fall apart not enough?" I walk, unable to sit, anger flowing through my veins, needing answers. "I walked away from her to keep her safe! I left her behind so she could escape any pain I might cause her, and you do this to her!" My hands are shaking, so I turn them into fists. "I love her, and you're going to take her from me, aren't you? I wasn't good enough. I know this, but I was going to give her everything! I … I was …"

I sink to my knees, looking up at the cross, just like the one my mother had.

I'm angry at God, my family, the farm, Sydney, everyone,

but most of all—myself. I have to live with the fact that she thinks I abandoned her. The guilt of her being disappointed in me.

"I am so scared," I confess.

I close my eyes and decide to talk to the only person who might be listening.

"Mom, please, if you're up there, don't let me lose her. I know my path. I'm ready to take my second shot, but I need your help. I need her, and I can't do this alone. Please, let me have another chance. I swear if you can just … give me this, I'll make you proud again. I'll stop running and be the man you've always believed I could be."

I stay on my knees in that chapel for a long while, letting the despair wash over me and then letting it go. I have to be strong for Sydney.

After another second, I rise and head out into the hall. If she's going to go through this, I'm going to be by her side the entire time. And whenever she opens her eyes, I'll be there. If anything happens, I'll be the one who sees it.

There's no other option.

As I get through the doors to ICU, I see people running toward Sydney's room. There are doctors, nurses, and a team of people going in and out. I start to move faster, my heart racing and throat dry.

Please God, no.

No, don't let this be happening.

Then I see Jane, her tears are falling, head shaking back and forth as she clutches her mouth.

My world ends as I pull her into my arms, hoping for a miracle but knowing I've just lost her.

thirty-two

People are everywhere, rushing around, and I can't focus on anything. It's as though I've been dreaming and have no idea how long I've been asleep.

I close my eyes again, trying to get my bearings. I know I'm in a hospital. There's a constant beeping of machines while nurses rush around me, and wires pulling at my arms. Not to mention, it smells like a hospital. A bit of antiseptic cleaner and rubber.

"Sydney?" A deep male voice calls.

I look to him and he smiles softly. "Yes."

The doctor lifts a light and shines it in my eyes while asking me a question. "Do you know where you are?"

"The hospital," I croak. My throat feels like I've swallowed knives. It's raw and scratchy and so dry.

"That's right." He continues to check me over, moving my body, squeezing my hands. "Can you squeeze back."

I do, and he nods approvingly. "Good. Do you remember me?"

Do I? I think I do. I know he's a doctor, and he looks familiar, but I am so tired and groggy. It's as though I'm in a fog. I can see things, but nothing is clear. Everything feels distant and hazy. "I just ... I can't remember."

He nods. "That's normal."

Normal? Normal for what? I don't know what's happening to me or my baby.

The baby.

Oh God.

My hand flies to my stomach as I scramble to remember what happened.

"The baby is fine." The doctor puts his hand on mine. "We've been monitoring him while you've been in a coma."

I've been in a coma?

"What? How long? My sister?" I barely get the words past my lips because my throat screams out in pain again.

I try to recall something about what happened. I remember going in for the surgery, and that's it. I don't ... understand what's happening. I don't feel like time has passed, but then again, I have no idea what day it is.

The nurse brings me a cup of ice chips. "Take it slow," she instructs.

"I'm Doctor Voigt, and I was your surgeon. I need you to stay calm so we keep your heart rate steady for the baby. Do you remember having the surgery?"

I nod. And now that I've heard his name, it rings a bell. I take an ice chip into my mouth and breathe through my nose. I won't do anything to harm the baby.

"Good. The surgery went well, the tumor is gone and the baby is healthy, but you've been unconscious for a week now.

We're not sure why, but we're very happy you're awake now. Your family is outside, they've been here the entire time. I'm sure you have a lot of questions, but I'd like to bring them in here to see you, if that's okay?"

The desire to see someone familiar is too great to pass up. "Please."

Dr. Voigt smiles and then heads out of the room. When the glass door slides open again, my mother walks in with tears streaming down her face.

"Oh, Sydney!" She moves quickly to my side, taking my face in her hands. "I've been so scared. We all have." Her hands fall, she looks back and then I see him.

Declan stands in the doorway, his eyes swollen, hair a mess, and God knows how long it's been since he's shaved.

He looks beaten.

He looks beautiful.

He looks absolutely terrified.

I turn back to my mother, needing not to look at him. Pieces of my memory flare up when I remember that Declan wasn't here earlier. He was in New York. He left me after I told him everything and begged him to love me.

It doesn't matter that he's clearly shaken now. It's too little too late.

"The baby, he's fine, right?"

She smiles through her tears. "Yes, baby, you and the baby are just fine. Everything is okay now, and the surgery went well. It's been … trying, to say the least, but you're awake and … oh, it's so good to see you."

I can hear the relief in her voice, and I hate that she was so worried. "I'm sorry I scared you."

Declan shifts, and as much as I try to focus on my mother, it's impossible not to notice him. My mom turns to Declan and then back to me before taking a step back. "I'm going to call

Sierra and Ellie. I think you two need a moment."

I don't take my eyes away from him as he steps into the room. The glass closes behind him, and the fog I was under before is back, only it's everything else but him that's out of focus.

Declan is here. I don't know why or what he hopes for, but he's here and he looks as though he's been through war.

His eyes are on mine as he moves toward me, hesitation flowing thickly between us.

"Say something," his voice rasps.

"Why are you here?"

His eyes close for a beat, and then he is at my side. "Because I love you. I love you more than any man has ever loved a woman, and I was coming to you that day. I went to the doctor's office after everything that could've gone wrong did. I missed the appointment, and I was … God, I was chasing you. Just like you asked. I've been here, and I'm not leaving you again, Sydney."

All the words I've longed to hear fall from his lips, but I can't think. I am so lost and confused. I rest my hand on my stomach and lean my head back. Right now, I have to digest the fact that I've been in a coma. "Tell me about the last week."

When I open my eyes, I see the hurt painting his features, but he shields himself quickly. "You didn't wake up after the surgery. They couldn't figure out why, so we just sat here, waiting and hoping, but you didn't respond. I talked to you for hours. We all did. Sierra, your mother, Ellie, and Connor … we were always here."

As much as I thought I wanted to hear this, I don't. I want to know why he wasn't there before. I need to know what was so much more important than the ultrasound. And yet, right now, he is here.

"Declan, I can't …"

My words drift away as my mother pulls the door open, but Declan doesn't turn to acknowledge her. He just moves closer and sits on the edge of the bed.

"I was coming for you, Syd. I've been here, and we have to figure this out." He finally looks to my mother and then back to me. "I'm going to make some calls and change my clothes, but I'll be back."

I nod, not really having the strength to do more. Declan leans forward, pressing his lips to my forehead, but I hold my breath. It's intimate and sweet. My head is a jumbled mess. So much has happened and I'm exhausted.

My mother touches his arm as he leaves before coming to my side.

"It's good to see your eyes." Her voice is soft, but I can hear the fear under it.

"Days?"

She nods. "It's been days since that man has left your side. He's been a wreck, but we haven't been able to get him to take a break."

That wasn't what I was asking, but the information is new. "You mean he hasn't left?"

Mom smiles softly and then sits in the chair beside the bed. "He's been here all day and all night. Every day that you were in the coma. He would leave to shower, usually after Connor browbeat him into doing it, and maybe to grab some food, but otherwise, Declan has been at your side every moment."

I lick my lips and let that information settle around me. "Why?"

"Because the man is in love with you," Mom says with a laugh. "He's been torn up about how it all happened. He's talked to you, begged for your forgiveness, and said a lot about his feelings while you slept."

A lot of good it does me since I don't remember anything.

"Seven days pales in comparison to the years that I've had to cope with being without him."

"Maybe so, but those years of coping did nothing to stop you from leaving the farm you love, your friends, and the life you've built. No, my sweet girl, what did that is the man out in the hallway."

I see his silhouette through the frosted glass, pacing back and forth, never straying far enough for me to lose sight of his profile. I would know him even in the darkness. Hell, maybe even blind.

"He lets me down. He doesn't choose me, ever. He's let me go, pushed me away, and abandoned me."

She seems to consider that. "Maybe that's true, but it's also a bit unfair. I know true abandonment. If Declan didn't love you, he would've left. He wouldn't have spent the last week as a fixture at your bedside."

"Obligation and duty are important to him. I'm carrying his son, so for all we know, that's what he cared about."

She laughs once. "You're a fool and a liar if you believe that. I've seen a man stay out of obligation, Sydney, and that wasn't what Declan did. He was devastated. Not about the baby, in fact, he and Sierra had it out about the baby and you. Declan would've let the entire world burn down and allow everything else to perish if it meant saving you. You don't have to forgive him yet, but at least listen to what he says before you make a decision you'll regret."

I let that sink in and worry my bottom lip. I still don't believe it completely. However, even after sleeping for what seems like forever, I'm too exhausted to think about Declan and his reasons for doing what he did.

If he loves me, he needs to do a lot more than sit at my bedside for seven days.

"Mom," I say while my eyes start to feel heavy. "I'm sleepy."

She rubs my cheeks. "Rest, my sweet girl, I'm right here."

I allow my lids to fall, and as exhausted as I am, I don't fall asleep. I drift in a muddled, dreamlike haze that is on the edge of unconsciousness. There's a shuffle in the background, tempting me to open my eyes, but I can't focus enough on it.

Just as darkness starts to overtake me, on the very edges of consciousness, I sense him. I feel his warmth, his scent of musk and spice meets my nose, and then the deep timbre of his voice fills my ear. "Thank you, Mom. I couldn't have survived losing her."

It's been four days of resting, trying to function, and being around Declan. He will not leave. He won't argue with me or go away, he's just always here. Each time the doctor encourages me to do something to regain my strength, there he is … pushing me to do it.

I want to hurl something at his head.

"You should go home, you have a job," I say as I lower myself into the chair, which is part of my daily to-do list.

Sitting.

Not walking or trying to do anything of great effort, but moving from the bed to this damn chair for more than forty minutes.

What does one do when forced to sit in a chair? Talk to the man who won't go away.

"I'm perfectly fine here."

"Yes, you've said this, but you *should* go."

Declan shrugs. "I'm good."

I groan and let my head fall back. "Our son is going to have your stubbornness, and I'm going to want to strangle myself."

"Yes, because you're the most accommodating person ever."

"You're the one who won't leave."

"Because I love you, and I'm not going until we figure our shit out."

He said that yesterday, and my response was to force myself to go to sleep to avoid this exact topic. I don't want to have it out. I want to go home and ignore him.

However, I know that isn't going to happen.

It's also the coward's way out, and I'm not a coward.

"You made your choice."

"I told you what happened," he replies. "I know you don't forgive me, and honestly, you shouldn't, but I'm going to make it up to you."

I breathe heavily and try to slow my racing heart. He has no idea how much I want this to all be true. But I think his promise is coming from a place of fear, and once I'm out of the hospital, he will take it all back and leave again.

"You don't have to do this." My voice is soft and strained.

"Do what?"

I open my eyes and let him see the truth there. "You don't have to stay here out of obligation."

He flinches and moves closer, eyes never leaving mine. "Is that what you think? That I'm here because I feel obligated to be?" His voice is low. "Because that's the furthest thing from the truth."

My pulse is rapid because he's close enough for me to smell his cologne. "I don't know what the truth is."

"Are you ready to have this discussion? Because I am trying not to push you and let you recover without adding to your stress."

I wish that were possible, but my stress levels aren't going down without this discussion. If anything, I can't seem to think about anything else. Why is he here? What does he want? When will he leave? And how the hell will I endure all of this?

But those answers can't come from me.

"I think we have to."

Declan crouches so his face is right in front of mine. "I was coming for you, Sydney. I was late, I know I was, and I'm so, so sorry, but I'm here now."

"For how long, Dec?"

"Forever."

I sit, staring at him, waiting for him to laugh or smile or something, but he doesn't.

"Forever?" I ask. Maybe I heard him wrong. Maybe there is some weird side effect from the coma that is making me hear things that aren't real.

"I'm not leaving. I'm not going back to New York City, not unless you're with me, and if I have to stay in Sugarloaf or wherever you go, I'll do that. You see, I lived eight years without you in my life. I existed by thinking that you were happy, better off without me, and I can't exist that way anymore."

"You can't?"

"No." His hand lifts and his palm settles on my cheek. "No, I can't."

I try to force myself to swallow and then pull in a deep breath. "You say this now, but why?"

"Do you know why I didn't make it to the appointment? What it was that I *had* to do in the city?"

I shake my head.

"Well, there was this thing I was buying, and it became really difficult out of nowhere. I had time—or, I thought I did, but the seller changed their mind."

Anger starts to build, and I can't hold it back. He missed the appointment, not because of something important or an emergency. No, it was because he was buying something he wanted. I don't know why he thought this wasn't going to be no big deal.

"So, you left me and missed the appointment to see our son over something you were buying?"

"Well, the buyer made an unrealistic demand that I needed to move the date up by a month."

I roll my eyes. "And this is supposed to make me feel, what? Bad for you?"

"You're asking the wrong questions, Syd."

I cross my arms over my chest and fight back the urge to flip him off. "Well, then why don't you tell me what I should ask."

He grins. "What was I buying?"

Because this conversation is exhausting and I'm not getting anywhere, I play his game. "Fine. What were you buying?"

"Your farm."

thirty-three

D id he just say my farm?

"What?" I ask on a haggard breath.

"I'm the buyer for your farm."

I blink a few times, waiting for him to correct himself, but he doesn't. This entire thing is so confusing. "I don't understand."

The property just went under contract a week ago. Before he knew about the baby or we slept together the second time. It doesn't make any sense.

Declan moves closer and his hand drops to mine. My chest feels tight. "Milo called me when you were going to take the deal with that company, and I knew it was wrong. I couldn't imagine you not living in Sugarloaf, and I couldn't handle the thought that your farm, the pond, the barn, the property line where we used to meet, wouldn't be yours. I knew that *I* was the reason you were leaving, and I couldn't let you lose anything else because of me."

My lip trembles as I feel the honesty in his words. "That was all before …"

"Before the baby. Before the night we shared. Before all of this."

He should've told me. I wouldn't have let him do it. "Declan …" Tears fill my vision, and I fight to hold them back.

"No, Syd, let me say this, please. I told you ten times when you were in the coma, but I need you to hear it now that you're awake too. I love you. I love you for the memories we made and the ones I want us to make. I wasn't running away from you, I was chasing you. I was buying the farm because I knew it was what would make you happy. I left you all those years ago because I didn't want to weigh you down with the baggage I'd bring. Everything I've done has been with you in my heart. And now …" He pauses and his head shakes. "Now, I can't leave you. Not because we're having a baby but because I *can't* live without you. And if I could, I wouldn't want to. I want to love you every day. I want to walk to the pond and make love to you in the sunlight. I want to kiss you just because I can. I want to raise our child together, and I want to do what I should've done eight years ago instead of walk away—marry you."

My breath catches, and that tear falls down my cheek.

He bought my farm.

He knew that, somewhere in my heart, it wasn't what I wanted, and he bought it. I drop my head into my hands and start to cry harder. It's all too much. How can he say all this now? Doesn't he know that my heart has always been his? Can he not see that my life has been waiting for this moment and it's just too … hard?

"Sydney," Declan's fingers wrap around my wrist.

I slowly lift my head and meet his gaze. "You bought my farm."

"I did."

"Because you love me."

"I do."

"And now you're saying you want to marry me?"

Declan nods. "Yes. I want to marry you, raise our child, and be a family. I want it all, Syd."

This big, broken part of me is rejoicing and telling me to leap into his arms and love him for all we are. I have loved this man for so damn long, and this is all I've ever wanted. The other part of me, the hurt part that doesn't trust him, is telling me to tread carefully. Yes, he bought the farm before, but then he let me go when I told him about the baby.

He let me walk away and didn't come after me.

"Why did you wait so long after the wedding to come for me?"

Declan's fingers intertwine with mine and regret fills his eyes. "Because I was an idiot. I wanted to chase you that night, but I was so fucked in the head after finding out about the baby. There's a deep fear in me that I have some of my father in me. I would rather cut myself out of everyone's life than inflict any harm on a child. I'm not proud of it, but the next morning, when I got my head out of my ass, I was going to you, but Milo told me of the new requirements."

"I was running away," I admit. "When you didn't come for me, I couldn't handle it. I can't handle another person abandoning me."

He rubs his thumb against the top of my hand. "I won't ever leave you again, Sydney. Watching you lay in this hospital bed for days were the lowest moments of my life."

This is what scares me. That all of this is drawn from fear. "What about when things get hard? What about when you're scared again? What about when you delude yourself into thinking you know what's best for everyone and you push me and the baby away?"

Declan doesn't say anything for a few moments. We just look at each other. He can deny that he won't do that, but we know he probably will. His desire to protect the people he loves always wins out, and he's usually wrong.

I can't pretend to believe otherwise.

"I didn't make the decision because I thought you were going to die."

"Do you understand why I don't fully believe you?"

Declan nods and then gets to his feet so he can cup my face. "I'm not asking for you to suddenly trust me. I've done a lot of things to prove otherwise." He brings his lips to mine in a soft kiss. "But I love you, Sydney, and I'm going to marry you. Not today. Not tomorrow. Not next week or even next month, but one day, you're going to be my wife, even if it means I have to chase you to the ends of the earth."

My heart pounds against my chest as I stare into Declan's eyes. "And if I keep running?"

He grins down as though he's really hoping that's the case. "Then I hope you never take a break because I'm ready for a marathon."

Well, then … I better get my rest so I can make it out of the gate.

"And how long until you're able to go home?" Ellie asks.

It's another day of physical therapy and they are rubbing my legs. They hurt so badly from the extra strain on my muscles. It's been tough this week. They're pushing me harder, forcing my body to do more each day, and with the slight pain from the surgery—it sucks.

"Hopefully the end of the week."

"And what are you going to do? You can't go home alone. Please come stay with Connor and me," she urges.

I love her, but there is no chance in hell that's happening. Their house is in total shambles since the construction on their new home is just about done, they just got married, and they have an eight-year-old running around. I love Hadley, but her energy levels probably won't help my recovery.

"Thank you, Els, but I'll just go to Sierra's if I have to."

"No! You can't!"

"Why?"

"Because my brother-in-law will die. And a dead Arrowood is really not something I'd like to deal with." Her smile is wide.

"I doubt he'll die."

She laughs once and then sighs. "No, but Connor might kill him."

My head tilts to the side as I wait for further explanation.

"When you were … sleeping … Declan was beside himself. I have never seen anyone so devoted to anything as Declan was trying to get you to wake. He talked to you almost constantly, and he just wouldn't give up."

I've heard this so many times that I can't help but believe it, but I don't fully trust it. Declan has proven me wrong time and time again. He's failed me when it mattered most, and he has a bad habit of pulling away when he thinks it's best.

There isn't a part of my heart that doesn't believe he has good intentions, but the sudden decision to repair our relationship has me most worried.

"It's not that I don't love him, because Lord knows that has never gone away for me. I worry about what kind of future I can expect."

"Once upon a time, a very good friend of mine told me I was being an idiot for letting Connor go. She told me about how she would give anything to have the other half of her heart back."

I inhaled deeply through my nose and ignore her tone. "Ellie, it's not that simple."

"It never is."

"And what happens if he leaves again? And did you know he bought my damn farm?"

"No. He told no one until the day of your surgery."

Seems I wasn't the only one keeping a secret from the people around us.

"Well, even if he told you, I wouldn't expect you to say anything."

She squeezes my hand gently. "I still would've."

I have the best friends ever. Between Ellie and Devney, I don't have to worry about anything. They've been here, even though they have their own lives to worry about, and have offered their unwavering support. "Are you feeling okay?" I ask her.

"I'm great. The baby is good, we decided not to find out the sex."

My eyes widen in surprise. "Uh, what?"

"I didn't know with Hadley and there was some fun in it. Connor said he was fine to leave it as a surprise. I think he's worried about the house, Hadley, you, his brothers … we haven't had time to fret over it. We know he or she is healthy and moving around in there."

"You've felt the baby?" I ask, sitting up just a bit. I've been waiting and hoping, but it hasn't happened.

"Yeah, it started a few weeks ago."

"Oh," I can hear the desolation in my tone.

"Syd, I've had a baby, so I know what it feels like. Do you get this butterfly type sensation at all? Like something is just … fluttery or bubbly but you can't tell if it's indigestion or gas?"

I nod. "Constantly."

"That's him!"

"Really?" That's sort of underwhelming. "I thought it would be more pronounced."

Ellie laughs. "Oh, it will be. I'm already feeling it more and more. Now that you know, it'll be more noticeable. At night, when it's quiet and I'm lying in bed, I feel it most."

Well, I've been in bed forever, and I don't feel anything all that wondrous.

"I'm happy for you, Els." She looks at me with a hint of puzzlement on her face. "I mean that you and Connor are happy. You have Hadley, the house, and the baby coming. It's the life you were always meant to have."

Ellie releases a breath through her nose. "I'm going to say this with all the love in the world. You're a dumbass. Declan wants to give you all the same. He bought the farm because he was worried you would regret it and knew that, if he owned it, you wouldn't lose it. He was by your side not out of obligation but because he couldn't be away from you. All the things you've ever wanted are right in front of you. He's there, Syd. His arm is outstretched, you just have to take it."

My heart knows she's right.

It's my head that holds the fear, though, and it's telling me that he's dropped it before too.

thirty-four

"Good afternoon, gorgeous," Declan says as he enters the room. His smile is bright, and he has another bouquet of flowers.

This time, it's hydrangeas—my favorite.

"Good evening is more like it."

He leans over and kisses my forehead before putting the flowers next to the other ones he brought. "When you bought the farm, did you also purchase a florist shop?"

"No, why?"

I look over to the row of flowers on the ledge by the window. One is from Connor and Ellie, one is from Jacob, and the other *twelve* are from Declan.

He laughs. "I just remember you liked flowers."

"I do, but we're good now."

"Noted."

He throws out the three dead bouquets and then sits in *his* chair. He left for a few hours to go home, get clean clothes, and get some work files he needed. When I told him he didn't have to return, he laughed as though I were an idiot and said he'd see me soon.

Soon is now, and I'm in a terrible mood.

The thing is that I missed him.

Even with all his hovering and driving me nuts, I don't feel alone when he's here. Sierra is being a mom and doing all the things she neglected when I was in danger, my mother had to go back to work, and everyone else's lives go on. Which I get, but … I felt the loss of him.

It was so great that I ached.

And then I decided I hated him and myself for being like this again.

Here I am, trying so hard to go slow, feel my way around this situation so I don't trip and face-plant, and the first second I have to deal with his absence, I crumble.

I'm pathetic and so deeply in love with the man, it isn't normal.

The doctor knocks on the door and smiles as he looks at the two of us. "Good, you're both here. I'd like to do another ultrasound, make sure that things with the baby are okay, and if they are, we can start discussing getting you out of here."

It feels as though the sun is shining for the first time since I opened my eyes. I can see my bean and then hopefully go home.

"Really?" Declan's voice rises with excitement. "We can see him?"

He missed the first one. Where I was able to see this precious life in my womb.

"Yup," he says with a grin. "I put the order in and you guys should have someone come get you very soon."

Declan's fingers entwine with mine, and he stands as the doctor leaves. "I missed it."

"Missed what?"

He looks at me, regret and shame in his green eyes. "The first one, when it mattered."

We have always faced adversity. Nothing in our relationship or lives has come easily, I've seen that, but there is little that can be done about what happened. He's here now. He loves me, and I have to find a way to trust that.

The choice is either dwell on what we haven't had or forge a new path.

I think about Declan's motto.

I know it because each time we went to his house, we recited it.

I like to think that Elizabeth Arrowood was magical. She knew what each of her sons needed in a way that still blows my mind. It was as though she peeked into their souls, saw the flaws, and tried to help them right their course.

Connor needed to take chances. Sean needs to learn that it is the shot that counts, and Jacob has to learn to adapt. Their mother somehow knew Declan had to screw it all up in order to make it right the second time around.

Which is what this is.

"Yeah, this is our second chance to see our son ... together."

Declan sits beside the bed, tightening his grip. I can see that he wants to say something, and then, I gasp as I feel the strangest sensation. "Oh!" My hands rest on my belly, and the entirety of my focus is on waiting to see if I feel it again. It's not the light flutters that Ellie talked about, it's much stronger and there's no denying what that was.

Declan jumps to his feet, eyes concerned as he moves closer to me. "What's wrong?"

My heart feels lighter than it has been in weeks. It's beating with a flurry of emotions—joy and hope and happiness and contentment. "I … I just felt the baby."

He rests his hand tenderly on my stomach. We both stay still, watching each other as we wait for something—anything—to happen. I move his hand to the area where I felt it last and hold his wrist. A few moments pass, and I will our son to move again, to show his father that he's okay.

Neither of us so much as makes a sound, and then I feel it once more. "Did you feel that?"

He looks to me. His eyes are filled with wonder and the biggest smile paints his face. "Our baby. That tiny nudge?"

"That was him."

"He's strong."

My vision blurs behind unshed tears. "He is."

Here in the hospital room where so much has happened, Declan and I share a moment so beautiful that I know I'll never forget it.

"I love you, Sydney."

"I love you, too."

And I do. I always have. To tell him otherwise or omit it would be a lie. While I don't know that we will be able to weather the storm, I know that I can't go out in it alone. Declan is who I want to be my shelter.

He and I move at the same time, and his hands cradle my face as mine rest against his chest. I can feel the steady thrum of his heartbeat as he kisses me reverently. There's passion, which has never been something we lacked, but this time, there's something so much deeper. There's love, understanding, and acceptance that passes between us.

We've been through so much, and somehow, we're here right now. I'd be the fool my people have said I am if I weren't able to see it.

He poured his heart out to me earlier, and I may not trust it fully, but I know it's true.

He deepens the kiss a little, and I surrender to him. Not only am I too weak to fight against the feelings inside, but I also have no desire to. I love him.

"Well, if this isn't a sight I never wanted to see again." Sean's voice breaks the moment.

Heat creeps up on my cheeks, and I look away. "You're a sight I wish I wasn't looking at right now," Declan says.

"Much easier to maul Sydney without an audience?"

I roll my eyes. "Hello, Sean," I say, wanting to break up this fight before it happens.

He smiles at me and then enters the room. "Syd, it's good to see you awake. I was worried."

Declan gets up and hugs his brother. "What are you doing here? Don't you have a game to play since your injury was nothing?"

"I do. We have a series here in *Philly*." He winks at me. "Some fan my brother is, huh? He didn't even know I was in town. Jackass."

"I've been a little preoccupied," Declan defends.

"You know, making sure I didn't die and take his unborn child with me," I say with a grin. "Baseball must have slipped his mind, I guess."

Sean shrugs. "I guess that's a good enough reason."

I laugh. "Thank you for coming."

He scoffs. "Please, I find out you're carrying my newest nephew, which reminds me that I need to have a talk with two of my brothers about safe sex, and you thought I wouldn't come?"

I laugh and then feel comfort from his embrace. Sean sits

in the chair that Declan was in and takes my hand. "How are you?"

Declan and I fill him in on all the medical stuff, tell him that we're waiting for another ultrasound, and then let him know that I'll likely be discharged. He smiles as I tell him how much I've improved. I went from barely keeping my eyes open to staying awake for hours at a time now. I can walk, but I'm still very shaky on my feet. If I want to get up, I have to have someone here to help.

It's incredibly irritating since I've never been dependent on anyone. I've run my farm, business, and been a damn volunteer without needing someone to take care of me. Now, I can't even pee without sounding the alarm.

I, for one, can't wait for the physical therapy to be over so I can go back to some sort of normal.

"You left me in the parking garage?" Devney huffs as she appears in the doorway.

"Dev," I say with a smile.

Her eyes meet mine, and her scowl fades away. "*You* have some explaining to do too, but for now," her voice softens, "I'm just so damn happy to see you."

I open my arms, and she rushes forward, shoving Sean aside as she passes him. "I'm sorry I didn't tell you."

"I'm more angry I didn't figure it out. You're pregnant and … with an Arrowood baby, no less. You should've told me, Syd. I would've helped you."

"I know, and I was planning to. I just felt that Declan should be the next person to know."

She looks at him and then back to me. "I get it. We all have our secrets I guess. Are you okay?"

"Of course she's okay," Sean breaks in. "She just had her tongue down Declan's throat."

Devney turns to Sean and huffs. "You're an ass."

"You love my ass."

She rolls her eyes and turns back to me. "This is what I get for agreeing to pick him up and bring him to see you."

One day, the two of them are going to realize just how perfect they are for each other, and then we are all going to be in trouble.

"I'm really sorry you both found out this way. I swear, it ... it just all got away from me."

Declan stands beside me, hand on my shoulder. "Nothing is going to get away from you now."

Devney's eyes twinkle, and her grin grows. "Does this mean you two have finally gotten your heads out of your asses and are back together?"

Are we? I know he loves me and wants a future, and it's all I've wanted as well, but this is all ... scary.

The man I thought abandoned me is at my side.

The baby I thought I might lose is safe.

And I'm not sure I'm really living in my current reality or if something insane has happened.

I open my mouth to say yes, but Dec speaks before I do. "It means that Syd and I have a lot to figure out, but I love her and she knows that. What we do from there is between us."

Well, isn't he just my knight in shining armor? I look up to him and grin. "That was very lawyerly of you."

"What was?"

"The way you handled them."

Declan chuckles. "I know how to manage people."

Sean snorts. "This kid is doomed with the two of you."

Maybe he is, but there's no one else I would want to have a child with. I look at Declan, wondering if he feels the same way.

His eyes meet mine and then he leans down and gives me a kiss. "I think the three of us are going to find a way to make it work."

"You do?"

He nods.

Sean throws his arm over Devney's shoulders and chuckles. "You owe me fifty bucks."

Both of us turn to look at him. "For what?"

"I bet Devney that he finally figured out how much he loved you and was willing to put the past where it belongs." Sean walks to Declan with a grin. "It's good to see it finally happened."

Declan punches his brother in the shoulder playfully. "Yeah, I think it's time we all face issues we've been pretending didn't exist."

I note the subtle jab at Sean's denial and lie back against the pillow. I gained a lot during the week I was sleeping. I got back the family I missed.

thirty-five

"I'm staying until I know you can go down the stairs without breaking your neck," I tell her as she tries, once again, to get me to leave.

This is her new favorite thing. Push me away, try to get me to go, and then cave when I refuse.

"I'm fine."

She isn't fine. She isn't even close to fine, but reminding her of that only pisses her off more. "I know you are."

Sydney's eyes narrow. "You know I don't believe you."

I smirk. "I do."

She left the hospital two days ago, but her balance is still a bit off and she tires very easily. I found her earlier this morning, as she tried to get to her room on the second level, sitting on the stairs panting and pale. That was the last straw. Ellie came over and sat with her while I packed my shit and brought it here.

It definitely is not the way I planned to get her to agree to us living together, but anything works for me at this point.

"You can't just move in here, Dec," Syd tries to reason with me again.

She's nicely tucked into bed, and I have my laptop on my lap so I can do some work while I supervise her. "I'll officially own the house in two days, so I sort of can."

Her jaw drops. I guess she forgot about that one. "And where am I going once the transaction is complete?"

"Nowhere."

If I have my way, neither of us will be going anywhere and this will be our permanent residence.

"Am I your hostage?"

"I'd prefer the title of wife."

Sydney's eyes widen and then she tosses a pillow at me. "You know, when you say shit like that, you make it really hard to remember I'm supposed to be upset with you!"

I hoped that would be her reaction, but I never know. I put the laptop aside and make my way over to the bed. "Does it help when I tell you how much I love you? Or how beautiful you are? Or how much I want to kiss you?"

She shakes her head. "No."

"What about if I were to do it now?"

"Do what?" Her voice is soft and there's a slight tremble in it.

"Kiss you."

Sydney's gaze turns molten, and she smiles. "Is that what you want?"

If she only knew. "More than anything."

I hesitate, not because I don't want to kiss her—hell, I want nothing more—but because I want her to choose me. I want Sydney to see that, while I'm the same guy I was when I showed up here months ago, there's something different inside me. Maybe it's because I've found some way to let go of the past.

My father was a bastard, there's nothing that will ever change that, but I don't have to be him.

I can be my own man. One who's worthy of the woman before him. I have a lot of healing left to do, and I'd be a liar if I didn't think there would be times I'd doubt myself, but for her, I'll push.

I'll fight to be the man she believes me to be.

"Sydney," I say as our lips brush.

I can feel her breath mingling with mine. "Yes?"

"Tell me you forgive me."

Her hand lifts to my cheek, and she rubs her thumb softly against the scruff on my face. "I have loved you my entire life, Declan Arrowood. I never stopped, and I don't know if I ever could."

I kiss her tenderly and then pull back. "But do you forgive me?"

When Sydney looks at me, the vulnerability in her expression would drop me to my knees if I weren't already sitting. I see the fear swirling in those blue eyes. "Will you leave me again?"

"No."

She sighs.

Unable to resist the sweet sound, I kiss her again.

I kiss her as though the world around us can crumble because I have everything I need right here. Sydney is what I fought for through all the hell I've endured in my life. She's the pot of gold at the end of the rainbow, and God help me, but I want her.

Her hands snake around my neck, and she pulls me tighter.

I smooth my thumbs against the soft feel of her skin and send another round of thanks to whoever answered my prayers.

"Uncle Declan! Aunt Sydney!"

I freeze, and Sydney pulls back. "What is it with my family and their timing?" I say quietly, but Syd laughs.

"Hey, Hadley," Sydney says around me to my niece.

"Mommy and Daddy are parking the car, and they said I should come in here and make sure you were okay. Are you okay? Was Uncle Declan and you kissing?"

I turn to her and shake my head. "What do you know about kissing?"

"Umm, I'm eight years old. I'm almost a teenager, and … I watch YouTube."

Great. "You should be playing with dolls."

"Well, she could be riding a horse, but her uncle hasn't gotten it for her yet," Sydney adds on.

I give her a playful glare.

"Yes! I need my horse, Uncle Declan."

The women in my life are trying to kill me. But, I did promise her one, and I know it'll piss my brother off, which is always an added benefit.

"How about we go visit Devney's parents this weekend and see what they have?" I offer.

Devney's parents run a farm that has horses and other animals in need of new homes, and they always have options for newer riders since the horse I was looking at from the Hennington farm still isn't ready for her. Maybe she is going to end up with two freaking horses.

"You mean it?" Hadley asks, her green eyes bright and hopeful.

"I mean it."

"What do you mean?" Connor asks as he enters the room.

"You're getting a horse!" Sydney tells him, ruining my moment of joy.

"I'm going to have a brother or sister and a horse! It's the best day ever!" Hadley yells and then launches herself at me.

I catch her, pulling her into my arms and laughing.

Yes, it really is the best day ever. I have everything going my way.

"Declan?" Sydney's voice is quiet in the dark as she pokes me in the chest.

I sit up, alarmed that she's waking me. "Is everything okay?"

"Yes, I'm fine. Are you sleeping?"

I look over at the clock sitting on the side next to the recliner I'm in. It's two in the morning. "Not anymore."

"Good. I wanted to talk."

I rub my hand over my face and try to shake off the drowsiness. "Now?"

"Well, I figured now was as good a time as any." Sydney stands in front of me, hands on her hips.

Yeah, that makes total sense. "Okay."

"Why do you want a relationship now? What's changed? Why didn't you realize how much you wanted this before the possible death thing? Also, why the fuck did you buy my farm?"

That's a lot of questions, and my brain isn't really working, but even in my half-asleep haze, I know I have to answer this without pause.

"Because I realize that my life is complete shit without you. What has changed is me? I've stopped trying to think I know better than you. You said you love me and want me in your life, and I'm really too exhausted to pretend that isn't what I want too." She doesn't say anything, so I continue, hoping I don't fuck this up. "As for why it took me so long? Well, it really didn't. It just took me a while to be able to accept it. I knew the minute I saw you again at the pond that I had never gotten over you and that I was still hopelessly in love with you, but didn't want to hurt you. As for your farm, I bought it because you wanted it."

She's still quiet, and the fear I had about fucking it up is growing. "It's millions of dollars."

"It's a good thing I have a really good job then."

"Declan."

"Sydney."

She huffs. "I don't know how you did it."

"I got the cash from my company line of credit and sold my apartment. Well, I'm selling it this week. I should accept the offer I got yesterday."

"You what?" she yells.

Here's where I had to really hedge my bets. "I'm not going back to New York. I am selling my apartment, so the options are either to live with you or in that tiny fucking house thing on my farm. And just so you know, I really hate that goddamn thing." I get to my feet and take her face in my hands. "I'd much rather be with you."

"You sold your apartment and risked your company just … to buy the farm?"

I lean in and press my lips to hers. "I'd sell it all for you, Syd. I'd give it all up if it meant I'd be with you. I've been a fool for a long time. Now, I have a second chance with you, and I'm not giving it up. We're meant to be together. You know that, and so do I. We're having a baby, and I swear to God, I'll make you happy." I feel a tear reach my thumb, and I wipe it away. "Why are you crying, Bean?"

She sniffs and wraps her fingers around my wrists before resting her forehead against mine. "Because I love you, and I have needed you so much."

"I'm here now."

"I want to trust you, but my heart …"

I lift my head back. I can't see her, but I can feel it all. Her tension and fear is like a living thing between us. "My heart is yours, Bean. It always has been."

"And mine is yours."

"Then let me love you. Let me prove it."

Heartbeats pass between us before she nods. "You chased me."

"I've never stopped. No matter what you thought, I've been chasing you, running but not willing to let myself catch you. It took me far too long to realize I'd been fighting for the wrong thing."

I pull her lips to mine and kiss her tenderly. The taste of her is something I've never forgotten. She's life and air and everything good in this world. Her fingers glide up my chest and settle against the back of my neck, gently stroking the skin there.

We kiss, languidly and tenderly, only breaking long enough for me to lift her into my arms. Sydney squeals and grabs on. I move to her bed, laying her down carefully before climbing in next to her. I don't expect anything to happen. Hell, I'm not even sure she is allowed to, but I want to hold her.

I need to feel her sleep beside me, knowing she's mine and she's chosen me.

She shifts closer, tilting my face to hers and then kissing me on her own terms. I give her what she wants, pouring everything into the kiss. Sydney moves so she's straddling me.

Her kisses become deeper, longer, more urgent.

"Syd," I croak her name, both wanting her to stop and never stop.

"I need you."

"We can't."

"I can."

God, she's going to kill me. I try once more to do the right thing … to hold her off until I can call her doctor and make sure. "We can wait. Holding you is enough."

She sits up, her long hair flowing around her. The moonlight filters through the big windows, allowing me to see just her profile. "It's not enough for me."

Her hands move to the hem of her shirt, and she pulls it over her head. She takes my hand and places it on the soft skin of her belly. There lies our child. The baby who brought us back to each other.

"You're so beautiful," I tell her.

"Touch me, Declan. Make love to me."

I lean up, practically growling and unable to stop myself at her soft plea. I want nothing more than to make her feel my love.

My hand moves up to her breast, lightly stroking the top of her nipple. It pebbles beneath my touch, and she lets out a breathy moan. I roll it between my finger and thumb, plucking, and then wrap my other arm around her, pulling her to me.

She braces over me, and I pull her nipple into my mouth while playing with her other breast. Sydney's head flies back, and I swear that I could fucking die at the sight of her.

"Lie down for me," I tell her.

Thankfully, she obeys. I pull my shirt off, hating that there isn't enough light in here for me to see her clearly. I want to watch her, see her face, bask in the desire that will swim in those blue eyes. I want it all. Remembering that she has half this house remotely operated, I lean over and grab the small remote that operates the fireplace and let that roar. Then I push the button she hit that turned candles on.

Now the room is set perfectly.

And then I look at her, watching the lights dance across her skin.

"I love you," I tell her.

"I love you."

"You have to promise me that if you feel anything …"

Her fingers graze the whiskers on my cheek. "I promise. I need you."

I need her more than air. I lean down, bringing our lips together, and kiss her with all the emotions in my heart.

Sydney is mine.

While she always has been, now it's different. We aren't kids making stupid promises we can't keep. This is a love that's strong, been through hell, and has found its way back to heaven. We've battled and won. She's the prize. She's everything.

I pull her so we're face to face, not wanting to put any weight on her. I slide her shorts off, slowly revealing her skin. A shudder passes through Sydney's body. The last time we made love, everything changed. This time, it won't be that.

Instead of her leaving, I'll hold her.

Instead of tears, I want smiles.

There is nothing of myself that's being held back. All of me, all that I can give will be hers to have.

I move her back and trail kisses down her body, push her legs open, kissing the insides of her thighs and drawing out the anticipation.

"Dec, please …"

"Please what, Sydney?"

"More."

I push her legs higher and run my tongue along the seam of her pussy. "More of that?"

She groans. "Yes."

I do it again and make sure I flick her clit. "More of that?"

Her fingers slide into my hair, wrapping around the strands and tightening. "Only you, Dec. Please."

That pushes me over the edge. I lick and suck, pulling her deeper into the abyss. She moves her hips, seeking more. I hold her down, wanting to control the pace. There's a great joy in drawing it out, hearing the whimpers escape her throat, making the moment last longer.

Sydney has always been fire in bed. She's never been afraid to ask for things or tell me what she wants. I know her body as well as I know my own, and when I feel her thighs tighten, I know she's close.

Wanting to be inside her but needing to have her climax beforehand drives me harder. I suck at her clit, flicking it over and over, rubbing small circles until I feel her body tighten further. I slip my finger into her, curling it slightly, and she screams.

Her body goes rigid as I do everything I can to make it better for her. I watch as she falls apart, and I know there's nothing in the world more beautiful than this.

I make my way up her body, shed my shorts, and then wait for her eyes to open.

When they do, my heart feels as though it settles back into place.

Where it was meant to be—with her.

Sydney smiles as her hand moves to my cheek. "Hi."

"Hi?"

She nods. "There you are again." A tear rolls down her temple, but her lips are still set in a grin. "I've missed you."

It's too much. My chest feels as though it's going to explode. The way she sees through me, knows what I'm feeling before I've been able to speak, is too much. I can't take it.

Her legs part, and I move closer, wanting to have no space between us anymore.

I'm coming apart and binding back together.

All because of this woman.

The one thing in the world that has always been what I've needed.

She runs her thumb along my lips. "Make me yours, Declan."

And then I slide into her, and it is not her who is mine … it's me who is hers.

thirty-six

"You don't understand, Jimmy, he's driving me insane!" I say as I dip another Oreo into milk.

"He's being cautious with you, that's all. You didn't see the man when he thought you were going to die."

I sigh, trying to remember that this was traumatic for everyone. I fail.

"Still not an excuse to keep me hostage in my own house!"

Jimmy laughs, lifting the coffee mug to his lips. "I think you mean both of your house."

I glare at him. "Traitor."

I may have originally sold the house, but a few weeks ago, he put me on the deed with him. So, we both own it … with his money.

"Aren't you supposed to be retiring?" I ask him.

"It's hard to stay off the farm when you can't do much, your boyfriend hasn't run a farm ever, and I haven't found someone competent enough to do what I'm capable of doing," Jimmy complains.

Dec and I think it's that he really doesn't want to retire and that he likes being around us. I don't mind. In fact, I would be content to never let him leave, but that is just me being selfish.

I know that I scared ten years off his life when I was in a coma, and since then, he's been just as protective as Declan.

I smile and then grab another cookie. "I guess you have a point."

"Damn right I do." He refills his cup and thrusts it toward me. "You know, you're going to be hard-pressed to get me to stay away once that baby comes. There will be a lot of things you're going to need done around here while you're both taking care of an infant."

I nod. "I bet we will."

"And not to mention all the things that still need to be taken care of."

I bite back the smile at how wound up he is. "Of course."

Declan opens the back door and smiles. "Hey, Jimmy. I thought you were going to take the week and stay home on your new retirement."

Jimmy puts the mug down with a clunking sound that reverberates, and I bite my tongue so hard I can taste blood. Oh, he's in for it now. "Kids thinking I can just retire," he mumbles under his breath as he walks out of the room. "Think they know everything until something breaks, and then retirement just means free labor."

Declan stares at the door he vacated through and then back to me. "What the …"

"Oh, you stepped in the shit, my friend."

"I said hello."

"And then you mentioned that he should be home."

"So you pissed him off, and I get the brunt?" Dec asks.

"Yup. I love the way that worked out."

He rolls his eyes. "I have a surprise."

"For me?"

"Yes, love, for you. Come on." Declan's hand is extended toward me, so I take it.

We get outside and I inhale deeply with my eyes closed. It feels so good to be out here. The sun is warm on my face, humidity is low since it's still early morning, and the sky is the brightest blue.

"You have no idea how much I hate feeling cooped up."

"I think I do." Declan stops me, facing me toward him. "I want you to put this on, and not complain."

I look down at the black tie and raise a brow. "You want me to put just this on? I mean, we're out in the open, Dec. Jimmy can see from the window and the farmhands are all over."

He looks heavenward and then back to me. "As appealing as the idea of you naked in nothing but my tie is, us being outside in the early morning while that happens isn't what I had in mind. I meant to put it over your eyes."

"Oh!" Now it makes sense. "A blindfold."

"Yes, love."

"Lead with where you want the tie next time." I pat his chest.

Declan laughs and then helps me tie it on. "Can you see?"

I move my head a bit, trying to see anything, but it's all black. "Not a damn thing."

He turns me around twice. "Am I pinning the tail on something?"

"No, but you're the worst person to try to surprise since you watch and note everything, so, I'm hedging my bets."

He's right. I am the worst. I'm having a baby shower in a few weeks. They tried to make it a surprise, but he was acting weird, so I snooped and found out about it. It was really sweet that he tried though. I did my best not to let on that I knew, but a few days ago I mentioned that the train theme was lame, and blew up my spot.

I'm pretty sure he wanted to choke me.

Still, we are now having a zoo theme, which is what I'm decorating Deacon's room in.

"Are we there yet?" I ask, hating the darkness.

"Just a little farther." Declan holds my hands, pulling me along. I have no idea what his grand surprise is, but the fact that I'm out of the house is enough to make me euphoric.

The last few weeks, I've felt wonderful, but my overbearing nurse has made me absolutely certifiable. I can't go to work, drive anywhere, walk too much, or stress because it's not good for the baby.

I swear, I could beat him.

Which leads me to try my hand at subterfuge to stay busy.

"All right," Dec says as we come to a stop.

I inhale, and can smell the just cut wood, fresh paint, and traces of hay. His hands move to the tie, slowly lifting it from my head.

My eyes widen in shock. This was my barn a month ago. It was a small office with farm equipment below, and stalls that we didn't use for anything other than storage.

Now, it's beautiful.

The walls are covered and painted a soft light gray, there's a subfloor and area rugs down. To the right, where the stalls were, is cleaned out and is now a sitting area with a couch and two big chairs.

It doesn't even look close to the same.

"Dec," I say, trying to take it all in. "This is incredible."

"Come this way," he says, placing my hand on the crook of his arm.

He pulls me deeper toward the back. "The bathroom there is redone and now is … clean and usable."

I would've peed my pants instead of using the one here. It was so gross. "I'm glad to hear it."

"I've instructed the entire staff that, if anyone uses it, they'll be fired."

I laugh. "Well, I don't know that they can't use it, but I'll go with you on that for now."

"Let me show you the best part."

"There's more?"

He nods. I allow him to take me all the way to the back side where there are now two rooms with barn doors that are open.

I gasp. "Is this an office?"

"That's yours, and this is mine."

I walk inside and my heart overflows with love for this man. It's beautiful. There is a large gray wooden desk with white built-in bookcases behind it. They're already filled with some of my law books that I know were in my office building.

Behind the desk is a white leather tufted wingback chair. It's classy, modern, and so very much me.

"I know you're miserable working in the house, and we both need space to do what we love. I'm overbearing and ridiculous, but at least here, you're safe and can be comfortable."

"Oh, Declan," I say as tears brim, ready to spill over.

"Now we can both work, and you can be out of the house without pushing yourself to go back to work at the office too quickly."

Not a chance, but I just smile at him. "This is really sweet. And perfectly done."

There's really nothing that I would change.

"I'm glad. I love you very much."

I lift my hand and rest it on his cheek. "I love you."

"I want to do and give you everything."

"You already have."

He's given me more than he can even understand. I have my farm, a baby on the way, and the man I love.

He gave me his heart, and I'm never giving it back.

epilogue

"What the hell are you doing here?" Devney asks as I step into my office building.

"Last I checked, I work here."

She rolls her eyes. "Yes, but you said you wouldn't be in for a while."

"I lied, and I escaped."

"You seriously need to seek psychiatric help."

It's been the best month of my life, but I can't sit in that damn house anymore. It doesn't matter that we converted the barn into offices. It's great, don't get me wrong, but he's always freaking there.

He brings me water, juice, food, and then doesn't argue when I'm picking a fight.

Declan has been the most doting and wonderful man that any woman—any sane one—would want.

But I'm not sane.

Nope. I'm a crazy, hormonal, unhinged lunatic per Ellie and Devney.

Instead of staying home, I drove to my office—without his damn supervision.

"Yeah, well … whatever."

She follows me into my office. "Do you need anything?"

I shake my head. "Nope, just wanted to stretch my legs, get some fresh air, and not be confined."

My doctor and surgeon have given me the all clear to go back to work on a very limited basis. I'm meant to take it easy and stay off my feet whenever possible. They advised me to limit stress as well … like that could ever happen as a lawyer.

I have done that though.

I don't take as many cases, and I've hired another lawyer to help out once I have the baby, but there are some things that just can't be done from home.

"You act like being around your doting boyfriend is the worst thing that could happen."

"It's not, but he's always fussing over me. There hasn't been a single issue since I woke up, all the ultrasounds have been great, and Deacon is growing at the perfect rate. Yet, his father seems to think I shouldn't walk more than ten feet without him checking my heart rate."

Devney grins. "He loves you."

"He does."

"You're lucky," she says with a raised brow.

"Please, like Oliver doesn't dote on you? In fact, shouldn't your amazing boyfriend be here in an hour to pick you up for your date?"

It's the first Friday of the month. And the first Fridays are for Devney and Oliver. It's so great that she has someone who loves her to the point of madness. He plans this for her and constantly makes sure she knows how much he loves her.

Devney looks away and doesn't say anything.

Well, that's a cue that I can follow. "What?"

She turns her head back to mine. "What?"

"Why did you look away when I talked about Oliver?"

"It's nothing. Let's talk about you."

I lean back in my chair, but the baby makes it look less like leaning and more like a balloon tilting. I may not have shown until much later, but I more than made up for it in the last two months. I've not just popped, I've expanded like a blimp.

Each day it's as if someone is inflating my stomach a bit more.

"There's not a chance in hell I'm letting this go. Do you know what my last month has been like? Boring. Completely lacking in gossip or anything fun. Sure, Declan ... entertains me ... but since Ellie is on total bed rest until she gives birth, I get a few video calls or whatever Dec relays, which is horrible. He's truly bad at telling me the town news."

She laughs. "There's no news. Nothing about anyone in this town at least."

I narrow my eyes. "Is it about Sean?"

Her lips part just a bit, and I internally smile. I knew it. He was here this week to drop off some stuff before he has to stay for six months. I got to see him for a minute or two, but then he and Declan went downstairs to talk. I don't know what it was about, but it was clear that Sean was not his normal, happy-go-lucky self.

"Sean?"

"Yes, your best friend. My boyfriend's brother."

Devney sinks down, head falling forward into her hands. "Syd ..."

Concern fills me and I get up, move around the desk,

knocking some papers off as I go, and settle into the seat beside her. "What's wrong?"

She looks back to me, tears brimming. "I don't know what happened."

"Did you guys fight?"

"I wish. I mean, we did … *after* … but, now? What am I supposed to do?"

The anguish in her voice makes my stomach hurt. "I don't know what you're saying, Dev. You have to tell me something. What does *after* mean?"

I really hope it isn't what I think it is. Although, it would be well overdue. Still, their friendship will never be the same, and Sean needs Devney as much as she needs him. They have been best friends forever.

"He kissed me."

I bite back the smile that threatens to form. Finally, the man has done something to give her pause to think the feelings are there.

"Like a friendly kiss?"

She shakes her head quickly. "No, we were drinking and … I don't know … I said something about how hot he is and he said something about how he is always attracted to girls who look like me. We laughed, and then I said, 'Well, it has to be tough kissing your best friend, right?'"

Yeah, I don't think it's all that difficult for him. She's ridiculously beautiful. "And?"

"And then he cupped my face with one hand, and it was like one of those movie frames where you know they're going to kiss. He said, 'I don't know, but I'd like to see if it's tough to kiss you.'" She plays with the hem of her shirt, and I can hear the confliction in her voice. "I looked up at him, and at that moment, I *needed* him to do it. *I* wanted him to kiss me. And God, when he did, I thought I would die. How can a man kiss like that? How can a woman ever be the same after feeling that way? It was like I couldn't think, breathe, or focus on anything but him. I was so lost that I didn't care about anything else."

I take her hand, offering her some support. "The Arrowood boys sort of do that to you."

"I have Oliver, Syd. He's great, and he loves me so much. He's been ... so good to me. He doesn't play ball and run all over the country, fucking God only knows how many girls. Sean does. Sean is my best friend who I bitch about Oliver to. It doesn't make sense, but ..."

Oh, this poor girl. She has no idea what she's in for. However, I know better than anyone that you have to talk it out sometimes. "But?"

"Since that kiss, all I want is to see him. I want to kiss him again and see if it was the drinks or ... more? And yet, he's called, but I can't talk to him. I love Oliver. I love him so much, and he doesn't deserve that. Oliver makes me happy."

I've never loved anyone else other than Declan, so I don't know if can I empathize, but Oliver does love her, and I know she loves him.

"What are you going to do?" I ask.

"I'm going to have to tell Oliver. I owe him that, and ... he was talking about marriage the other day. I was telling Sean that he was going to propose soon."

Jesus. Is that what finally pushed Sean over the edge? I wonder if he knew that, once she was married, he'd never have a chance with her.

"What would you say?" I ask her.

Devney releases a heavy sigh and shakes her head softly. "I don't know ..."

I would bet my ass a week ago, the answer would've been clear as day.

"Maybe take some time," I suggest.

"There's more, Syd. I mean, not with Sean, but more that I need to tell him and you and everyone really, but I can't."

"Why?"

"Can you just give me some time?"

Of course I can, although a part of me is chomping that the bit to know what she has to tell us. "Can you assure me you're okay?"

Devney nods. "I am, but it's … hard to talk about, and I'm not ready yet."

"I have no room to push anyone to admit something before they're ready." My hand moves to my stomach where my secret hid for quite a while.

"Thank you. I need to sort out whatever I'm feeling for Sean and then I can deal with everything else."

My hand reaches out to take hers and before I can say anything else, I hear a crash in the hall. "Sydney!" Declan's roar comes from outside my office door.

Great. He came home early. Damn it.

"Can you cover for me?" I ask sheepishly.

She stands and goes out to the waiting area. "Hey, Dec. Long time no see? Aren't you supposed to be in New York?"

He is quiet for a second. "Hey, Dev, yes, but it seems I have to put a tracking device on someone."

"Yeah, I could see you doing that."

I stay quiet, hoping he won't figure out I'm here.

"Where is she?" Dec asks, a bit of the anger dissipating from his tone.

"Oh, she's in there." I hear Devney say as the door flies open. And then I hear her laugh. "Next time don't lie to me."

"Lie?" I yell. "What the hell did I lie about?"

"You said you didn't know you were pregnant when you

did."

I should fire her, but then I'd really be screwed.

Declan steps into the door frame, brow raised, and a look of relief and irritation mixing in those green eyes. *Like I'm screwed right now.*

I smile at him.

He doesn't return it. "Really, Syd?"

"What?" I ask innocently.

"You couldn't help yourself? You couldn't just stay home?" he says, entering and then tosses a folder onto my desk.

I shrug. "I needed to do some stuff here. Calm down."

"Calm down? You promised you would stay home and work in the barn so I could go into New York without worrying."

I smile at him and his loose tie around his neck—the one we had a lot of fun with last night—and his hair, which is pushed back as though he's run his hands through it a hundred times, and I see love.

"Yes, well, I got bored, and you weren't supposed to be home until after dinner."

He looks heavenward and groans.

My hands rest on my protruding stomach as my son flips around. "You're upsetting Deacon."

He steps closer and then squats in front of me. "I'm sorry, Son, but your mother is an exasperating woman and I am going to tie her to the bed."

"She might like that …"

He looks up at me, a sly grin painting his face. "Not for pleasure."

"What a pity. We can even use this tie again." I take the silk between my fingers and pull it tight. "It worked well last night."

"Woman."

Declan and I have a lot of things to work out, but together, we're happy. Sure, he drives me crazy with being overprotective, but I love having him with me. So much so that we've made big moves to make our lives permanent.

"Did you get the paperwork?" I ask, hoping to smooth his ire.

He gets to his feet and then pulls me into his arms. "Yes, Milo had a courier meet me outside of the city, which is why it didn't take me the extra time you thought you had to deceive me."

I roll my eyes. "I didn't deceive you. I merely failed to mention my outing."

"Right. We'll go with that. Anyway, as soon as you sign the paperwork, we'll be one step closer."

He kisses me quickly and then grabs the folder he brought with him. I take a seat and then pull out the documents. I read them and then smile when I get to the end.

"You're sure about this?"

Declan crouches in front of me again. "I'm wondering if we filed the wrong paperwork."

"What?"

He has doubts? I don't understand. He's the one who wanted to approach his brothers about entailing his portion of his family's farm once it's eligible. It would give us more land, and protect Connor and Ellie from having anyone around them. Since Connor decided to stay in Sugarloaf, we thought doing the same deal with his brothers was kind of perfect.

Does he regret it? Did he fall back in love with New York City an hour ago?

"I'm thinking that what we set up is fine, but I'd rather sign a different paper."

"And which one is that?"

"A marriage license."

My jaw drops, and my breath hitches. "What?"

He pulls a little black velvet box from his pants pocket and then repositions himself to be on one knee.

"You see, I had this big thing planned to propose today, but someone … went and altered it by leaving the house, causing me to chase her. You see, Sydney Hastings, I have loved you since I first laid eyes on you. I knew, even at my young age, that I could never be good enough for you, but I couldn't imagine not trying. I've failed. I've faltered, but my heart has always been yours. I want to wake up each morning with you, sleep each night beside you, and raise our kids as husband and wife. I want you to be my wife. Will you do me the greatest honor and give me my second shot? My path is clear—it's always the one that leads to you."

Tears fall down my face, and my heart is so full it could burst. "Yes! Yes! Yes! A million times over!"

He pulls me into his arms, kissing my lips as I breathe him in. This wonderful man. This man who I love so deeply it isn't even normal is mine, and I'm never letting him go.

Thank you for reading Declan and Sydney's story. I hope you love them and the rest of the Arrowood Brothers as much as I do. Sean and Devney's story is coming next and you are in for one heck of a ride with those two!

Preorder The One for Me!

acknowledgments

To my husband and children. You sacrifice so much for me to continue to live out my dream. Days and nights of me being absent even when I'm here. I'm working on it. I promise. I love you more than my own life.

My readers. There's no way I can thank you enough. It still blows me away that you read my words. You guys have become a part of my heart and soul.

Bloggers: I don't think you guys understand what you do for the book world. It's not a job you get paid for. It's something you love and you do because of that. Thank you from the bottom of my heart.

My beta reader Melissa Saneholtz: Dear God, I don't know how you still talk to me after all the hell I put you through. Your input and ability to understand my mind when even I don't blows me away. If it weren't for our phone calls, I can't imagine where this book would've been. Thank you for helping me untangle the web of my brain.

My assistant, Christy Peckham: How many times can one person be fired and keep coming back? I think we're running out of times. No, but for real, I couldn't imagine my life without you. You're a pain in my ass but it's because of you that I haven't fallen apart.

Sommer Stein for once again making these covers perfect and still loving me after we fight because I change my mind a bajillion times.

Michele Ficht and Janice Owen for always finding all the typos and crazy mistakes.

Melanie Harlow, thank you for being the Glinda to my Elphaba or Ethel to my Lucy. Your friendship means the world to me and I love writing with you. I feel so blessed to have you in my life.

Bait, Stabby, and Corinne Michaels Books—I love you more than you'll ever know.

My agent, Kimberly Brower, I am so happy to have you on my team. Thank you for your guidance and support.

Melissa Erickson, you're amazing. I love your face. Thank you for always talking me off the ledge that is mighty high.

To my narrators, Andi Arndt and Sebastian York who I swear I heard talking as I wrote this book. You always bring my story to life and always manage to make the most magical audiobooks. Andi, your friendship over these last few years has only grown and I love your heart so much. Thank you for always having my back. To many more concerts and snowed in sleepovers.

Vi, Claire, Mandi, Amy, Kristy, Penelope, Kyla, Rachel, Tijan, Alessandra, Meghan, Laurelin, Kristen, Devney, Jessica, Carrie Ann, Kennedy, Lauren, Susan, Sarina, Beth, Julia, and Natasha—Thank you for keeping me striving to be better and loving me unconditionally. There are no better sister authors than you all.

about the author

Corinne Michaels is a *New York Times*, *USA Today*, *and Wall Street Journal* bestselling author of romance novels. Her stories are chock full of emotion, humor, and unrelenting love, and she enjoys putting her characters through intense heartbreak before finding a way to heal them through their struggles.

Corinne is a former Navy wife and happily married to the man of her dreams. She began her writing career after spending months away from her husband while he was deployed—reading and writing were her escape from the loneliness. Corinne now lives in Virginia with her husband and is the emotional, witty, sarcastic, and fun-loving mom of two beautiful children.

books by corinne

The Salvation Series
Beloved
Beholden
Consolation
Conviction
Defenseless
Evermore: A 1001 Dark Night Novella
Indefinite
Infinite

Return to Me Series
Say You'll Stay
Say You Want Me
Say I'm Yours
Say You Won't Let Go

Second Time Around Series
We Own Tonight
One Last Time
Not Until You
If I Only Knew

The Arrowood Brothers
Come Back for Me
Fight for Me
The One for Me
Stay for Me

Co-Write with Melanie Harlow
Hold You Close
Imperfect Match

Standalone Novels
All I Ask

CPSIA information can be obtained
at www.ICGtesting.com
Printed in the USA
LVHW080306170620
658316LV00016B/286